Raves for Pamela Ribon's "witty, wonderful, and wise"
(*Maryland Gazette*) novels

WHY MOMS ARE WEIRD

"Hilarious and heartfelt. *Why Moms Are Weird* tackles the absurd morass of family with joyful wit and brutal honesty. I barreled through this book."

—Jill Soloway, Showtime's *United States of Tara* and
Six Feet Under; author of *Tiny Ladies in Shiny Pants*

"Compassionate. . . . fans will identify with this kind, imperfect heroine." —*Publishers Weekly*

"[A] joyous, single-sitting read. . . . Ribon is a sparkling talent."
—*South Florida Sun-Sentinel*

WHY GIRLS ARE WEIRD

"Chick lit at its most trenchant and truthful."

—Jennifer Weiner, *New York Times* bestselling
author of *Best Friends Forever* and *In Her Shoes*

"Light and entertaining." —*Booklist*

"Irresistible. . . . [L]ike hanging out with your best friend just when you need to most."

—Melissa Senate, author of
See Jane Date and *The Secret of Joy*

Going in Circles is also available as an eBook

ALSO BY PAMELA RIBON

Why Girls Are Weird

Why Moms Are Weird

Available from Downtown Press

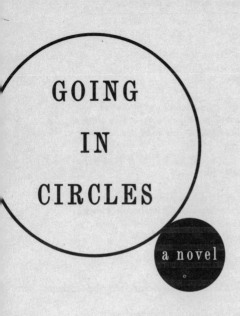

GOING
IN
CIRCLES

a novel

PAMELA RIBON

D

DOWNTOWN PRESS

New York   London   Toronto   Sydney

Downtown Press
A Division of Simon & Schuster, Inc.
1230 Avenue of the Americas
New York, NY 10020

This book is a work of fiction. Names, characters, places, and incidents either are products of the author's imagination or are used fictitiously. Any resemblance to actual events or locales or persons, living or dead, is entirely coincidental.

This Downtown Press paperback edition May 2010

DOWNTOWN PRESS and colophon are trademarks of Simon & Schuster, Inc.

For information about special discounts for bulk purchases, please contact Simon & Schuster Special Sales at
1-866-506-1949 or business@simonandschuster.com.

The Simon & Schuster Speakers Bureau can bring authors to your live event. For more information or to book an event contact the Simon & Schuster Speakers Bureau at 1-866-248-3049 or visit our website at www.simonspeakers.com.

Cover design by Susan Zucker
Cover photo by Andy Reynolds/Stone/Getty Images

Manufactured in the United States of America

10 9 8 7 6 5 4 3 2 1

ISBN 978-1-4391-9346-4
ISBN 978-1-4391-9390-7
ISBN 978-1-4391-6925-4 (ebook)

For my wives:

Anna Beth Chao
Cat Davis
Sara Hess
Allison Lowe-Huff
Dana Meller
Allison Munn

And for the
kick-ass, badass,
superhero rock stars
of the LA Derby Dolls

Did my ring burn your finger?
Did my love weigh you down?
Was the promise too much to keep around?

—*Solomon Burke*
(lyrics by Buddy & Julie Miller)

I've been working on a cocktail
called 'Grounds for Divorce . . .'

—*Elbow*

Paranoia may be the most natural response to the feeling
of love, to fully valuing another and hence growing aware
of the ever-present potential for their loss.

—*Alain de Botton*
The Romantic Movement

GOING
IN
CIRCLES

I've done the thing where I'm awake but I haven't yet opened my eyes. I'm in that twilight haze where I know I'm not asleep but I can't move a muscle. I've only got a second or two left before the panic will set in that I've some-how slept myself into becoming a paraplegic, that during the night I wrestled in some kind of nightmare that caused me to twist in horror, snapping my own neck, dooming me to an eternity of immobility.

Naturally, this will then trigger a second wave of fear. If I have separated my head from the rest of my body there's no real way that I can let anyone know this has happened. I will have to remain useless and numb, stuck in this position until someone figures out I've gone missing. I fear that it won't be a matter of hours, but perhaps days or weeks before anyone truly notices. My office mate, Jonathan, will eventually get bored with this unexpected man-holiday and will finally ask someone if I died.

But first, there's this special just-up time, when I can't move and I can barely think, when everything is perfect. I'm half in the real world but still able to clutch on to whatever dream I'm reluctant to depart. That makes this person I am—this Charlotte Goodman, age thirty, a skinny brunette with absolutely no singing voice and a deep aversion to paper cuts—nothing more than a concept. I'm not a real person and I don't have to be. Yet.

The dream I just fell from was gloriously mundane. I was sitting in seat 16A of a Continental flight somehow headed to a Starbucks, where I was to pick up a DVD for Sandra Bullock. This was supposed to be important. I was sitting next to a college frat boy who was singing the words to . . .

No, wait. I was sitting next to a sorority girl who was talking about her boyfriend who was the lead singer for . . .

No.

Damn. Nothing. It's gone.

Eyes open.

Morning, Sunshine.

Matthew used to say that every morning. It was a sarcastic dig at how terrible I am for the first hour before I get three good cups of coffee into me. It's not new—back in high school my parents would sometimes find an excuse to leave the house rather than wake me up early. They became avid churchgoers just to avoid my morning wrath. I know it's not right to hate everything before nine in the morning, but I don't understand how everybody acts like it's okay to be up at that hour. If we all got together and took a stand, we could all sleep in and force mornings to become a time for sleep and sleep only.

An early riser, Matthew would be well into his day, coffee brewed, having sometimes already gone for a run, taken a shower, and eaten breakfast before I waddled into the room, half-asleep, half-dressed, usually with only one eye open.

"Shh," he'd say, cradling my face with one hand. "Half of Charlotte is still asleep. Right Eye needs more dreaming."

And he'd whisper, pretending to tiptoe around the right side of me, the one that could wake up with a roar. "Shh. Right Eye is such an angel when she's sleeping."

This was before we were married, when there wasn't a question as to whether we were supposed to be together. Now I hear Matthew say, "Morning, Sunshine," even though he isn't here to say the words.

I've had to come to accept the fact that every morning my eyes will eventually open. I will wake up, and then I will have to get out of this bed. I'll brush my teeth, take a shower, put on clothes, and do all of the things almost everybody else seems to be able to do every single day no matter what is happening to them. I used to be one of those people, the normal ones who would make coffee and go to their jobs and joke with their friends and be productive members of society. Not anymore. At least not now.

Now I've had to develop a few defense mechanisms, tricks to accomplish a real-life calendar day without too many setbacks. Since I began employing these tactics, I have a 75 percent chance of making it to the next time I'm in this glorious bed without a full-on breakdown. Yes, there are still crying jags and the occasional panic attack. And sure, one time I kind of lost my shit at a Ruby Tuesday. But in my defense, that waitress knew what she had done.

Defense Mechanism Number 1 is crucial and happens every morning without fail, right here in this bed. Before I leave the safety of my crisp, white sheets and the soft, warm comfort of my purple flannel duvet, before I head out into that harsh, cruel society known as Los Angeles, California— home of the beautiful and the clinical—I make a plan.

This plan is important. It is the plan of the day. It doesn't take long, but I have found without The Plan, horrible things can happen. I'm likely to end up sitting on a curb beside a taco truck on Sunset Boulevard, crying over a carne asada burrito, wondering where my marriage went. It doesn't matter how much pain I'm in, I still have an awareness that people can see me, and I couldn't take knowing that to someone I'd just become the Weeping Burrito Girl.

The Plan keeps me from tangents. It keeps me from having to just float out there. Ironically, I learned this from Matthew. He liked planning, order.

Likes. I have to stop talking about him as if he's dead. He's still here. Just not *here*.

I hope he's not dead. First of all, that's going to look really suspicious. And second, I'm not really sure how I would be supposed to act at the funeral of my estranged husband. Would everyone think that I was secretly enjoying myself? Of course they'd think that, deep in the evilest parts of their hearts. Who wouldn't?

Look, as far as I know, today, right now, Matthew is alive. And if he's not, I had nothing to do with it.

Okay, so I've definitely decided I need to figure out what I'm going to do about my marriage before my husband dies.

I suck in my cheeks and tilt my head back on my pillow, trying to stretch out my face. For the past two weeks, I've been waking up with a feeling that someone has slammed a hammer into my skull. It has gotten worse every night, and this morning it hurts to open my mouth even the slightest bit. I wonder how long I can go without talking to anybody. Could I make it through an entire day, even if I left the apartment? That sounds like such a glorious luxury, being a mute. How wonderful not to have to keep answering the worst question on the planet: *How are you holding up?*

I lurch myself up and over until I'm in a seated position.

I make my feet touch the floor as I decide on the plan for today.

Okay. Leave the bedroom. Make coffee. Write email that you will be late for the office. Do not check your email to see if Matthew wrote. Go to Dr. Benson's office for this jaw pain. Go to work. Come home and hide.

Once The Plan is firmly in place, Defense Mechanism Number 2 will often be itching to take over.

Defense Mechanism Number 2 is a little more complicated. It took a while for me to be comfortable with it, and I've pretty much sworn myself to secrecy about it. If anyone else learned about Defense Mechanism Number 2, I would be put in the rather vulnerable position of having said person possibly think I was unhinged. Certifiable. But when I tried suppressing Defense Mechanism Number 2 I learned that it's not really up to me. I mean, it's me, but it's not me.

Sometimes, for no other reason than to get through This Hour Right Now, I have no choice but to pull myself out and narrate my own life, to myself, in the third person. I know it's me, but somehow, this way, it can also *not* be me, and that makes it so much easier to deal. That's Defense Mechanism Number 2.

So, look. I sleep, I drink, and sometimes a male voice in my head tells me what's happening to me. Perfectly understandable, considering.

In my head he sounds like a dad. Not my dad, but someone's dad. Half folksy, half serious, a man who's already lived a life and knows that this one I'm in is just going through a rough patch, nothing more. He kind of sounds like Craig T. Nelson. Well, really he sounds like John Goodman. This is probably because when I was a kid I told a bunch of my friends at school that I was related to the dad on *Roseanne*, and if they didn't believe me they could just check out our last names, which were *exactly the same*.

So when things get rough, when I don't know what's going to happen, when The Plan can't protect me, I let Uncle John do the talking. I let him go on in his stomach-stuffed voice like I'm tucked into bed waiting for one last story before I close my eyes, and soon everything's going to be okay.

Sometimes I even start to believe him.

2

Charlotte Goodman lets the voice in her head take over as she swallows three ibuprofen with her second cup of coffee. She sits down to her laptop with the intention of sending an email that says she won't make it to the office until close to lunch. At some point Charlotte will send that email, but not until she takes a quick, masochistic glance for a name in her inbox she has absolutely forbidden herself from checking for.

It is the name of one Matthew Price, a man who is her legal spouse. This means he is her husband. For now. And the last thing she should be doing is waiting for him to write. She shouldn't wake up in the morning hoping that this time there's communication from him. It is getting rather embarrassing how Charlotte wakes up every morning with new hope that somehow she will know without a shadow of a doubt that he wants her and needs her. So right now, Charlotte shouldn't be looking for Matthew's name. In fact, the whole point of having The Plan was to follow it, and one of the items on today's plan was not doing what she's now doing.

Charlotte quickly scans the names in her inbox, squinting the entire time. This way it doesn't count. She didn't look right at it.

She barely registered the names that were there. She didn't even take the time to delete the spam.

So why does Charlotte continue to search for a name she actively tries to avoid? Our beloved heroine would love to know the answer to that question herself. She's tried all manner of ways to break her addiction to information on Matthew's whereabouts.

This has much to do with why Charlotte has been popping anti-inflammatory medication for breakfast. It is also why she is currently letting the caller trying to reach her on her cell phone go to voice mail. Charlotte knows the only person who calls at this hour is her mother, a woman whom Charlotte is unable to deal with at this particular time, or that particular time, or any particular or unparticular time.

Charlotte feels the need to think to herself at this point that the narration of her life by John Goodman most likely doesn't sound like the actual John Goodman, but it's how the voice feels inside her that's important.

Charlotte isn't sure whom she's trying to placate when she makes mental excuses for her own strange behavior. She supposes it's not unlike how people check behind them after they stumble, in case someone saw them almost fall, so that everybody silently recognizes that the one who tripped had something tangible to blame, and isn't just bad at walking.

The narration of Charlotte Goodman's life is important for times like now, when she's driving across the city to Dr. Benson's office. Sometimes she wishes she could montage the boring, mundane parts of her life when she's alone with her thoughts. Skip ahead to the next part and get the day over with in a matter of forty-seven minutes. To be honest, Charlotte doesn't prefer spending time with people; it's just that they make the minutes pass faster than when she's on her own. Other people are distractions.

Roughly an hour after Charlotte has swallowed those ibu-profen, she's in Dr. Benson's cramped office. This is where she no longer needs her narrator.

Dr. Benson has his hands on either side of my face, pressing my temples, threatening to cause a cerebral cave-in. Standing inches from my head, he's staring me down like he can see through my skin. Like he's scanning my insides with robot laser eyes. The intensity of his gaze has caused me to stop breathing, worried that even a single exhalation could cause the results to be skewed.

Toned, tan, thin, with the kind of face on which you have to actually go searching for a physical flaw, Dr. Benson's exactly what one imagines a Beverly Hills doctor would be. While I find it very comforting to have my health observed by a perfect example of The Human Body, it's still amusing that someone would bother to get a medical degree when he's already successful at resembling a Hollywood actor. What a decision Dr. Benson must have had to make at one point in his life. *"Do I make a lot of money saving lives with these hands, or do I make a lot of money pretending to save lives with this face?"*

I force myself to detach from the hypnotic pull of Dr. Benson's apparently well-calibrated ocular diagnostic tool and focus instead on my file folder, which is tucked underneath his arm, jammed dangerously close to the dampness at his pit. For a moment I consider reaching out to snatch the folder to safety.

"TMJ," Dr. Benson concludes, breaking the silence in the room.

The disappointment in my sigh is unmistakable, but it's nice to finally breathe again. "Really?"

"TMJ," he repeats, with a distant tone in his voice, as if TMJ is a girl he used to know who doesn't come around anymore, one who never knew how much he loved her.

For the briefest of moments, I do worry what people are going to say when they find out my jaw pain is due to something associated with excessive gum chewers and those who give blow jobs. Anybody who knows me knows I didn't get it from either. At least not recently. But that doesn't stop me from being offended when Dr. Benson concludes: "You must be grinding your teeth in your sleep."

I rub my left temple for what must be the hundredth time this morning, still hoping to find a way to crush the pain. "I've never been told I grind my teeth," I say.

The doctor sits in a nearby chair. He grips his pen like a toddler holds a crayon, as if he's pretending to write words into my sweaty file. "Well, does your husband notice?" he asks. "Did he say anything about the noise waking him?"

Every time this happens, I feel like I'm breaking the news of a death. "Matthew and I . . . We aren't together right now."

Dr. Benson briefly looks up and glances at my left hand, to confirm. Like this is the secret test only he's smart enough to conduct. He points at my wedding ring with his pen, and even though I knew he was going to see it, I still cover my hand, feeling like I've been caught lying.

"We're still . . . trying to figure things out," I continue, wondering why I need to give him any explanation at all. "It's complicated." I stare at my shoes and kick my feet, knowing I'm way too old for this childlike gesture to be endearing. I silently count the grommets in my tennis shoes, hoping it makes me look lost in thought.

Dr. Benson runs a hand through his healthy hair, then rests the back of his perfect right hand against his flawless lips.

He closes my folder and shoves it back against his ribs, deep into his armpit. "You'll want to get a mouth guard to use at night," he says.

I know vanity shouldn't come into play when you're a woman who goes to bed every night alone. But I still have no desire to look like a hockey player when I'm in my pajamas. What if there's a fire in my apartment building and I run outside and everyone sees me in protective gear? What if one day I get my most recent favorite wish and I do actually die in my sleep? With my luck I'll get that wish by suffocating on my mouth guard, and I will become famous for having the most awkward accidental death of all time.

"How long have you been separated?" Dr. Benson asks, laser eyes beaming straight toward my wedding band. I get hopeful for a second, thinking that maybe his "oculoscope" will decide my jaw pain is related to my emotional pain. Then I'd be diagnosed with a devastatingly romantic condition, and I could call Matthew to whimper, "Please don't worry about me. It's just . . . the doctor said if we don't work things out . . . I might *die*."

Then I'd quickly hang up with an air of mystery; perhaps I'd faint and fall perfectly to the floor, and now it would be up to Matthew to jolt into action.

Unless he didn't jolt. Unless he let me die.

"We've been going through problems for a little while," I say. "Living separately for about three months."

All the euphemisms used for a marriage torn apart are lousy. The only reason I even try to use gentler words is because most people seem to immediately take some kind of responsibility for my situation. They seem to want to grab guilt from my heart by the handful.

But in this case, Dr. Benson isn't taking any responsibility for my pain. He gives a little grunt, nodding. I'm not sure if that means he's been through this before or if he's just seen it a million times and he no longer cares. Most likely it's the latter, and for him hearing someone describe a divorce is about as rare as hearing someone complaining about a sore throat. *We could run some tests, but usually with this kind of thing it's best to just wait and see.*

Dr. Benson stands, finished with the consultation. I'm just about to thank him for his time when he adds one last prescription.

"You should think about getting a therapist."

Diagnosis: Charlotte Goodman has a broken head, inside and out.

3

I t wasn't when Matthew declared he no longer wanted to be my husband that I started losing my mind. It hurt, absolutely, like a train slamming through me, circling back only to slam me again. It wasn't even how he did it, which must go down in history as one of the clumsiest break-ups ever.

It was six months ago. He had brought home Chinese food, and we were in the kitchen, dropping noodles into bowls, when he said, "I think I'm going to move out."

I laughed, knocking into him, briefly resting my head near the top of his shoulder. The soft fibers of his blue T-shirt rubbed against my cheek. "Jeez, so you forgot the hot mustard," I said. "I'm not kicking you out. *This time.*"

He was motionless, holding a paper container over a bowl from our wedding registry, noodles and marriage in mid-drop, when he said, "No, I mean: I'm moving out."

I saw his words written out in front of my eyes, complete with punctuation.

No
COMMA

I mean
COLON
I'm moving out
PERIOD

An announcement. Meaning it wasn't spontaneous. After the colon, there's information. I had thought my night was going to consist of Chinese food and backlogged television programming. New information. COLON.

I was being left.

"What are you talking about—'moving out'?" I asked.

He started arranging everything on the counter, aligning objects at right angles, all of his attention directed at the white origami boxes of chow mein and tofu. Someone who didn't understand my husband's obsessive-compulsive disorder like I did might have thought he was being flippant. How can a man announce he's moving out and then immediately dive into what appears to be a rather serious scientific experiment to determine exactly how far from the edge of the counter the packets of soy sauce should be? But in truth, his distraction was crucial information. His obsession over the placing of objects, the need for control over the things that couldn't control themselves, was tattling on him. I knew that no matter how rehearsed and cool he appeared to be on the outside, inside he was freaking out.

Finally he said, "I don't think this is going to work."

And then he lowered his hand onto the counter, splaying it from wrist to fingertips, like a wave, a presentation.

I placed my hand on top of his, letting him know I knew what the outstretched fingers meant. A signal that inside he'd just said something the way he wanted to say it.

What I'd just done was so absurd I had to laugh. Matthew

was the one leaving me, but yet I was trying to make him feel better, wanting to ease his inner turmoil by letting him know I understood the secret language his body used to speak to me. I should have been screaming with fury, on a rampage, but instead I was taking time to communicate with both sides of Matthew, the two parts of his brain—the half that used his mouth to make words that didn't match the situation, and the half that used his body to make movements that didn't match the situation.

I made myself scoff, trying to get angry. "You're breaking up with me?" I asked. None of this felt real.

"I should have said something earlier," he mumbled, sliding his hand out from under mine, holding it against his stomach protectively. "Things haven't felt right since—"

"You can't break up with your *wife*." I went back to the Chinese food, needing my own sense of order. I clenched a wad of noodles between two chopsticks and tried to toss them into a bowl, but they slid out of my grip, splashing me in sticky brown sauce.

"I'm sorry," Matthew said.

I kept attacking the noodles with those useless sticks, stabbing a meal I wasn't going to eat. "No, it's too late," I said. "We got married. End of story."

"I thought I could get through what I was feeling. But I still feel it."

"Feel what?"

"I don't know."

This is when I learned that chopsticks most definitely do *not* look cool when you throw them for dramatic effect. They flipped uncontrollably like I'd finished a wicked mini drum solo, one bouncing back to hit me square in the face. I knew it looked hilarious. That's why I knew it was bad when

Matthew ignored it. It was the one moment when maybe everything could have eased up. If he'd laughed, we could have taken a breath, taken a step back. But he was determined. Rehearsed. He said, "Please just understand that I'm sorry and I'll do everything I can to get this over with quickly."

This. Over with. I was a *this.* He wanted nothing instead of *this.*

"Can't we talk about it? Don't I get to be a part of this decision?"

He left the kitchen and kept walking, grabbing his keys and wallet from the coffee table. Just as he reached the front door, his hand on the knob, I said the only thing I could come up with at that moment that I knew would hurt him.

"You're really going to leave instead of staying here to talk about it like a real man?"

I thought it would get him fighting, keep him in the room a bit longer, just so I could fully grasp what was happening. It didn't work, and my husband of five months walked right out the door with a slam. I didn't hear from him for a week after that. He called only to let me know that he was staying somewhere, and he was fine, and he didn't want me to worry.

I guess it happens every day, probably much like that every day. Probably the other people don't end up smacking themselves in the face with chopsticks, but maybe they have similar awkward moments. That would make me feel better, I think, to know there are people other than me who can't have a dramatic moment without a comedic twist. I can't be the only one who trips, spills, flops, and drops through all of her most important moments.

I was still getting used to calling him my husband. My wedding gown was still hanging in my closet. I couldn't get over the feeling that he would walk back through the door with that grin of his that took over half of his face, shaking his head, saying, "I can't believe you *fell* for that!"

Instead, what happened was one month later Matthew came back from what turned out to be a motel hideaway to announce that he'd changed his mind. He did want to be my husband after all.

Ta-da! Who wants cake?

I'm sure this is when "good wives" are supposed to leap into the arms of their spouses, covering them with kisses and gratitude. The woman has been deemed worthy, and that means the marriage will never, ever suffer any more strife. How lucky, friends would say, to have such a big test early on in the relationship. How common, family members would say, to have the relationship strained in its early years. How fantastic that we survived it, and of course Matthew would never really leave, and, *"Are we back on for Game Night on Thursday? Yay!"*

And at first I did celebrate. Who wouldn't be relieved to find out she wasn't being abandoned after all? I think it lasted about as long as a weekend. Two days of snuggling and nice dinners in restaurants as familiar to us as the feeling of our fingers intertwined. After that, I supposed we were expected to just go back to normal, but I didn't know what normal was. In my defense, I didn't know things weren't normal to begin with. Following that logic, at any moment I could be left again.

Matthew didn't want to talk about what had made him leave. He said only that it had been a mistake, and that he was sorry. Over and over again he said that, like he'd read somewhere that it was the way to fix what he'd done. That's what I got for marrying a lawyer. He knew how to answer only the questions that would get him off easy. My cross-examinations were a complete failure.

"Did you stop loving me?"

"No. I'm sorry."

The words were real. They were what people were supposed to say. But out of his mouth they seemed remorseless, mechanical. Computations devised to soothe me. It was like picking a fight with an ATM: you get only so many responses.

"NO. I'M SORRY."

"Did you want someone else?"

"I AM HERE NOW. THAT IS NOT IMPORTANT."

"Do you think you might change your mind again?"

"I WANT TO BE HERE. LET'S LOOK FORWARD. WOULD YOU LIKE AN ACCOUNT BALANCE?"

At night Matthew would be happily snoring beside me, but I'd be spinning with panic, my eyes raw like sandpaper from staring at the ceiling, as I wondered *why, why, why.*

Why did he go? And why did he come back?

The only way I can sufficiently explain what happened next is to say that I cracked. I cracked right in half.

Yes, he wants me.

No, he doesn't.

I felt both of those thoughts, and I felt them both equally. Relief and anger. Security and panic.

He wants you now.

Yeah, but he didn't.

One night I couldn't take the wondering anymore. He was asleep next to me, happy like everything was fine, and all I knew was that somehow it wasn't. "Hey," I said, pushing him to the point of an actual shove. It wasn't nice, but I wasn't completely in control of myself.

He rolled toward me, opening a groggy eye. "You okay?" he asked. "Bad dream?"

I could have curled up into the crook of his arm, snuggled my cheek against his warm skin, and thanked him for being there for me when I needed him. Thanked him again for coming home to me. I could have slid my foot between his calves and called him my Snugglebutt. I could have rewarded him for coming home, for being in my bed again. For making it *our* bed again. I could have chosen to make this moment a loving one.

But I was cracked, so I couldn't do that. Instead, I said, "*This* is the bad dream."

A side effect of being cracked is that you say lines that would get cut from even the cheesiest of films.

"What do you mean?"

"Matthew." I had to say his name even though he was the only other person in the room because again, I was living a cliché. "Matthew, did you come back for me or for you?"

When living a cliché, always make sure to repeat a person's name at the beginning of every question.

Under the cover of darkness he thought I couldn't see him think through all the possible answers, his eyebrows furrowed as he feverishly narrowed down the possible responses, searching for exactly the right thing to say at this hour, in this situation.

"I came back for *us*," was what he landed on. The right answer on paper, as long as that piece of paper was from the cheesy movie script being written in my head.

I wished I hadn't asked, because the answer didn't ultimately matter. I was the one who had to be able to live with it. And Matthew didn't realize, couldn't realize, that when he had come back, he'd created an invisible monster that grew inside me. Like those little gummy toys that get larger from adding water, I'd swallowed a tiny dinosaur. It mixed with my stomach juices, poisoned by anxiety, frustration, unanswered questions, and abandonment, and now a T. rex was roaring inside me, ready to burst.

For the next couple of weeks, everything Matthew did drove me crazy. The most innocuous act could set me off on a mental tirade. He could flush a toilet, and my cracked brain would rant, "That man has the *nerve* to just come *waltzing back here* and *flush that toilet* like he *didn't just dump* me a few *weeks* ago?"

I'm pretty sure my head was involuntarily bobbing on every fifth word that went through my mind. I must have looked like a pigeon, swiveling my neck around, wobbling and weaving with indignation.

"As if *I* were someone you could just *leave* without *warning* and then come back here and just *ask* me if I wanted to eat Chinese for dinner tonight? Like we can ever have Chinese again when the *last time* we tried to eat it you walked out on me? Like anything will ever be *normal* again? As if I'm someone you just *ask* questions of and then wait for an *answer*— as if I have *answers* instead of a thousand questions? Like: *where did you go/who did you see/did you sleep with someone/ did you sleep with someone and decide you'd rather sleep with me?*"

That's another thing. Once Matthew left me, I imagined he did everything he could do while being away from me. It didn't matter if he told me the truth or not. In my mind, there were women. Lots of women. Naked, glistening, horny, dirty women who did everything I didn't want done to me. These hot women would cook for him and then beg him to do illegal activities on them, all of them. Giant hordes of whores and skanks wiggling all over Matthew. That's what I saw. And for some reason, I saw this happening in Cairo. *Everything's hot and beige and cannot be duplicated by me. I am nothing compared to what Matthew could have Out There. I will never be as good as Hot Sex in Egypt. I know that, but now he must know that, too.*

So why had he come back? There had to be a catch. Trying to figure it out was ripping me apart. If he couldn't get everything he wanted from me, then what was it he was getting from me that he couldn't get anywhere else? What did I do for him that even the dirtiest of girls was saying, "Oh, *hell, no*" to? Maybe I needed to be more like one of those Cairo orgy girls. Make some boundaries that didn't involve sex acts.

Sometimes I marvel at what the female body can endure. We can create life, giving our bodies up to grow another human being, one who takes things from us we need, like vitamins and nutrients. We become a host, a vessel of life-giving blood and shelter, only to be torn practically apart by the childbirth process. Afterward, we are never the same. Our bodies change, stretched and worn, scarred. We can never go back to the person we were before we were two.

My body might not have just gone through the miracle of life, but grief can create the same internal split. Sometimes you can be hurt so deeply, so badly, that there's another thing that lives inside you, beside you. A monster of anger, of regret. One that breathes and grows and feels.

And so, about a month after Matthew had come back home, I left.

People have asked why I didn't fight to stay in the house. I couldn't. I was leaving. Not for a day or two during which I could hang out in a hotel, ordering from room service and reading magazines until I'd decided to go back to domesticated life. Not long enough to have the lady version of the pornfest I imagined Matthew had had. I knew that I was getting out of there for a while, possibly forever. Once I felt I couldn't live there anymore, it was as if I'd accidentally seen the last page of a novel. I knew what was coming. I had to go.

I knew it would be hell on everyone. I thought about all of the people who had been involved in the uniting of our lives—everybody from our families, to the attendees at our wedding, to the country's legal system. Everybody was going to have to make a change in how they saw me, how they treated me. Or at the very least, where they went to visit me. I couldn't live in the house-minus-Matthew again. It had been too hard the first time.

I was angry. I was sad. I was cracked. And for some reason I knew without a doubt that I needed exactly what I had just gone through hating: isolation.

ext item on today's plan: get to work.

My job is the most monotonous, unenviable, lame, boring job in the entire world.

I love it.

I love it so much, I wish I could kiss it. I would take it out at night and get it really drunk and whisper in its ear, "You stupid, stupid waste of my life. Oh, how I need you. Never leave me, you soul-sucking zombie factory."

I'm a technical writer for a software company. This means I help create entries for the Knowledge Base, our web-based tech support. When I was happier, in the year or so I worked here back when my life wasn't broken, this place was the source of all my misery. I would drive to this fist-size building with my stomach clenched in knots, unsure how I was going to make it through the next eight to ten hours. I knew if I remembered I was a real person, one with flesh and blood and a beating heart, sitting in this puke-green shoebox of an office with no other function than to write words that described how computers worked, I might have driven straight into a tree.

These days, the fact that my job doesn't really need me to be an active participant in it—and actually goes better when

I have exactly zero emotions or original thoughts—helps me to live the majority of my life in an intentional coma, an encouraged numbness that requires absolutely nothing from me other than to keep my fingers moving.

Another thing I love about my work is that there's one right way to do it. There's no wondering, no questions to ponder. My job is to provide answers in a clear and precise manner. When I'm really in the zone with my writing it doesn't even feel like it's me typing the words. I become a machine, a word producer. A human manual. I am a collection of answers.

I do have one emotion when it comes to work: sympathy for my office mate, Jonathan. Being in the unlucky position of having his desk exactly three feet behind mine, he's had to deal with my personal issues for a long time. Proximity has forced him to overhear every phone call, every deep sigh, every tear that has plopped onto my desk. He knew when I had spent the entire day crafting an email to Matthew instead of working on copy. He heard me break down when I called my realtor to ask how exactly I would go about getting my name off my own deed. He pretended not to notice the time I broke down sobbing at my desk after someone wandered past our office whistling INXS's "Never Tear Us Apart."

The first time I apologized for my behavior was the only time he allowed it. "I've been through this before, Charlotte," he said. He's on his second marriage—one that he says "looks to be sticking." I haven't met her, but from the picture on Jonathan's desk, she seems fake. I don't mean that as an insult, I mean she looks like Jonathan designed her. He ordered up the pretty, skinny, blonde with the white teeth, pill-free sweaters, and arms-that-never-flap. Even her name is too much. *Cassandra*. Who's named that, honestly? Not even Cassie or Cass. She's so pretty that people still call her by her full name. *Cassandra*. People call me Char. Like someone who's been scorched.

Actually, people around here have apparently taken to calling me The Ghost. That's what Jonathan told me the other day. Frankly, I think that's a better name for the tiny girl down the hall with the sullen face who always dresses like she's just come back from a funeral. Francesca is her name. Which, come to think of it, is exactly what you'd call the tiny Goth girl down the hall with the sullen face and funereal clothes. She gets to keep her name, too. The gorgeous and the pseudo-tragic, they get to own their elaborate, fancy full names. Not me. Jonathan said even sad-faced Francesca calls me The Ghost. That can't be good. When you're bumming out people who spend all day intentionally trying to look sad, you must look pretty damn pathetic.

• • •

As soon as I remember that my mother called this morning, I try to forget it. For a fraction of a second it starts to work. I almost rewrite the morning away, changing it into a completely different experience. This morning I got up, jumped out of bed, went to the gym . . . and then on my way to work I saved a child from being hit by a car. Something fantastically honorable and noble like that, something that would either excuse or erase the fact that the truth is I'm the kind of girl who lets her mother's phone call go to voice mail and then completely forgets about it for the next three or four hours.

I can't rewrite the truth away. I have to check my voice mail.

I do it with my eyes closed, as this somehow shelters me

from harm. Because it's not just a phone message from my mother. It is a reminder that no matter how much of a victim I might try to play sometimes, there's no escaping the fact that I am a terrible person.

Charlotte Goodman is a terrible person. Only a terrible person would leave her husband and not tell her mother about it. That's right. Charlotte Goodman's own mother doesn't know that her daughter is probably about to get a divorce. Worse than that, Charlotte is the kind of rotten daughter who will lie to her mother, to her face, and act like she still lives in the house where she hasn't been in months.

In her defense, the only person possibly more terrible than Charlotte Goodman is Elaine Goodman, the woman who raised her. This is because Elaine has two emotional settings: none and all.

When Charlotte didn't make the high school cheerleading team, Elaine got rid of Charlotte's beloved dog, Shoelace, blaming the pet as a distraction from her daughter's future.

For most mothers, a daughter's engagement is cause for celebration. Not so with Elaine Goodman. When her daughter got engaged, Elaine's first reaction was to say, "Oh, thank God. I truly feared the only time you'd ever say 'I do' was when someone asked, 'Do you want more potato chips?'"

Charlotte was only five when her mother told her she'd grow up to be an awkward-looking woman, as years ago her father got her then-pregnant mother drunk and took her on a roller coaster, hoping to get rid of the baby.

One of those stories isn't true, but I don't want to say which one my narrator made up. The answer won't be flattering, and besides, this way I don't have to dwell on the two terrible stories that are completely true. Otherwise my daily plan will have to include "Find a Way To Sue Your Mother for Emotional Trauma."

It isn't that we don't love each other, my mother and I. It's more like we try to keep our love for each other a secret. We never hug. We don't say "I love you." We do tell each other when we're disappointed in each other, because that's important. Criticism makes you a better person for other people. Plus, if you find a couple of hours when you have less disappointment in each other than usual, you can note the banner day in your relationship.

This is why I haven't told my mother about my marriage. I don't think I'm prepared to handle the criticism. I figure as long as I keep Mom in the Emotional Zero zone, everything should be okay. We will both pretend that neither of us has any real thoughts or feelings about anything. Like we always do. We will discuss the weather, other people's problems, anything interesting we got in the mail, and—if things get really crazy—one will tell the other about a newfound breakfast place where you can get a phenomenal glass of freshly squeezed grapefruit juice.

My parents have been married for thirty-five years. This is how they handle problems or conflict: they don't. There are no problems. Problems don't exist. There are *situations*. There are *unfortunate moments*. There are *mistakes*. There are *bad patches*. They are only referenced as past events, and even then they are glossed over to the point where I cannot tell you a single thing that my parents have fought over. I can barely remember times when it seemed they weren't getting along. They never looked like they were in love, really. I can count on one hand the number of times I saw them kiss, and each time it was an accident when they thought they were completely alone. Their love was intentionally kept away from my view. Like it was none of my business. They were Mom and Dad—two people in charge of keeping me adhering to the rules of growing up. Basically, I have no idea what it looks like to be a married couple. But if someone needs me to take a kid's bike away for the weekend because she jumped on the bed, then I know exactly what to do.

If I tell my mother that I couldn't handle half a year of marriage, there's no telling what might happen. She could set my hair on fire. This is not a random hypothetical. This is something she actually did to her cousin when they were six and fighting over a spoon of raw cookie dough.

Mom's voice mail:

"Charlotte. I asked your father and he said he hasn't heard from you in a while. You shouldn't do things like that. He's old and will be dead before you know it and then you can spend all the time you want not talking to him.

"I got these shorts the other day but I don't like how they make my knees look, so let me know if you'd want them and I won't return them. You've got thicker legs, so your knees might not look as funny in them.

"Oh, and you'll have to talk to your father again because now he's insisting on having some kind of production for my birthday next Friday. Anyway, it's the four of us. Dinner. Tell Matthew that work's no excuse this time, and he can't skip out again. Bring a couple bottles of that wine you brought that one Christmas, the one your father liked but you drank most of.

"Okay, that's all. I'm hanging up now."

Charlotte Goodman takes a walk around her office building and wonders if anybody would really mind if she just ran away and disappeared. Maybe she'll go to Iceland. Make a brand-new start in Reykjavik. She'll be a modern-day Björk, a pioneer out there in the cold, reinventing herself. She'll take an interest in modern design, or sewing parkas, or whatever it is that Björk does.

To be honest, I'd rather go to Italy than Iceland. But I can't go to Italy, because that's the place where Matthew and I were supposed to go. *Are* supposed to go. I don't even know the tenses anymore. I'm not sure. I just know it was the honeymoon we were saving up for, one that we haven't taken and now most likely won't.

I couldn't have been happier with the way we had our wedding—just friends and family, hosted by our best-couple friends, Pete and Petra, in their backyard. We had already thrown all of our money into buying a house, a lovely little one-bedroom we nicknamed The Fort. It felt like our secret hideout. We treated it like one, too; the day after our wedding we made tater tots and hot dogs and sat on the floor of our kitchen to eat them, like we were having our first meeting in our clubhouse.

"For richer or poorer," Matthew had said, raising a tater tot as a toast.

"Let this be the poorer," I added, knocking a ketchup-smeared potato bud against his.

We spent that first weekend as a married couple in bed, making love and eating hundreds of tater tots.

In this memory, Matthew looks larger than life in my head. All the best parts of him are illuminated, highlighted. I see his strong hands, the small upturn of his nose, his glasses. That's how I know it's not a true composite; Matthew had gotten Lasik surgery before the wedding. But the Matthew who wore glasses is the man I fell in love with, and when I see him in my most cherished memories, I see him in his specs, pushed up too high on the bridge of his nose, always smudged on the lower right corner from his constant straightening. Black square frames that gave him a look of superiority that he often used to his benefit.

I didn't know how to tell him that after the surgery, I missed his glasses. He was so excited to be able to see everything, that there was one less thing for him to fiddle with, to worry about. He could wake up in the morning and jump right out of bed, if he wanted to. I loved how excited he could get about things. It didn't happen often, but when it did he had this little-kid face, full of wonder, so happy that something he had planned had worked out even better than he had assumed it would. That was when he was at his happiest—when he was absolutely as correct about something as possible. It's how he used to feel about us.

I still think we weren't a mistake, being together. At least not at first. When we first fell in love I kept feeling like I'd found something I'd been looking for. We had so much in common. Lots of *things* in common. We liked the same books, movies, music. We thought of visiting the same places. That's how Italy came to represent the place we'd go once we got hitched. Our dreams meshed into one, our goals singular. It was no longer, "I've always wanted to go to Italy." It would become, "We went to Italy together."

I can't go to Italy now, no matter how much I want to disappear. Like the books and photographs and that one blue hoodie we traded back and forth, ideas and places and emotions are also being divvied up right now. Regardless, I can't afford to go, as I spent half of my savings moving into my own place, and the other half I'm going to need while I find out what's going to happen to me.

Matthew would be rolling his eyes right now if he could hear what I am thinking.

One night, right before we'd gotten engaged, we were in bed talking about what the next year might be like. There was a possibility we'd do some traveling, or we'd spend most of our money attending his cousin's destination wedding. That was when my work was first starting to take off. Not my job, which was a way to pay the bills, but a possible career in something I'd never thought I could make a living doing. An actual future for what it was I'd rather do.

I make miniatures. Well, I used to, anyway. It started when I was little, with my dollhouse. We couldn't afford to buy a lot of doll furniture to begin with, but that didn't bother me. What I wanted was for my doll to have the same things in her house that I had in mine. I spent hours at the kitchen table with colored pencils, construction paper and glue, making sticky, lopsided couches and toaster ovens. My early origami-like representations were sufficient enough to get the point across, but would be destroyed by the end of one afternoon of Today Barbie Has Hot Sex with the Cable Guy.

I stole the little plastic inserts from pizza boxes used to keep the cardboard from meshing with the cheese. For me, they were perfect bases for coffee tables. Where some kids saw broken sunglasses, I saw the possibility of a full-length mirror, or a vanity. A juice-box straw was a fantastic find; it could be fashioned into a lamp, a shower curtain rod, or—for the more adventurous doll—a poolside stripper pole.

My mother, of all people, was the one who encouraged me to keep making miniatures. I think it was mainly because it kept me quiet and out of the way for hours on end. Still, she was the one who took me to the crafts store on weekends. I loved that grown-up feeling, mom and daughter entering the store together with projects in mind. I was so content being just like all the other women wandering the aisles of crafts supplies, browsing through seemingly infinite possibilities, each lost in her own artistic world. I wasn't tagging along like those other little kids, those *babies,* bored and whiny, who could be mollified with a coloring book and a package of puffy stickers. I had a real reason to be there, to touch the rows of unfinished wood, to sift through yarn balls and doll parts. I was a creator.

Once back at home, I'd work until my little fingers felt spiked with splinters from breaking hundreds of Popsicle sticks into what I thought of as wood scraps. I ruined the carpeting in my bedroom with Krazy Glue mishaps.

It was all worth it for my mom's thirty-fifth birthday present. I made her a shoe-box version of our dining room, with her table and her centerpiece and all the chairs, including the one with a broken leg spoke. The pink wallpaper was perfect, complete with the swirly white flowers just above the chair guard. The chandelier was fashioned out of a paper clip and cotton swabs. No dolls, no representations of people. Just the room, empty and silent, clean like company was coming, waiting to be useful. The way my mother liked to keep it.

I remember her reaction as she perched the old sneaker box on her lap and peered inside. She looked afraid to move an inch, like she might jostle something out of place. She held my hand so tightly I almost allowed myself to tell her she was hurting me. But then I saw the look on her face, and even though I was young, I knew that look wasn't because she was proud of me, but because I had surprised her. I had done something she hadn't known I was capable of. I had made something way better than a turkey hand drawing or a traced picture of a duck.

Mom grabbed my face by the chin and stared into my eyes. I stared at the tiny dark line between her eyebrows, the present her face had bestowed upon her for her thirty-fifth birthday.

"God has given you a gift," she said, her thumb too rough against my jawbone. I could feel her nail digging into my skin, but I didn't dare move. "Don't waste this."

All that seriousness directed at a ten-year-old. Mom was always hard on me, wanting to make sure I did things the way she thought they should be done, that I knew my life wasn't just important to me, but represented everything she had given up in her own life to have a baby. Always these stories about this *child* who stole her dreams, this horrible burden she was suffering with this *kid* someone apparently forced her to create and then raise.

Oh, wait. That's me!

I might have let the miniatures remain something I had done in the past if it hadn't been for Matthew. I guess that was because it seemed like a useless talent. I could make tiny things. Big deal. Then one weekend my mother asked me to clean some stuff out of the garage and I found some of the miniatures I'd done in high school. They were very "I'm a sad teenager" pieces, things like miniature cemeteries glued to algebra books. Matthew thought they were fascinating, and insisted on putting them out on display. When people would come over, he'd ask, "Can you believe she can do that with her hands? I can't do anything like that."

It was that same feeling I'd had when Mom paraded me around the crafts store. It wasn't so much validation as it was the confirmation that I was special. Someone I loved thought I was unique. And being unique confirmed what I needed to be true: that I wasn't replaceable.

That night in bed, as I was babbling on about the next year with Matthew, I mentioned that there was enough interest in the photographs of my miniatures I'd posted on the Internet that I might be able to get my miniatures seen in the real world, in bigger places. Maybe I could get a show going.

"That sounds exciting," he said. "Get seen outside our living room."

I liked the way he dressed for bed, in actual pajamas. He'd comb his blond hair over to the side and tuck himself in like a dad from the fifties, complete with the day's crossword puzzle from the newspaper. I often wanted to buy him a little pipe he could stick in the corner of his mouth after he fluffed his pillows. It made me smile, how he always seemed very official. *This is bedtime.*

I tapped him on the newspaper. "I wonder what's going to happen to me," I said.

Matthew lowered his crossword as he jammed his pen into his mouth. He stayed that way for a while, long enough that I decided he was pondering the answer to nine-across, and not my future.

But then he said, "You never say, 'I wonder what I'll do,' or, 'I can't wait for this to happen.' You sit and wonder what will happen *to* you. As if you have no choice. As if life just does things to you. You have free will, you know. You can make things happen for yourself." He picked up the crossword and whacked it back to upright, concentrating again on the lower right quadrant.

With as much drama as I could muster, I fairly levitated off the bed, like I was consumed with the spirit of indignant outrage. "You're right," I said. "I *can* make things happen for myself. So I'm going to use all my free will to go sleep on the couch."

He leaned his head back against the wall and made a sound deep in his throat, as if I were somehow being unreasonable. "Charlotte . . ."

"No, you seem to think it's okay to talk to me like a parent. But I am not interested in sleeping with my mom," I told him.

"Don't you mean your dad?"

"Not when you sound exactly like my mother. It's creepy. And stupid. Good night."

I made sure to make my motions in the living room as noisy as possible, so he would know that I wasn't finished with our conversation. It worked, and Matthew came out to the living room a few minutes later to apologize. "Don't sleep out here. Please."

"Why would you talk to me that way?"

"I'm sorry" was all he said. Because back then, that was all it took. One smile from Matthew, one apology, one touch of my lower back, and I would find a way to get back to how I had felt just before I got upset.

When it comes to problems or misunderstandings, I'm like a sitcom character. I want anything bad or uncomfortable to be over within twenty-four minutes. Less than half an hour later, I want us to be swapping apologies, each of us insisting we are more to blame, but have learned "something very important" from all of this. I want things resolved so the credits can roll, so that I can find rest.

More than likely, things went bad between Matthew and me because I rushed the sitcom ending. I rushed through our problems so quickly we rarely discussed what was actually wrong. Things got ignored, or at the very least diminished. They got squished down and shoved inside me, piling up higher and higher, until one day I guess they clenched my jaw shut.

That night, after I'd left the couch and once we were back in bed, I curled around Matthew. He stroked my hair and whispered, "What's going to happen to us?" We kissed, and then answered that question together, silently, in the dark.

There was a time when I looked at Matthew and only saw All Things Good. I pushed everything else aside. I saw him and I smelled him and I felt him and I wanted that to be my future. But then.

Two words that hurt: "But then."

I once had hope.

But then.

5

When I get back to my desk, I find a McDonald's bag sitting on my chair. A Happy Meal, with a Hello Kitty toy.

Jonathan enters. "What are you doing?" he asks. I don't get tricked; I know he's on the phone, his tiny glowing earpiece on the side of him I can't see. If Jonathan isn't actually sitting at his desk, he will be on the phone with his wife. Cassandra likes him to give constant updates on his life, apparently worried that if he has a single minute to himself, one that hasn't been thoroughly dissected with her, he will morph into a different person and they will grow apart. Mostly Jonathan spends his time placating Cassandra about whatever it is that's currently spinning her world into chaos. I would try to convince Jonathan that this is no life, but first of all I am not one to be giving out relationship advice, and secondly it appears Jonathan likes feeling needed.

"No, don't try to fix it," he says to Cassandra. "We'll go buy a new one."

As he lowers himself into his desk chair, I notice the tag from his khakis poking out over his waistband. It's making his shirt ride up, exposing a tuft of dark back hair.

Jonathan's not very tall, not very fit, not very smooth, and always just a tad sweaty. I don't exactly know how, but he makes this work for him. There's something about this that comes off as confidence rather than having given up, which is much closer to the truth. It doesn't make any sense. The unhappier he is, the more people like him. The ruder he gets, the more people laugh. I've tried to figure out his secret, because if I could determine whatever it is that makes this short, damp, hairy man one of the most popular guys on our floor, I would be a bajillionaire.

I rap my knuckle on my desk to get his attention. I point to my bag of McDonald's and mouth a thank-you. He shakes his head, eyebrows up, like he doesn't know what I'm talking about. "Whichever one you want, my love," he says into the air. "And if that lamp isn't good enough, then we'll get another new one, and another, until I buy you the sun if I have to." He pauses. "No, I'm not being sarcastic. But I have to go."

He flings the earpiece at his desk, but it lacks the flair of slamming down a phone. "Half an hour I've been hearing her complain about a lamp," he says. "I need my wife to have more friends. Do you girls honestly call each other and complain about lamps? How do you stand each other all day?"

"Thank you for my lunch."

"Honestly, I didn't do that."

"Okay, play it that way," I say, as I turn back toward my computer. I glance at the screen and then freeze.

For the first time in a long time, there's an email from Matthew. Subject line: PLEASE READ.

This can't be good. Lots of other subject lines out there he could have chosen. This one needs attention. *My* attention. My hand trembles as I drag the mouse and click.

C—I was trying to make some room for my weight bench, and I was wondering if you would come pick up your sewing machine. I'll put it in the closet if you don't want it, but I thought I'd offer before I moved it.—M.

When I read the message to Jonathan I can't help the sarcasm that pours out of me. I practically shout the initials Matthew used as placeholders for our names. As if anybody ever calls me C. As if that's how we talked to each other. "Oh, C, my darling. My sweet. My one and only. I love you. I love you, C."

But somehow Jonathan doesn't get how flippant and arrogant Matthew's message sounds. Instead he asks, "So, are you going to pick up the sewing machine?"

"I think there are more important things to talk about than the sewing machine," I scoff.

He slumps down in his chair, the heel of his right hand mashing his forehead. "Oh, no. Don't go crazy."

I play with the mouse cord, bending it into little loops. "I'm not. I won't."

"You *are*. I see your loony brain working. You're making a big deal out of a couple of sentences."

"Well, in those couple of sentences he's saying a lot."

"He's saying he wants to make room for his weight bench."

"Obviously he wants to exercise more."

"What an asshole."

I rip open the Happy Meal bag, stuffing cold french fries into my mouth. As the only thing that truly soothes a woman scorned is chilled salty potato.

"I know you know what this means," I say.

"He wants to be in better shape?" Jonathan snakes his hand up the bottom of his shirt to root around his belly button.

The friendship boundary between us has long been clearly defined and is constantly reinforced.

"Exactly. To impress someone. Someone obviously not me, because he wouldn't want to move my things to do it."

"Where does he keep his weight bench now?"

"That's the thing. He didn't have a weight bench when we were together. This is new. This is New Matthew, the one who works out with a weight bench."

"I think if he was really looking to meet chicks, he'd go to the gym. Not work out at home. How lazy is that dude?"

I shove more fries into my mouth, enjoying the mushy-salty feel against my tongue. I shrug. "He's trying to claim territory in the house. That's why he wants me to go get my sewing machine."

"You don't have to go get it. He said he'd put it in the closet."

"Oh, great. Off to the closet with memories of me!"

He leans over to steal one of my fries, and then steals five more while he's chewing the first one. "When was the last time you used that sewing machine?"

"That is not the point."

"I'm done with this," Jonathan says, turning back around to his desk.

My computer dings. More email. This time it's from Petra.

R U COMING 2 MY GIRLS NITE PARTY TOMOOROW NITE?—P.

Shit.

Besides being functionally illiterate, Petra is a friend and coworker. Well, she started as Matthew's best friend's girl-friend, which made her a forced friend (but one I genuinely enjoyed) whom I helped get a job here. Then Petra and Pete got married and she got a promotion, and then Matthew and I separated, so these days she's Matthew's best friend's wife and my boss. Petra is my supervisor and awkwardly estranged friend. It's *great*.

Add to that the fact that once Petra got her promotion, she worried people would accuse her of giving me special treatment, so when we're at work she acts like she barely knows me. She's all business, not wanting to have personal conversations. Her emails to me, if they aren't about work, are extremely brief, almost in code:

TONIGHT: 8 PM. THE PLACE WHERE WE SAW CREEPY GUY. I'LL BUY.

I can't skip out on Petra's party, because then she'll tell Pete I wasn't there, and he'll tell Matthew I wasn't there, and then Matthew will think I'm either too sad to go to Petra's party or too busy having fun to go to Petra's party, and I don't know which is worse. I turn to ask Jonathan, but he's busy looking up lamps on the Internet. I've bothered him long enough.

I write back to both Matthew and Petra, telling each I'll be by tomorrow night. I'll stop by Matthew's for my sewing machine, and then I'll swing by the liquor store, and then I'll go to Petra's and get superdrunk.

And *that's* how this girl spends her Friday nights.

On my way to the break room to throw away my Happy Meal bag and get a cup of coffee, I run into Goth-Girl Francesca. I mean I actually bump right into her, turning a corner. Our heads come so close together, I almost accidentally kiss her. Her dark eyes widen as she laughs.

"Oh, sorry," I say.

"It's fine," she says. "Don't worry about it." She wipes her bangs back with the palm of her hand. I see black scribbles across her skin, snaking up her forearms. Phone numbers written in pen. She points at my empty McDonald's bag. "Did you like your lunch?"

Is this small talk? "Um, I did. Yeah."

"Cool," she says, and walks away.

I take some comfort in knowing I'm not the weirdest one in this building.

6

I blame Matthew," Andy says, pushing my hair behind my ear to inspect my temple.

We are standing in the kitchen, getting ready to make the mouth guard I bought on my way home from work. I'm grateful Andy is here to keep me from wallowing in what could be a rather pathetic evening.

He briefly kisses the soft spot where my jaw meets my ear. "I blame Matthew for lots of things," he continues. "Things that have nothing to do with you and your sadness. The other day someone knocked over the recycling trash can outside my place—broken glass everywhere—and I raised my fist to Heaven and shouted, 'Dammit, Matthew!'"

"I get it," I say as I turn toward the stove, hiding my smile. I'd thank him again for being here, but I know he's having a fantastic time at the event he has crowned my "Dorkination."

Andy and I became fast friends our freshman year of college, when we were stuck waiting in line for our IDs. It was aggressively hot that day, and we were on our second hour outside in the unwavering, unforgiving Los Angeles sunlight. Before we ever spoke a word to each other, a silent bond had already formed between us as our mood dipped from grumpy to spiteful. I think he was the first to make fun of the girl a few feet ahead of us, the one who was losing a desperate battle to save her hair and makeup. I joined in, pointing out the ones who were obviously hungover. By the time we reached the end of that line, we were the proud owners of two horrible IDs and a friendship that would last forever. We never dated, but we kissed once. It was a New Year's kiss, it felt inexplicably incestuous, and we agreed never to do it again.

We did get really drunk and go skinny-dipping once, the one time he'd gotten me to go camping. We were in some spot outside San Diego, a city where I would have been much happier in a hammock near a swim-up bar, but he wanted to show me how fun it could be to "sleep under the stars." I know this because I remember asking him then, "Isn't that why people live in Hollywood?" and he has still not given me the proper amount of accolades I feel that joke deserved, considering my response time.

There were a lot of things I didn't like about not having shelter for an entire weekend. It's pointless to list them, as they were the things that any normal human being would crave during the course of a day. I don't really understand why people would willingly wander away from plumbing or pillows. But I did like the sense of discovery, imagining we were exploring a brand-new world. I think I only truly enjoyed it because I pretended Andy hadn't already been here before and didn't know every step of the trail we were hiking. It made me able to get into the spirit of things while still knowing in the back of my mind that absolutely nothing unpredictable was going to happen. Like bears or coyotes. Or bears *and* coyotes.

At one point Andy led us to a private swimming spot where we could splash and play in the dark. Whenever I was out of the water, I would shelter my body with my hands, trying to be modest, until Andy said, "Don't worry. You do nothing for me."

"Thanks."

He was floating on his back, staring down at his tiny toes jutting out of the water. "It's not that you're not pretty," he said. "But I think of you as my sister."

I swam over to him, touched that he felt that close to me. As an only child, I'd always wanted a sibling, someone closer to me than anyone else who would be stuck with me forever. A twin would have been perfect.

"You really think so?"

Andy nodded. "Mostly because you look like my brother."

I grabbed the top of his head with both hands, trying to push him under, but he was stronger and ducked out of my grip.

"You kind of even have the same mustache," he continued, his laughter echoing off the cliffs, bouncing around us in the dark.

Andy dates lots of girls. They rotate in, they rotate out. The only thing I can find in common about them is that they all have voices like singing mice. I've made him promise not to introduce me to another one unless he's sure she's The One. Like, they must already have wedding invitations in the mail.

But who wouldn't fall for Andy? He's got that dark and broody look without the accompanying dark and broody personality. He's one of those freaks who actually likes working out. He also takes advantage of the parts of California one usually enjoys only in theory (hiking, surfing, tai chi in the park). Most people never actually do these things because it's hot and sunny and tai chi is boring. But Andy will throw himself into anything that might involve taking off some or all of his clothes, as he thinks a body as nice as his shouldn't stay under wraps. It would be a crime to cover such hard-earned perfection, and quite frankly rather unfair to people who have working eyeballs. Being familiar with the mostly naked version of Andy, I have to say he's got a point.

I'm so glad I'll never be Andy's girlfriend, because if I gained even three extra pounds I'd feel like a monster next to him. It is hard for Andy to find women who don't feel at least slightly physically insecure next to him, so he tends to end up with the most vacuous pretty girls in this city. Although I might be giving him too much credit here. He could be dating the most vacuous pretty girls in this city because there's no shortage of vacuous pretty girls in this city. Girls you wish you could hold down with one hand while you slice open their foreheads and jam some brains in with the other.

So while Andy plays around with all those girls, for about the past decade or so the woman in his life has been me. Lucky me.

"You should try saying 'Dammit, Matthew,' too," Andy says to me now. "Say it. 'Dammit, Matthew!' Just once. Please."

"I would, but I'm very busy." Using a pair of tongs, I dunk the mouth guard into a pot of boiling water, softening the plastic.

Andy frowns. "Blue? Why a blue mouth guard?"

"I thought it would be cuter," I mumble.

Andy gives a quick whistle, placing his hand on my shoulder. "That is sad to me. You are breaking my heart. Truly."

I know Matthew would have had a great time making fun of this, too, probably calling out football plays as I climbed into bed. *"SLEEP-97! DREAM-97 HUT HUT HUT!"* But now it's just going to be me, my pillow, and whatever book I'm trying to read in order to blank out the fact that these days I sleep completely alone.

I still reach for Matthew. I wake up sometimes with a pillow between my legs and one over my head, like I've been trying to swim through the bed in my sleep to find him. Actually, first I'd want to swim to the past, find *that* Matthew, put us both into a coma, and stay there.

The next step in my Dorkination must go quickly, or I'll have to start over. I pull the mouth guard from the water and cool it briefly in a nearby bowl of lukewarm water. Then I pop it into my mouth, jamming it against my upper palate with my tongue, trying to form a mold.

"Push! Push!"

It's Lamaze class for my face as Andy reads from the instructions in his hand. I stare at the little white flakes of skin that arc his thumbnails. Once he's eaten his nails to bloody chips, Andy moves on to his fingers, ripping the flesh away with his front teeth. He's embarrassed by this habit, so he hides the skin he pulls away in his front pockets. I am pretty sure he doesn't think anybody knows he does this, including me.

"Howph dah?" I try to ask, but my mouth is filled with the unfamiliar.

"Hot," he says.

I try to smile, but I start to cry. *"I'm hideoth!"*

"No. Come on. Divorce looks awesome on you."

I yank out the mouth guard as I take a step back. "Don't say that word."

"I *am* going to say it," he says, rubbing his chin with his hand, running his fingers over his lower lip in frustration. "And I'm going to keep saying it until you get used to it. He sucks, and you are getting a divorce."

"He doesn't suck."

Andy takes the mouth guard from my hand and places it gently in my mouth. "He kind of does. But mostly he sucks for you. Look what he's done to you."

He's not just referring to my mouth guard. I used to be considered rather slender, but I've become gaunt and bony. It's not from dieting, or doing one of those I'll Show Him ridiculous crash-exercise routines designed to make you look as fantastic as possible. I'm not doing anything; I'm simply falling apart. My stomach won't hold on to anything for long before it churns and rips with anxiety, making my appetite disappear entirely. My complexion used to elicit compliments from even passing strangers. I was so proud of my skin, pink and glowy and rarely in need of any makeup. But these days it is blotchy and angry, cracked and chafed from crying fits. I look like I've been lost in the Alps for weeks—raw and jagged, inflamed and weak. It's only getting worse: lately the bathtub has become clogged with clumps of my hair. As I dislodge the globs of wet, brown twists from the drain I can't help but think, "Good. There's less of me."

I'm watching Andy watch me and I realize how small and helpless I must look. Self-conscious, I tug a brittle strand of my hair behind my ear, hiding it.

"You don't know—," I croak, before the mouth guard halts my speech. The muffled oddity of my voice is pathetic, and I am stuck between a laugh and a sob as Andy pulls me hard into his arms. He smells like coffee and spearmint gum. I clasp my fingers together behind his back and hang on, leaning into him, my face smashed against his perfect chest. The mouth guard is pinching my gums, a thick hunk of plastic at the back of my tongue. I have to concentrate if I want to be able to breathe.

I'm outside of myself, like I'm standing in the corner, watching this beautiful olive-skinned man hold the bony, weary brokenheart in her tiny, white, understocked kitchen. The superhero embracing the damsel in distress.

I want to thank Andy for being here, to let him know how much it means to me that he's been beside me even as I've fallen apart in front of him like a paper doll in a rainstorm. So I finally say something he will appreciate, or at least I try to say it. The words Andy wants to hear tumble out of me, smothered and strained, almost a whisper.

"Namiht, Madtew."

7

Continuing his dominance in the category of Super Best Friend, Andy has brought me a present. Actually, he has brought a present for my mouth guard. He pulls a tiny pink box from the pocket of his jacket. It's a mouth guard holder, complete with a sticker of a unicorn.

"I want you to always feel pretty," he says.

I thank him by opening a bottle of wine, from which I pour a hefty glass.

After giving my mouth guard box a home on my night-stand, I find Andy wandering around my apartment, glass in hand. "What I like about your place," he says, "is that you didn't wait to make it look like you live here. You aren't living in a pile of not-yet-unpacked boxes."

"Thanks. And just so you keep feeling that way, don't go in the closet."

The closet is where Charlotte has hidden all of her not-yet-unpacked boxes. She hasn't opened them because she doesn't know what to do with their contents. When she thinks about exactly what she has stored away, fear sets in. Actual fear. It only took close to thirty years, but Charlotte finally has a monster in her closet. To be more accurate, it's hundreds of monsters, all in hibernation, waiting for their moment to attack.

The wedding pictures are in there. This beast of burden Charlotte did to herself. She didn't want to part with some of the best photographs ever taken of her. Maybe one day she will be less emotional over these pictures and will find someone skilled enough in Photoshop to make this album look like she was the life of the party at someone else's wedding, but until then, the box stays hidden. And since we're revealing secret monsters here, it's time to admit that a good percentage of the real reason Charlotte took that box of pictures was so that Matthew couldn't have it. She wanted Matthew to go looking for it one night and realize it was gone, just like she was. Yes, Charlotte took that box on the off chance this fantasy sequence would play out someday—a scene she will never actually get to see, even if it happens. Matthew is more likely to realize Charlotte packed the thesaurus. If she really wanted her money's worth on a moment when Matthew realizes all he truly lost by her moving out, she should have taken the coffeemaker.

Most of the boxes of books remain unopened, because each book tells a story more personal than the one within the pages. Charlotte was still happily attached to Matthew when she was reading the book, or he bought it for her, or it's one that belongs to him and she packed it—either accidentally or with extreme purposeful spite. Charlotte thinks that if she keeps the spite boxes safely sealed shut, she won't have to return their contents. They simply won't exist. This way she can start to make everything be in limbo. Why should it just be their relationship? Put the world on hold! First possessions, then careers, then exhaling after inhaling—make absolutely everything wait to see what happens next.

Charlotte has created an apartment that looks like the home

of someone who isn't falling apart, and it's commendable she did it in such a relatively short period of time. But she actually has a little secret. The reason nobody seems to notice that her apartment is more functional than comfortable is because everyone is blinded by her most impressive new purchase. Charlotte spent the majority of her moving money on something that would capture all of anyone's attention. Not normally a gadget girl (she still prefers holding an actual map in her hand to a picture of a map on a PDA, and somewhere in that Closet of Exile there's a box of cassette mix-tapes), she surprised herself at her tech-lust for this piece of electronic wonder.

It's not just a television. It is the Fuck You Television, and there are no regrets. Just one look, and there are no questions. There are only whistles of awe. It is the main attraction of the apartment, a constant companion for what Charlotte knew would be countless nights alone. This television is wondrous.

The Fuck You Television is bigger than any other television Charlotte has ever owned, and was the largest she could find that wasn't designed for a screening room or a conference hall. One tap of the power button and the Fuck You Television plays a little chirpy song, announcing its arrival. "Hello, I am ON!"

It is white. Not black, not silver. White. This alone seems to be impressive enough to most people. But that doesn't stop the Fuck You Television from offering features Charlotte never even bothers to investigate, like how it can become a gigantic computer monitor for her laptop. This television wants to have a meaningful relationship with her iPod. The Fuck You Television can be seen from the street outside the windows of the apartment, which prompted the purchase of Fuck You Curtains.

See, the "Fuck You" in Fuck You Television isn't directed at anyone in particular. There's no "you," exactly. It's more of a feeling, a thought. It comes from when Charlotte first moved into *this apartment, when she looked over her list of everything that needed to be purchased in order to make it through one day of life in her new home. Bed, towels, toothpaste, table, television, hangers, storage boxes, Scotch tape, pencil sharpener . . . it was overwhelming.*

You don't realize how many things you've acquired in life until you separate yourself from someone else. When you leave, you feel like you don't need or want anything. That's for the best, because if you choose to take some of the things, sorting through to determine what's essential, you'll never finish packing your home. You'll never leave. Instead you will stand amid empty moving boxes, growing increasingly furious as you ponder important life decisions such as which whisk to pack and which one to leave. Do you keep the one from the wedding gifts, or the one from when you first moved in together? Which Whisk-o'-Love-and-Commitment won't reduce you to tears whenever you decide to make pancakes? (Answer: get a new whisk. They're everywhere.)

Besides, why would you want something that you used to share with someone who's currently killing you from the heart out? No good. Start from zero.

But starting from zero meant that when Charlotte wanted to make a peanut butter sandwich, she'd reach for a knife, only to find: no knife. Also: no peanut butter.

This would have Charlotte angrily marching the aisles of the supermarket, thinking, "Fine. Fuck you, Peanut Butter. There. Never have to buy that again. And here's a knife. Fuck you. Now I have a knife. Fuck you, Knife."

Now she's got the Fuck You Trash Can, the Fuck You Shower Curtain, and the Fuck You Lamp. These things only have to be purchased once, and the more you slash items off your list, the easier it gets. There. Done. Fuck You Scrub Brush. Fuck You

Weird Little Bowl I Need by the Bed for When I Take Off My Earrings at Night.

The Fuck You Television was her finest purchase. There was no doubt that it was new, no doubt that it was hers, and there was nothing anybody could say about it other than, "Wow, look at your television!" In fact, the best part of the Fuck You Television is that Charlotte doesn't have to do anything to entertain people when they come over other than turn that beautiful machine on. It is an instant crowd-pleaser. Right now, Andy's adoring it, watching an episode of House, wearing a grin almost as large as the screen.

"This thing is amazing. The resolution is so ridiculous I can count Hugh Laurie's pores!"

I crawl onto the Fuck You Couch beside him and bury my head in his lap.

"Thank you for my mouth guard case," I tell him.

"*Mnuh*," he says, more to the television than to me.

"Can I ask you something personal?"

"That's the best kind of question."

I roll toward him, burying my face in his stomach before I ask, "Do you know a good therapist?"

He kisses his palm and places it on the back of my neck, his gaze still transfixed by the Fuck You Television. "Of course I do, *mamacita*," he says. Then he nudges my chin with the tip of his finger, his eyes finally meeting mine as he says with rare sincerity: "I'm really glad you asked."

8

I'm spending my lunch break auditioning for a therapist. Apparently my health insurance will cover therapy sessions only if the counselor and randomly assigned caseworker decide I'm in need of mental guidance. As if it's not humiliating enough to ask for help getting through the day, now I have to find out if I'm the only one who thinks I need it. What if they're both, like, *"Suck it up. Other people have actual problems, you baby"*? I think the trick is to sound just crazy enough to make this therapist find me entertaining in a weekly-visit sort of way, but not balls-out-crazy at the level at which I need to be institutionalized.

The irony does not escape me that in Los Angeles even the shrinks make you go in for an audition. Maybe I should bring a head shot and résumé: *"Hi, I played Girl Who Loses Her Shit at a Ruby Tuesday about six months ago for the Santa Monica Third Street Promenade Players. Here's a CT scan of my skull, a list of past boyfriends for references, and the last birthday card I received from my mother, the one that says, 'Soon you won't be able to make me grandchildren.'"*

Andy reluctantly admitted that he knew about this therapist from an ex-girlfriend who had gone through a divorce.

"She seemed completely healthy about the marriage breaking up," he said as he handed me Dr. Hemphill's number. "But luckily she was still riddled with self-doubt. It's much easier to break up with them that way."

"Maybe he's not such a great therapist, then."

"He's a *psychiatrist*," Andy said, pausing for a second as he got distracted by his own arm muscles. He squeezed his right hand into a fist as he watched his forearm flex.

"So?"

"It means he can give you really good drugs. Which you should insist he do. Tell him you can't sleep, you can't eat, you can't stop crying."

"That wouldn't exactly be lying," I pointed out. "But you don't think it's weird to take pills that will make me trick myself into thinking everything's okay?"

"At this point, I don't know how you could think that would be a bad thing."

This morning, when I made today's plan, I made sure to insist I follow through on this therapist thing. I told myself I could at least go and see what it's like. One session. Today's plan also includes going to my house where Matthew lives and making it through Petra's party, so honestly, this is the easiest part of the plan. I might as well get it over with.

As I stand in the lobby of this nondescript corporate building, searching the directory for the correct office, it dawns on me that I'm not nearly famous enough to have all the same problems as the celebrities in this town. At least let me have the fun part of their lives too, like the rooftop parties and the drugs and random sex scandals. Or the clothes and limos and photo shoots. I get the doctor's appointments and the divorces? Lame.

This building houses chiropractors, accountants, and the occasional questionable pseudobusiness, like life-coaching. Dr. Hemphill's office is on the third floor, but when I first enter the elevator, for a second I debate pushing a different button, taking my chances telling my problems to some random tax assessor rather than face the specialist. I'm a bit nervous as to what's going to happen once I start talking to someone who deals professionally with the things I'm dealing with personally.

I hope he tells me exactly what I need to do. You know, like a doctor would. "Apologize three times a day with meals. Stay away from alcohol for a few weeks. Get lots of rest and take these pills to kill the voices inside your head." I could do that; I could follow a doctor's orders.

In the waiting room, there's a little red button I'm supposed to push to let Dr. Hemphill know I've arrived. There's also a chart with my first name scrawled across the top. I push the button and get to filling out my paperwork. This takes much longer than it used to. Grief has made me stupid, or perhaps the constant debate going through my head has left me permanently distracted. All I know for sure is that my brain has decided it no longer cares to remember my driver's license number or Social Security number. Instead it prefers to let a single lyric from a song I hate play over and over again in my head. That's what it spends its time doing. Not remembering what medications I'm allergic to, not remembering a series of directions when I'm driving somewhere new. It would rather just hang out wailing, *I got a little change in my pocket, going jing-a-ling-a-LING!*

"Charlotte?"

"That's me!" I don't know why I just cheered like that. Like I've won at bingo or something. Do I want him to think I'm this happy, chipper girl? Well, maybe it would help me land the part. *"This girl should be terribly depressed about her life, but she's got this scary-crazy smile on her face, so . . . medication time."*

I follow him through a tan, heavily carpeted hallway into his office. It's stuffy in the room, which is smaller than I would have expected, with a glass coffee table in front of a purple velour couch. He gestures for me to have a seat as he eases into a small, black seat that looks like an ottoman with armrests. Does he sit on that all day? It looks so uncomfortable. I suppose I'd do the same thing to myself if I had to stay awake while people droned on about their problems for hours on end.

I drop my purse by my feet, then wonder what that says about me and how I treat my belongings and opt to place it beside me on the couch instead. I am aware that the audition has already started as I watch Dr. Hemphill look over the paperwork I filled out, perhaps assessing my penmanship. Do I write crazy enough? Maybe I should have done it in crayon. Maybe I'm supposed to bark, or perhaps eat the orchid he's got on the coffee table between us.

Dr. Hemphill is taller than I would have thought, and younger, with this wild patch of blond curls on top of his head that needs some attention. One of the buttons on his shirtfront is undone, and I practically have to sit on my hands to keep from walking over there and fixing it. It's not like his skin's exposed—he's wearing a T-shirt underneath—but it makes me feel like I've rushed him, that he doesn't have time for me. That I'm in the way.

Dr. Hemphill hitches his pants at the knee as he crosses his legs and asks, "So, Charlotte. What brings you to therapy?"

His casual tone is off-putting. Do people come to therapy

with a chummy vibe? Isn't this serious business, the delving into life crises and behavior patterns? Shouldn't he have more of a solemn tone? At least appropriately solemn enough for someone who feels desperate and lost enough to seek help? *Seek!* That's the word we use! A word we use for blind people, for the starving, for refugees. Seeking is urgent! I am at such a low place in my life that I'm actually seeking the advice of someone on how to simply *be*. So it would be nice if he treated this meeting with a bit of gravity.

It occurs to Charlotte Goodman at this moment that perhaps she shouldn't worry so much about the audition, as she's crazy enough without having to embellish even the slightest bit.

"I thought I told you on the phone why I'm here," I say to Dr. Hemphill.

He leans over on one elbow, pulling at the back of his curls with his hand. "I know you're struggling with decisions about your marriage," he says. "But that has to do with a third party, someone who isn't here. I meant what specifically about yourself brought you here?"

"Well, Doctor," I begin.

"Call me Gary," he says.

First of all, that's not a doctor's name. *Gary* is the name of the guy at the pet store, the one who keeps trying to talk you into buying that electric litter box. I need this man in front of me to be a doctor all the time. I'd rather call him Dr. Doctor. "Dr. Doctor, MD." I want this to feel as medical as possible. It already bothers me that he looks like anybody else.

"Well, *Doctor*," I say firmly, letting Gary know exactly what kind of relationship we're going to have. "I guess I don't know, then."

He nods. Maybe that was the right answer. "Why don't you start by telling me why you left your husband?"

"Because he left me first."

"And what was that like?"

"When he left me, or I left him?"

"Your choice."

So I tell him.

9

Charlotte Goodman spent her final night in her marital house packing and alone.

Matthew didn't want to be a witness to her exodus and had wisely chosen to go to a poker game with some friends. Before he left, as he stood at the door with his hand still grasping the knob, he said as a good-bye, "I'm going to stay at Pete's tonight. I don't want to see tomorrow."

It was their last moment together, in their home as husband and wife, for at least a while and possibly forever. Charlotte found herself rubbing her wedding band inside her palm with her thumb.

He had given her this ring in front of the restaurant where they'd had their first date. It had all gone so wrong for Matthew, his proposal. The restaurant had been closed for repairs, they'd gotten rear-ended as they were parking the car, and a hungry Charlotte had become grumpy and bickering, intentionally antagonistic with every new topic Matthew started. He was trying to get her to be quiet long enough so he could drop to one knee. Finally he realized the gesture would shut her up. And it did. Until she said yes.

As Charlotte watched her husband stand in the doorway,

ready to leave for not the first time but perhaps the last, she couldn't shake the feeling that this wasn't truly happening, that this was happening to other people, that she was playing a part in a movie about some other sad life.

"Wait," she said. She went to him, putting her hands on his face, where they'd rested thousands of times before, the familiarity of his body sending an instant message through her own:

This is your husband.

She knows this man. She knows this face. This head. This hair, these warm green eyes. The scar under his chin she's noticed every time she's looked up at him. His smell, soapy and clean, like he just stepped out of a shower.

This is your husband. What are you doing? What are you risking? Why?

At this moment, memories flood Charlotte's head. She sees him at their wedding, staring at her as she walked down the aisle like she was his answer, his face overcome with elation, the happiest she ever saw him, before or since.

Somehow Charlotte can hold this image in her head while also feeling Matthew's kiss, both on her mouth and on the bridge of her nose—memory kisses, tender moments of affection surrounding her, reminding her, embracing her as if begging her to stay.

Another memory: a scribbled drawing he once made for her of a hopeful-looking little stick figure standing next to a childlike rendition of a house with an open door, six wavy lines forming a square topped by a triangle. Written underneath in a scrawl: "Will you live with me?"

These memories take boxer's swings at Charlotte's heart, her organs tiny punching bags. Why does the brain do this to us when we leave a relationship? What sense does it make for it to spend seemingly half its time reminding us of all the things we will miss? Perhaps we are worried about the ramifications of sticking to our own decisions. When the mind stays semifocused on the possibility that things don't have to end, there's always another moment when everybody could stop all of this nonsense and pretend they were just kidding, that it was all a mistake. There's still time to sit down, swap apologies, and then make out like crazy. You just have to grab it, but you choose not to.

Or rather, more importantly, you both choose not to.

In their last moment together as husband and wife in their home, both Matthew and Charlotte stood still, most likely so as not to shake each other in frustration. As much as she wanted him to produce a time machine from his pocket that could jettison them back at least a year, he must have been wishing she'd step out of her lunatic costume and go back to being the woman he had thought he'd married.

But they couldn't do either. So they did nothing. Once something that huge is in motion, perhaps nothing can make it stop.

She kissed him, lightly, before he pulled back with a sniff, shoving his hands into his pockets. "Figure it out," he said. And he left.

Charlotte stood alone, staring at the space where Matthew had just stood, a place where not long ago he'd carried her over the threshold. And now she was about to cross that line again, in the other direction. All she could hear in her head was, "You can't take this back."

Dr. Hemphill has been scribbling as I've talked. He stops at this point to ask, "And do you want to take it back?"

How can he not know I ask myself that every day? "It doesn't matter," I say to him. "I can't."

"Maybe because you've crossed the threshold," he says, and I detect a slight smirk.

"You're proud of yourself for that one," I say.

"A little." He grins.

It was a good word for what was happening. *Threshold.* Matthew and I were both pushed to the edge, and now we're challenging each other. A line has been firmly drawn between us, and it's possible we're both stubborn enough to remain separated for the rest of our lives.

There's a box of Kleenex on the table beside me. I grab it, pulling the box close to me, hugging it in my lap like it's a pillow or a kitten. I'm not crying, but my nose has started to run from the dry air in the room. Dr. Hemphill keeps the heater on too high.

"So, what is it that's really worrying you?" he asks, his foot making a lazy bounce as if we're in the middle of a leisurely Sunday morning brunch and we're waiting for our second round of mimosas.

"Not to sound too dramatic," I say, "but I think I broke my life and I don't know if I can do the thing that will make it right again."

"You're saying there's only one right way?"

His question makes me snort. Of course there's one right way. One way is wrong, and then there's one way that's right. People live their lives the right way or the wrong way. He should know this; his job is supposed to be to make sure people live the right way.

Instead of saying any of this, I shrug.

Dr. Hemphill shapes his hands into a little tent and rests them under his chin. He actually does that, like he's impersonating a therapist. I bet in sign language that's the symbol for psychiatrist, that little hand tent. Is that something they're forced to do, or something they pick up in shrink school? Maybe he does this all the time, whenever he's pretending to know everything. Probably even at poker games it's his tell.

Once he busts out the Shrink Tent, then everyone knows this man is completely winging it.

His ottoman-turned-chair creaks under him as he adjusts it to sit higher. He asks, "What would happen if you were to fail at something?"

The question confuses me. "What do you mean, fail?"

"Fail. Not do it right. Get it superbly incorrect."

"Well, I suppose I'd do it right the next time."

"What if there was no next time?"

"There's always a next time. I would get it right eventually."

The Shrink Tent unfolds, and this guy named Gary crosses his arms. "What if you were not just bad at something, but horrible? And what if your failure caused others to experience pain or suffering? What if you really fucked up?"

The question takes my breath away, not because he has cursed, but because instantly I know with complete conviction that for the rest of my life, whenever I have a moment to myself, when I'm at a red light, when I'm waiting for conditioner to finish working through my hair, when I'm reaching for a cardboard sleeve for my to-go coffee cup, I'm going to hear that question in my head.

What if you really fucked up?

"Are you saying I fucked up with Matthew?"

"I'm not talking about your life right now," he says. "I'm just wondering what would happen if you . . ." He points a finger at me, pausing for effect. ". . . just you, made a huge mistake. If you fucked up. Would the world end?"

"Yes."

He writes me a prescription for Lexapro.

10

I'm staring at my old house. Our old house. But now it's not our house, or my house.

It's *his* house. And I can't get out of the car.

I know exactly how many steps it will take to reach the door, and which step will creak as I get there. The key to the front door will appear between my thumb and finger without a single glance at the ring in my hand. It will feel like I've come home again. I'm afraid I won't be able to handle it.

I once cried so hard in that house I blew a blood vessel in my eye. It happened in the middle of the night, a few days after Matthew had come back home. This is probably more information than needs to be shared, but I had woken up from the middle of a . . . sexy dream. I guess I wiggled myself awake. I was still turned on, but the only person next to me was this man who had just put me through emotional hell. I didn't want to wake him up, because having sex would make him think everything was okay, and it wasn't. I couldn't take matters into my own hand right there, as Matthew was too light a sleeper.

I tried to go back to sleep, but my body was ready to go. In the dream I'd been touching myself, which is disappointing as far as fantasies go. *The one place where I'm allowed to fool around with anybody, and I'm choosing to play with myself? My dream brain is useless!*

I was left with only one choice: covert masturbation, teenage-style.

I tiptoed to the bathroom, the tiles cold under my feet. There's a fan that whirs when you turn on the light, so I left the switch alone. I grabbed a washcloth and jammed it into my mouth. I didn't want to make a sound that he could hear. *This is how prisoners must do it*, I thought to myself.

Easing myself to the floor, panties around my ankles, my back mashed hard against the cool porcelain of the tub, I concentrated on the feeling between my legs. Still, no matter how good it felt to rub up against myself, I was fully aware of where I was: hiding in the dark, on the floor, trying to get some kind of pleasure in the middle of this mess I was in.

No wonder I couldn't stop the sadness from creeping in, soaking from my heart to my lungs, down to my belly, getting closer to where my fingers were desperately trying to get a job done.

No. He doesn't get to have this part of you. This is all yours. Don't let him take it. This is your body. Claim it.

There, in the dark, during the weirdest masturbation session of all time, I heard those words. I don't know if it was my voice or the opening statement from my narrator. And I'm thankful I didn't stop to think about whether or not I was hearing the voice of John Goodman as I had my hand between my legs. I rocked, keeping my breath steady and low, until I felt far away. My teeth ached from clenching terrycloth. My tongue was bone-dry.

Afterward, I stayed in a ball on the floor, waiting for my heartbeat to return to normal, trying to keep my breath quiet.

But when the peace settled within me, it left room for more sadness. I saw myself on the floor of my dark bathroom, saw what I'd go through to get away from my husband, and I broke open again. The washcloth fell from my mouth as I silently wept and wondered what I needed to do.

The saddest thing about hitting some kind of emotional breaking point, about having a moment when you are reduced to an animal state—rubbing yourself and crying, naked and fetal and feral—is that eventually that moment ends. Reality sets in. Now you're just a woman with her underwear tangled around her ankles, huddled on the floor of her pitch-black bathroom. In order to cope with this tragedy, you start having very normal thoughts about this rather un-normal place you've put yourself in. Like:

I wonder how long it's been since I cleaned this floor.

Even being quite kind to myself it had to have been at least a month. This meant I'd just had the dirtiest orgasm of my life. I instantly felt germs crawling all over me, around me. This is why Matthew found me at three in the morning in the bathroom, wearing only my underwear, scrubbing the floor with a bucket of bleach.

No telling what must have gone through his head when he discovered me. Regardless, it was still better than if he'd known the whole truth. After he left the bathroom, shaking his head and muttering, I wondered what I looked like. I stood up to check myself in the mirror, and that's when I saw the burst blood vessel. It looked like I had Ebola in my right eye, blood pooling from one corner toward the dark brown curve of my iris, the other side bloodshot. Half-naked, reeking of cleanser, hemorrhaging from the skull—I had turned into a zombie. *"I am sad zombie crazy wife-lady. Why won't you love me?!"*

If only Matthew had known what I was going through, the things I didn't tell him. Would that have made him reach for me? Could that have broken through his pride?

I'm in my car now staring up as the house looms above me. I grip the steering wheel, convinced I can't handle finding out what my home looks like without me.

Never mind. I'll get a Fuck You Sewing Machine. And maybe while I'm at it, a Fuck You Weight Bench.

Or, more accurately, a Fuck Your Fuck You Weight Bench.

Petra has incense burning that I can smell from the sidewalk outside her apartment. She cheers as she opens the metal gate that guards her front door. "You're here! Thanks for coming."

"I couldn't miss it," I say, accidentally telling the truth.

She's wearing a paper party hat with a too-tight elastic band that's sure to leave marks on her fleshy cheeks. The corners of her mouth are stained in little dashes of purple. Clearly for Petra, this party started some time ago. She's in a flirty red dress that makes her look ten years younger. A tiara crowns the long brown hair that flows over her shoulders, down toward her tiny waist. Petra has a hot coed's body attached to the face of the girl who hates what she sees in the mirror. You can see her past sadness mapped across her skin; how she became one of those women who spend a lot of money to change anything that once made others judge them. There are acne scars under her jawbone, the tip of her nose angles in a way that tattles on her plastic surgeon, and the space between her eyebrows hasn't moved a centimeter in the past three years. Petra is trying to freeze an image of herself that exists only in her head, and unfortunately she is losing the battle.

This birthday party is not a celebration but her defiant rebellion against turning thirty-one.

"How are you?" she asks, tilting her head in that way people do when speaking to those in mourning.

I don't have an answer she's going to like, so I nod while swallowing, pulling my lower lip into my mouth. I find this gesture gets me off the hook. People prefer to project their own feelings onto my face, anyway. Right now, no matter what I'm actually feeling, Petra has her own opinion of how she would feel if she were in my situation, and therefore she'll treat me the way she thinks she'd want people to treat her if she were me.

"Let's get you drunk," she decides, putting a heavy hand on my shoulder. It seems it's less in support of my emotional state and more for supporting her determination to stay upright.

If there's one thing that everyone in the world seems to agree on, it's that I have license to be a complete lush, pretty much twenty-four hours a day. I'm sure that won't always be a good thing, but for right now I'm happy about it. That means if I end up sobbing in a corner, people will assume I've had too much to drink.

Within a minute, I'm holding a glass of Merlot, compliments of Suzanne, the boisterous girl in sales who only talks to me when she thinks Petra's watching her. She's both impossibly tall and impossibly blond, shiny all around, not just in her hair but in her twinkly spark-blue eyes, sheen glaring from her taut, tanned skin. Her beauty is so shocking that every time she looks at me, I feel I'm reacting as if a policeman's flashlight is in my face. I'm squinting from the intensity.

"I've decided my job tonight is to make sure you keep drinking this," Suzanne says, all *twinkle, twinkle.* "Don't let it get empty or I lose two points."

"Two points where?"

Suzanne floats her free hand into the air as her eyes close. "In the game of life." As her hand passes in front of her face, I see the sparkle of her diamond. Even more twinkle. I forgot Suzanne recently got engaged, but I know she's about to remind me, as she finds a way to work her wedding plans into just about every part of every conversation.

Sure enough, she asks, "Do you like this wine? Because I think we might have it on the table during our wedding dinner. Do you think this wine would go with fish? Does fish need white wine? Because the fish is red. Well, pink. It's salmon. Maybe that's boring, but it's the one thing that doesn't seem to conflict with all the food issues everybody has now. You know what I mean? Oh, of course you do. You're married, you've done this."

I nod, smile, and gulp my wine, pretending it's filled with all the words I'm swallowing.

Suzanne's whole face changes, and it's like a supernova. It's stunning. She goes from twinkle and shine to a black hole of remorse. I know she's trying to move her face into a shape she recognizes as grief, but since she's never had one bad day in her life, she's only mimicking the pain she's seen in others. It looks painful, as if the muscles a face would normally use for sadness have atrophied due to lack of use, and are now twitching and writhing in useless confusion.

"God, Charlotte, I'm sorry." She clamps her hand down on

my arm too tightly. "I shouldn't be having these conversations with you, when I'm getting married and you're getting . . . going . . . what you're doing . . . through."

That's kind of the best thing I've ever heard. That's exactly what it feels like. I'm *getting going what I'm doing through.* My failures force others to think of themselves as more fortunate, and therefore they need to choose their words carefully as they talk to me, as if I'm a *c-h-i-l-d* who might *u-n-d-e-r-s-t-a-n-d* what they're really saying.

"It's cool, Suzanne," I say.

"You're better off without him."

Eventually that statement was coming, but it still drives me nuts every time. What a terrible thing to say to anyone who is going through a separation or a divorce. It's as bad as the opposite clichéd phrase people fling at me all the time: *"If you're meant to be together, it'll work out."* What Disney fairy godmother came up with that twisted logic? If you can even buy into the concept of "meant to be together," which implies that people are destined for one another, paired off in the future beyond their own control, abandoning the idea of free will and reducing us to molecule bundles bouncing around until we bang into the other fated atom ball. To me, that isn't romantic. Taking out the element of choice means that no matter what happens, no matter what anyone does in life, there's only one way things can be, all because some other thing or being or force or whatever declared it to be so. We're all just human puppets dancing on the invisible strings of an unknowable creator. How depressing.

What I really don't understand is how anyone can look someone in the eye and say it'll only work out if you were meant to be together. Why would anyone dare to sound that ominous with someone's heart? It seems cruel to make such whimsical predictions that could go horribly wrong.

And on that subject, there's one more seemingly optimistic line of bullshit people keep giving me.

"At least you don't have kids."

Let me go ahead and expand that to any sentence that begins with: *"At least you . . ."* I don't need to hear people say how it could have been even worse, or rate my "luckiness" in this terrible situation. Whenever someone says to me with that wistful, patronizing squint, "At least you don't have kids," I want to look her (always a her) right in the eye and say, "We tried for years. It's because I'm barren. But thanks for reminding me of another reason why my husband might have left me." I just want to watch them suffer.

I'd rather they said, *"At least you were never in a car accident in which you lost your legs."* That sounds like something I should be giddy over. But being grateful over the lack of having a child with someone I love sounds twisted. I understand splitting up would be harder on everyone if there were children involved, I do, but there would be children, which sounds much more . . . I don't know, *hopeful*.

If I never go back to Matthew, there will never be a family. Our family. He'll slip away, wander off, and someone else will find him. Someone else will love him. Someone else will start a family with him. Which means one day she might whisper into his ear, *"At least you never had kids with her."* And right then no matter where I am or what I'm doing, I will feel those words like bullets through my stomach.

So now I try to stop listening the second anyone begins a sentence with: "You're lucky . . ." They are going to finish it up with something so insulting I will feel smacked in the forehead with their shortsighted observation that minimizes my life decision into something as trivial as the voting-off of a reality show contestant.

There's really only one sentence someone can say in this situation that is 100 percent accurate and appreciated. It takes only two words, but they go right to the heart of the matter, and while they can't heal, they can at least empathize.

"That sucks."

It's the only sentence that's appropriate.

I'm afraid Suzanne thinks I've blacked out or gone into some kind of schizophrenic personality shift, so I rejoin the conversation by changing the subject. "I like your new hair color," I tell her.

Her hand flies to her locks, and she pulls. "I hate it. It's all wrong. Robert hates it, too, although he's too nice to say it."

"Where is Robert tonight?" I ask. "You got him at home stamping invitations?"

"I wish," Suzanne laughs. "He's off at some poker game with Pete."

"Ah," I nod. "Probably with my husband."

And then we stand there enjoying the thirty or so seconds of awkward silence I've just accidentally created.

The funny thing is, I never call him "my husband." Never. Not to people. I always call him Matthew. Because that's his name. *Matthew.* Not Matt or Matty. He's not into nicknames, and he doesn't care for the baby talk of sweethearts, so he's not Babe or Honey or even Sweetheart. He was Matthew. He *is* Matthew. But I didn't mean to bring him up in front of Suzanne. It's just the truth. Robert plays poker with Petra's husband, Pete, and therefore plays poker with Matthew. So if there's a poker game going, odds are they're together right now.

Abandoning the job she so recently assigned herself, Suzanne finds a reason to be in any other room in the apartment immediately. I step outside for some air and silence. I decide not to speak for the next twenty minutes. It's the least I can do to help these other people.

Squished onto the tiny back porch, smoking a cigarette like it needs her full attention, is the Goth girl from work, Francesca. Her tiny fingers are pressing a closed cell phone to her lips; her nails are flecked with bits of red nail polish. She's peering through her dark bangs into the back window of the neighboring apartment. I follow her gaze to see she's watching their television. Letterman is interviewing someone I don't recognize. For some reason I find Francesca's presence to be very comforting, like that of an old dog napping on a porch.

It's good I'm in the middle of a twenty-minute vow of silence, or I might have just told her that. She nods at me, but that's it.

I roll the stem of my wineglass between my thumb and forefinger as I think about Suzanne's ridiculous conclusion.

"You're better off without him."

It's as if suddenly everyone feels free to tell me I've been making a terrible mistake all this time. Were they all thinking that when they raised champagne glasses at our wedding? Did they take bets in the bathroom between dinner courses?

Every time someone tells me that Matthew isn't good enough, I can't help but worry that at that moment someone, somewhere, is trying to talk Matthew into believing the exact same thing about me. Someone is saying monstrous things about me, confessing their utter contempt and disdain for my personality, my voice, my figure. Do they tell him he's lucky he didn't have kids with me? That I would have made a lousy mother? Do they rip me apart and dismiss me with

Matthew the same way some of my friends act as if I'd broken things off with a casual fling?

When those words come at me, someone else's judgment of the kind of man Matthew is, I want to stomp them, deflect them. I find myself defending Matthew's actions, even the things that drive me crazy, things that upset me or hurt me. I don't want to be told we outgrew each other, like one of us is stunted, malformed.

No matter what, he's still my family. He put a ring on my finger and became my family. Nobody gets to talk smack about my parents, so why do they think they have the right to talk about my husband in such a manner? These women say kinder things about my hips than about Matthew, and my hips have done way more damage to my self-esteem over the years than Matthew could ever achieve.

From inside the apartment, Petra's yelling for everyone to gather. "You have been ordered by the birthday girl!" she adds.

"Shit," Francesca mutters, flicking the cherry off her cigarette before jamming what's left of the butt into the front pocket of her jeans. She then holds the door open for me. "Hey," she says. "You really don't have to be here, you know. You've got this free pass. I don't know why you aren't using it. I'd be as far away from this mess as possible."

One of the million things that's supersensitive on me right now is my Bullshit Detector. I can spot insincerity in the slightest inflection, the tiniest of twitches.

The flip side is that when someone is being legitimately compassionate, it goes right to the core of me. Francesca wasn't just trying to convey empathy; I felt it. It's real. Empathy is my Kryptonite. I can't even thank her because it'll make me break down like I did with Andy in the kitchen. Instead I nod.

"Feel free to tell me to shut up," she says. "I just figured if you're hiding on the porch with me, you're rethinking being here. You should bolt."

"No, I'm okay," I say. "It's Petra's party. I can make it through a party, can't I?" This is how my life goes now: asking a near stranger to tell me if I'm going to be okay.

"I'm sorry I weirded you out in the break room earlier," she says. "I should've told you I brought you that Happy Meal."

When she realizes I'm too shocked to say anything, she shrugs, blushing. "I thought you needed some Happy."

• • •

Petra's standing at her dining room table above a massive display of crafts materials. Markers, glitter, poster board, and stacks of magazines cover the middle of the table. "Come on, everybody," she says. "I thought we'd all have fun doing this."

Everybody has their own notion of what makes up a party. For some it involves alcohol, mingling, and music. For someone like Petra, it's bonding and soul celebrating. She tells us that we're each to take a poster board and create a "Wish Collage." She's put out all these magazine clippings and leftovers from her scrapbooking phase to make us goop together a visual representation of all that we haven't yet accomplished in our lives. Bright side: at least I won't be the only one focused on what's missing from her life. It's a real good thing there's booze at this party.

We sit at the table, most of us reluctantly. But *twinkle-twinkle* Suzanne dives right in, holding up a bridal magazine, laughing. "I don't need this one anymore!" The heavy tome bends around her knuckles as she looks for someone to congratulate her. But the only sound is the rapid-fire snapping of pages and pages of glossy magazines flipping in determined focus. A blonde eating from a bag of popcorn snatches the magazine out of Suzanne's fingers without a word.

Petra pastes a magazine cutout of a hammock onto the poster board. "This year, I will focus on being relaxed," she says. "I'm going to put this up in my office, and I'm going to remember this year that peace is only a mental decision away."

Only the rich can have this kind of impossible, selfish life wish.

I watch these women scratch their heads, staring at advertisements of happy women, thinking, "*Do I want that underwear she's wearing? Would that make me happy? Getting new underwear this year is a realistic goal.*" With one well-intentioned project, Petra is undoing years of collective therapy.

I recently heard that 40 percent of Americans say they don't worry about anything at all. I don't understand how that's possible. There are things to worry about everywhere. Fine, get past the major things, like health or traffic or the sudden changes in weather or wars or the possibility that one day there will be no such thing as TiVo. Maybe most people don't spend time worrying about the personal decisions their friends and family have made, or about when to do laundry, or what's for dinner, or if they remembered to lock the back door when they left to do laundry. Almost half of America says they never spend a second worrying about why they can't fall asleep or what will happen when they do fall asleep and end up sleeping through the alarm because they're so tired from staying up late worrying about not being able to sleep. Then what do they spend their time thinking about? Do they just walk around all day with dial tones in their heads?

I'm worried about what to put in my wish collage, and I'm worried about what *not* to put. If I focus on one thing, something else is going to suffer. If I layer a ton of pictures on top of each other, something's going to get smothered. What if one picture being bigger than another makes it more important? What if one font grabs the universe's attention more than another? What if I can't find a picture of the thing I really want?

And if I knew what it looked like, wouldn't I have figured out a way to have it by now?

I can worry about all of this and 40 percent of Americans don't even come close to thinking about these kinds of things? Well, then I'm really worried about *them*.

I've got Monkey's Paw–level anxiety over this wish collage. It has become the most important series of decisions I'm being forced to make, and even doing nothing is doing some damage to my future.

After half an hour, my wish collage contains only one image: a bottle of sunscreen.

A skinny girl I recognize from the break room looks over my shoulder. "That's so great," she says. "A very simple message to your spirit. 'Take me out of here.'"

Skinny girl, you are reading my mind.

The women around me are clucking and chuckling to each other, trying to make jokes about their unfulfilled needs. At some point there was a shift in which the women began focusing on tangible things. Objects. New cars. Shoes. One girl plastered a picture of a laptop to the corner of her poster board. "This is the year I'm going to change jobs. And maybe write a book." Then, realizing she has just announced her desire to leave the company to a room filled with coworkers, she adds, "I mean, once I write the book, maybe I can change jobs. Otherwise, I'm so happy getting to hang out with all of you every day."

Francesca elbows me, peering out from under her dark

hair. "I wanna hide the word *herpes* in all of their wish collages. So a year from now, they have the man they want, the house they want, the job they want, and raging, fiery herpes."

This makes me laugh. "See, I'd rather hide a surprise pregnancy in there," I tell her. I switch to a ditzy voice: "Well, I got everything I wanted, but then I got this baby, so now my carefully planned life is over."

"What are you two giggling about?" Petra asks suspiciously, glaring over her bottle of glue. "Don't make fun. Some of us take this seriously."

"So do we," Francesca says, turning her wish collage on edge so it's on display. "Extremely seriously. I made sure to include everything I want to happen for me in the next year."

She's assembled a sentence, ransom-note style: MAKE SURE LUNGS AND HEART KEEP DOING THEIR JOBS.

"I've never been very ambitious," she explains.

Suzanne clicks her tongue against her teeth. "This thing really works, you know," she says. "Last summer, I swear to you, I wish-collaged Robert into existence. He wasn't there, I made the collage, and two days later I saw him on Match.com, saw he was looking to get married as well, so I asked him out and now we're getting married."

"Romantic," Francesca murmurs under her breath, but a couple of the other women near us also hear her, and they are unsuccessful at stifling their giggles.

Suzanne's face falls into something that seems like disappointment but is probably more like pity. "I would think that you two, of all people, would want to give this a try. I mean, no offense, but you both could use some help."

Petra lifts her head from her project, trying to decide whether or not to intervene.

Francesca says, "I didn't see the porno magazines on the

table. But I guess you did, since you clearly put a picture of a vagina on your wish collage."

The shocked sound that comes out of me is so sudden and uncontrolled, I think I just barked.

Francesca raises both of her fists and shakes them in celebration. "And hey, look, Suzanne! It does work! Your wish came true! You're a total cu—"

I clamp my hand down onto Francesca's arm, forcing her to change her curse word into a yelp.

The other women quickly dip their heads back into their work, a silent ring of brown-rooted blond crowns moving in unison, as Suzanne's face flashes crimson with fury.

"Just be careful," I hear myself say. "What you put on there, I mean."

Now the eyes in the room are back on me.

Charlotte Goodman should probably shut up right now, but unfortunately she hasn't even filled that Lexapro prescription yet, so she's completely on her own here. Let's watch as she ruins yet another night of her life using only her voice and her complete lack of self-control.

"Because you could get everything you want and then realize it all came at a cost. Like, by the time you finish renovations on your bathroom, your husband is having an affair. That might sound a little extreme, but I'm warning you. You don't get something for nothing. Make sure that car is really something you want, because you could end up being very alone driving in it."

It is remarkable how Charlotte Goodman can condense what would appear to be the entire series of "Monologues from Emo-

tional, Pathetic Women" into one speech. This isn't amateur hour, folks. She's quite advanced in her ability to be her own worst enemy. All we have left now is for Charlotte to run from the table, crying.

And there she goes.

I excuse myself and run to my car with the familiar, unstoppable tears streaming down my face. I am upset mostly with myself for being unable to hold it together in public yet again.

"Ghost Girl, wait!"

I stop in my tracks, surprised the nickname worked on me. Francesca is quickly by my side.

"I can't believe you were going to ditch me back there," she says, putting a hand on her hip. "With the crazy bitches. I don't want to be at some work birthday party. Take me with you."

"You don't have a car?"

"No, my boyfriend dropped me off. He's out and won't be picking me up for hours. Please, Ghost Girl. Save me from this place. If I have to collage my future I will end up gluing a gun to that thing."

She lights another cigarette and I watch her, small and smiling, the moonlight making her look like a teenager. Yesterday I never thought of her, and now she's the girl who put a Happy Meal on my desk and is running away with me from Petra's crap birthday party.

"Where do you want to go?" I ask her.

"Anywhere there's coffee."

"Get in."

12

Four cups of coffee and two plates of fries later, Francesca has a diagnosis.

"You need to go outside."

"It's cold out there. It's November."

"I mean with capital letters. Go. Outside." She makes jazz hands in front of me, like the world is dazzling.

I've told her as much as I can handle in the hour and a half we've been inside this diner. Other than repeatedly leaning over to check the time on her cell phone, she has listened without the patronizing pity face. Whenever she has interrupted me, it was only to say, "That sucks." Just like I've always wanted to hear.

"I am outside right now. With you. And I went to Petra's party."

"That was a work function. Going to the apartment of your sorta-ex-husband's best friend's wife who also happens to be your boss is not a normal party. That's fulfilling every obligation at the same time. I mean go out and do things. Act like a single person."

I wrap my hands around my coffee mug, wishing it were warmer. "But I'm not a single person."

"Kinda, you are," she says. "And if you don't try it, you'll never know if you don't want it."

"Sounds like no fun."

"And definitely don't take the Lexapro. I think drugs are a last resort."

"This isn't my last resort?"

She drops her head into her arms. She's got her sleeves pushed up, and I notice a bruise near her elbow, on the top of her forearm. It's one that's been there for a while, swirled with shades of green and yellow. "Trust me," she says, "you are not there yet. I know what that looks like."

I believe her. There's something in her eyes that makes her seem like she's lived through something I am only starting to understand. "You okay?" I ask.

She pulls herself back in her chair, arms folded at her chest. "What if I told you I knew how to get you on the other side of this, but you'd have to do exactly what I told you?"

"Oh, really? You can do that?"

"I can." She hands me the straw from her drink. "Can you make something out of this?" she asks. "Make me a miniature, like you told me about."

"What do you want?"

"I don't know. You're the artist."

"I'm not. I haven't made anything in months. Not since my gallery show." That's a lie. I made things after that. I stopped after Matthew left. I put everything away one morning and didn't touch it again.

"See? You were a real artist. When are you doing another show?"

"I'm not. It kind of messed things up in my marriage."

"I thought you didn't know why he left."

"It's complicated."

"I like hearing about complicated things."

Francesca's cell phone lights up, buzzing so fiercely that the table hums. She lunges for it, opening it like it's Christmas and the phone holds the one present she's been waiting for all year. She reads a message, nodding and smirking.

"Sorry," she says to me. "Just a second."

"No problem." I start bending the straw in my hands, trying to figure out what it wants to become.

As she types a reply, I'm impressed with how quickly she's got her thumbs flying. Her mouth forms half words as she types, smiling. After a few seconds, her phone buzzes in her hands again. She silences it with a button and quickly writes something back.

"Boyfriend?" I ask.

She scrunches her nose. "I feel like an asshole doing this in front of you. I'm just going to tell him I can't talk to him right now, as I'm busy saving the life of my new friend. I mean, I'm just guessing I'm your friend. Don't tell me I'm not. You might decide you want to be friends, and Jacob will be happy if I tell him I have a new friend, so don't say anything that'll make my boyfriend sad, and I'm sorry that I'm gushing like this, but it's kind of new and still very exciting and not messed up yet, so cut me some slack and then we'll get back to your mess of a life, okay?"

I can't believe how much more animated she got from a shot of attention from her boyfriend, and it makes me ache a little, missing the way a message from someone you love can instantly make everything seem brighter.

"It's okay," I say. "Other people can be in love. It doesn't offend me."

She finishes her text and puts her phone down but not away. "So," she says, flushed and grinning. "Will you do what I tell you, if I promise it'll make you feel better?"

"I don't like promises."

"You're not cool enough to get away with that sentiment," she says, arching an eyebrow.

"I don't. Promises just tell you how someone's going to let you down."

"Yes, I believe I read that on a Hallmark card."

"You don't have to tell me you're going to do something if you're going to do it, but if you *promise* me, that means you know there's a chance you won't do it, and then you won't."

"Are you talking about me, now? Or Matthew?"

"Everybody."

"Fine. Can I guarantee? Is that the same thing?"

It makes me nervous to be forming a potential bond with a near stranger. One day it might be that she no longer wants to be in this, and I will have to separate myself from her.

"I guess you can guarantee. You're offering me a service, not a relationship."

"Charlie," she says, "I'm offering you both."

"I don't know."

Francesca opens a sugar packet and dumps it on the table. She dips in a finger and sucks on it. "Listen, rule number one is easy. I already said it. Go outside. All caps. You can't keep falling asleep in front of the television. That'll send you back to your husband because you feel pathetic, not because you want to be married to him."

"I guess."

"Do you want to be married to him?"

"Mostly." I twist the end of the straw and form it into a

circle, tying a knot. I take her empty sugar packet and work it through the circle until it forms the shape of a bowl.

"If I were in your position, I'd be living the ultimate girl life right now. Have fun, have a fling, get drunk, go sing. And other things that rhyme. Do whatever it takes to become your own woman. Then you can decide if you want to share that person you are with someone else."

"That sounds exhausting. And like I might need anti-biotics."

"I'm not saying skank out and get VD. Jeez. Isn't Matthew seeing someone?"

"I don't know."

"If that guy was my boyfriend, I'd be totally stalking his house. And for the record, it's total bullshit that you don't live in that house anymore."

"For the record, I'm the one who left."

"You're the woman. You're not supposed to be out on your ass. He should be a man and find someplace to live. Because, *for the record*, you're only in this situation because his ass left you to begin with." Francesca takes the last fry and drops it into her mouth. Ketchup hangs on her upper lip as she grins. "Having fun yet?"

I am. It isn't just that she has listened, but she has made me feel like things could be okay. She's in front of me because she has chosen to be, not because of an obligation. Over the months my other friends have been whittled down to just Andy, mostly because he's the only one with absolutely no connection to Matthew. And there's only so much more I can ask of his patience.

I take a breath. "Okay, Francesca. I will Go Outside."

"Great. And once you master that, you'll learn the next rule."

"Going outside is less of a rule, and more like a task."

"*You're* more like a task," she snaps back.

"Can the next rule be Do Laundry? My closet is a mess."

"Yeah, it won't be that. We're gonna get you a life, Charlie." She yawns. "Let's bounce. I'm finally tired."

I hand her the straw miniature. She gasps, shaking her bangs out of her face as she balances the twisted white plastic on the tip of her finger. "It's a coffee mug!"

"You like it?"

"I love it. You're amazing."

She pretends to take a sip from her tiny mug and then toasts my giant one.

"To new friends."

"And to Going Outside."

13

O ne day I will find out who taught my mother how to send a text message, and I will force that person to read every text my mother ever sent me until he or she breaks down into a puddle of regrets and apologies. Because whoever it was didn't teach my mother anything about what kinds of messages are appropriate for texting. He or she must have said something like, *"It's easy, Elaine. You just push these buttons to write whatever's important, and then push this green button here, and as long as you make it sound like you're trapped in a flaming car, then the person you want to talk to will immediately call you back."*

More important, this person must have told my mother that she didn't have to worry about spelling or punctuation, and that you could make a word as short as you wanted and nothing about your message would be confusing.

It leads to moments like right now, when I'm walking into my office and I get this series of mind-jarring texts:

YOUR MOM WANTS 2 KNOW IF U R CUMMING.

MATTHEW SHOULD CUM 2.

FRIDAY. OLIVE GARDEN.
CUM 4 MY BIRTHDAY.

My mother's text messages are like spam from Mexican Viagra suppliers. It's beyond disturbing.

I send a message back to her: "HI, MOM. WILL CHECK WITH MATTHEW, BUT I WILL DEFINITELY BE AT YOUR PARTY. LOVE TO YOU AND DAD.—CHARLOTTE"

I know it seems weird to sign my text, but twice before my mother has replied with, "R U REALLY MY DAUGHTER?" and it was too tempting to write back, "I HOPE NOT."

I call Matthew, but it goes to voice mail. I hang up before I leave what would only have been a babbling message that would no doubt have included an unfortunate tangent about my mother asking me about his orgasms. Instead, I opt to text him, letting him know the time and place, asking if he'd like to be there.

This time, I do get a text back: "YOU STILL HAVEN'T TOLD YOUR MOTHER ABOUT US."

I can hear the accusation. This isn't a question. This is enough to let me know that he's told his family. Most likely he won't be able to attend my mother's birthday dinner, not because he feels awkward but because he'll have a previous engagement. Overjoyed by the good news, his mother must be throwing celebratory fests every night.

He sends another text: "I HAVE PLANS THAT NIGHT. SORRY."

Plans. Just "plans." He's got plans. Things to do. Matthew's very important out there, with his *plans.* Matthew, who used to come straight home after work, do extra work in the spare bedroom until dinner, then watch exactly one hour of television before getting into bed with his nightly crossword puzzle, now is too busy with *plans* that keep him out on a Friday night. Not to mention wherever he was last night when he wanted me to pick up my sewing machine.

I know I'm probably not supposed to care, or at the very least it's supposed to make me want to make my own plans and have my own fun. But right now, I just want to know what Matthew's doing with his post-Charlotte life. How can I find that out?

Crap. I'm gonna Google my husband.

You know how you have to click through a million things to get online, to get a new version of iTunes, to buy a book on Amazon? Since there's already a million clicks and agreements you have to go through, there might as well be one more. One giant pop-up window that says:

ARE YOU SURE YOU AREN'T GOOGLING AN EX?

But there's no pop-up, no warning, nothing that keeps me in check. Nothing that adds an extra second to decide if this is really what I want to do. So right now, in front of me, I have found Matthew's Facebook page.

That's new.

Matthew doesn't usually bother with online social networks. He doesn't really bother with any kind of social network, if I'm being honest. His core group of friends goes back to the third grade. They all still hang out, play fantasy football together, and get dressed up once a year for a wedding or funeral.

I'm not exactly sure where to start being angry about this site. Okay, the easy one right off the bat is the photo he's using, the one right next to his name. It's a great picture of him—he's laughing, leaning against a wall with his hands in his pockets. He almost looks like a model. I know why he looks this good. Because *I took this picture.* Right before I snapped the shot, I said, "Okay, give me Hot Model." At first he tried to get me to get rid of it, because he thought it made him look like he liked boys. Someone must have informed him that I wasn't the only one who found the picture to be hot.

Matthew has a few fun facts listed about him. He graduated from Harvard Law. He loves football, beer, and "chicks who can whistle using their fingers." Didn't know that. Also: I can't do that.

"Is that him?"

I jump in my chair with a yelp. Francesca has a way of walking into my office without making a sound. I suppose it's because she's so tiny, but honestly, I don't know how she can get herself through what's basically a crack in a doorway, just sliding into a room like an envelope under a closed door.

She pushes me aside, leaning over to grab my mouse. "No offense, but I really thought he'd be cuter. What with the way you're going on about him all the time."

"He *is* cute." I sound entirely too defensive.

"I thought he'd be taller. And it says here he likes jazz music."

"He does."

"I just can't imagine you sitting next to this short dude all the time, listening to jazz music."

"He's not short. His knees are kind of bent in that picture."

"Well, what's with the 'chicks who can whistle' thing?"

"I don't know." I feel resigned. "I didn't know about this page. I just found it."

"You mean it's new?" Francesca's leaning closer to me now, leaning onto my arm as she pores over Matthew's page. The collection of metal bracelets on her wrist jangles as she moves the mouse, making her sound fairylike and magical. Her eyes dart back and forth, making the tips of her eyelashes catch on her bangs, the dark hair jolting in spurts like spider legs across her brow. Her mouth hangs open as she memorizes all this information.

I rub my eyes, suddenly feeling how long I've been staring at my monitor. I'm not sure how much time has gone by, but I think I've missed lunch. "Yes, it's new."

"Do you know all these people he's linked to? All his friends?"

"Some of them. Not the girls."

"There's a lot of girls."

"I know."

"They're young."

"Yes, I see that."

Francesca lowers herself to her knees in front of my desk, her chin resting just behind the keyboard. "This is why Jacob and I have a no-Facebook policy. We only share ourselves with each other."

Turns out Jacob is kind of a long-distance boyfriend. He's based here in Los Angeles but goes to New York every other month for weeks at a time. So while they've been dating for six months, it's really more like three. They spend much of the day sending and waiting for communication. It's why she's always got her cell phone in her hand. She says it's hard but worth it. He takes naps when he gets off work so that he can talk to her through the night. That's such a great time in a relationship, when someone will still organize his sleep patterns around a chance to hear your voice.

"Do you want my chair?" I ask, but she shakes her head. She clicks through Matthew's other photographs, his friends, all the messages they've left each other. She goes through everything I've been doing for the past couple of hours, but much more quickly. Still, she comes up with the same questions I have.

"Who is this girl who says she likes his eyes?"

"I don't know."

"And who the hell is this bitch who put up a picture of her undercleavage?" Francesca cups her breasts and poses at me, face twisted in mock innocence. A spot-on imitation of the girl in the picture.

"Also don't know."

She turns back to the computer, apparently determined to click through the entire Internet. "How's Going Outside working for you?"

"It technically hasn't happened yet."

"Okay, maybe that was too difficult a first rule for you," she says. She rubs at her wrist as she stares at the monitor, wincing. "You need to change your focus. It isn't about how you feel *with* Matthew, it's about how you feel without him."

"Do you write self-help books in your spare time or something?"

"New rule: Quit the Internet. Think you can do that?"

I don't, actually. So I try to change the subject. "You okay?" I ask, nodding toward her arm where she's been rubbing.

She points at the screen. "Look. This is the damn truth, right here. Did you see this?"

Under "Relationship Status," Matthew has: "IT'S COMPLICATED."

She's still nursing her wrist as she leaves my office. "You both seem to love that word," she says. "Quit the Internet."

14

I'll quit the Internet tomorrow. Tonight, I've poured a giant glass of wine and created a Facebook profile, complete with a fake name so that I can get to the bottom of Matthew's Undercleavage girl. It comes as no surprise that she's so desperate for attention she "Friend"-ed me back immediately, giving a complete stranger access to her profile.

I head straight for her photographs.

Predictably, Undercleavage is a skinny girl with huge fake boobs and a bad blond bob. I didn't even know they still made colored contact lenses, but I'm pretty sure this chick wasn't born with lavender pupils. She likes her jeans low-slung, her eyeliner blue, and—if there's a camera around—her tongue pointing down toward her chin.

Here she is holding a margarita, pretending to lick her own cleavage.

Here's one where she's with a group of girlfriends. She's the one in the middle with her hands throwing up devil horns, tongue licking her own face.

There's a picture where the woman next to her must be her grandmother, and yet, the tongue. It is still out of her mouth, this time pointing right at her grandmother. What woman threatens to lick her own grandmother in a photograph?

Occupation: pharmaceutical sales. Oh. One of *those* girls. A drug pusher, someone who gets prettied up and flirts with doctors until she finds one to marry her.

Status: IN A RELATIONSHIP.

Oh, really, Undercleavage? That's a big word, don't you think? Aren't you more like a rebound? More like Matthew's marriage is on the back burner, and you are what he can easily make in the microwave. Get it? You are nothing more than a Hot Pocket. And just like a Hot Pocket, one day he will regret putting you anywhere near his mouth.

Charlotte Goodman is rarely grateful to be alone, completely by herself. But the fact that there's nobody around right now to hear her call someone a Hot Pocket is truly a blessing.

Undercleavage has a name. It's Kallie. I'm sad to lose her nickname.

Kallie writes that she did her undergrad at Cal State Fullerton, but she's still trying to figure out what she wants to be when she grows up. *Adorable.* She likes surfing, sunshine, going vegan, going topless, and chickening out right before she gets a tattoo. She wants to meet Chris Martin someday.

I get an evil thrill out of the fact that Matthew is spending so much time with a Coldplay fan. I hope he has to hear "Clocks" every single day of his life. I hope she can't fall asleep without the sound of "Viva La Vida" playing on her nightstand. I hope she's forced him to watch DVDs of concerts, and downloaded every track they've ever made onto his iPod, demanding that he love Coldplay if he wants to be with her.

I hope he's drowning in Coldplay. I hope he's choking on

it. And when she's done, when he's at what he thinks is the end of it, may she start up with Dave Matthews Band.

I search through ten pages of photographs of this girl playing centerfold before I find one with Matthew in it. The two of them aren't alone. It's a group shot. They're sitting around a poker table, game in session. Her arm is slung around his shoulders and she's leaning into him for the picture. I can't see her outstretched tongue because it's covered by Matthew holding his beer up, toasting the photographer. There's a glint on his hand from his wedding ring.

Our wedding ring.

Wait. Stop everything. This girl has a blog. I click on the link.

She wrote "were" when she meant "where." Twice. She misspelled "San Francisco." She wrote an entry about how hard it is to maintain her bikini wax, lamenting the fact that her "pubes are out of control." She wants me to believe she loves having threesomes, but I'm calling bullshit on that.

Her dad died three years ago. I stop reading her Father's Day entry before I start to care about her, before I think of her as a girl named Kallie.

She claims to love to cook, but every night she appears to be going out to another restaurant or bar. Actually, she might have a bit of a drinking problem, as she often starts her entries by saying how drunk she is, or how hungover she is, or how she can't wait to be done working so she can start drinking. A drunk, Coldplay-loving prude. I wonder what Matthew's firm will think when he takes her to the Christmas party.

I click more links and find myself on another girl's page, one where Undercleavage has written a comment. "Shels! It's been so long! Can't wait for you to meet my boyfriend."

The word *boyfriend* is underlined. A link.

My finger acts completely and immediately on its own, clicking.

A new page opens. A Facebook profile.

But it's not Matthew.

It's some other guy. And he's got Undercleavage in every single picture. They're together—on the beach, at a bar, at poker. Both of them with their tongues wagging, devil horns flying, holding each other so closely their tans have meshed. His interests: "Kallie, Kallie, Kallie. What can I say? I'm in love!"

The upper corner of my laptop blinks, letting me know my battery is almost dead. I've just spent three hours learning the entire life of some girl named Kallie, a girl with an epileptic tongue who loves booze, Coldplay, and a gym-addicted frat boy named Wes.

Okay, so maybe Francesca has a point. Maybe it's time to quit the Internet.

15

Francesca can't stop laughing. "Please, you don't have to tell me the entire story again. But please repeat the part where I was right."

"You were right."

"Again! When will you realize I'm the only person who knows what's best for you?"

Francesca came straight over. She claimed she was here to seize my laptop, but she arrived armed with a full bottle of wine. That was a couple of bottles ago. I'm currently face-down in a pillow on the floor of my own apartment, drunk in ways I didn't know were possible.

"I am intoxicated," I say.

"Me too." Francesca slaps at her face with both hands. "I can't feel any of this," she says.

"Kallie would be so proud of us right now."

"Let's call her."

"We should."

"I feel so close to her. She'd love us."

"She would. We're great."

"We can't, though. She's out tonight."

I push myself up onto my forearms. "How do you know that?"

"I found her Twitter page. She's currently partying big time with her friends At-MarcyLand and At-Bootytown. I think there was a 'Woo' in there somewhere."

Francesca is also on the floor, lying a few feet away from me. She scoots down and holds up one foot. Her black sock is dotted with small white skulls and smells like the inside of her combat boot.

I swat at her foot. "Move that."

"No." Instead, she kicks her foot closer. Her toes touch my face.

"Quit it," I say, hitting her ankle with my palm.

"Better," she says, truly impressed. "I like it when you get mean."

"Then keep kicking me in the face."

She laughs. "That is exactly your problem, Charlotte. You don't get mean enough until someone is actually kicking you in the face."

"I can be mean."

"No, you can be a martyr. It's completely different."

Francesca wiggles on her hands, stumbling on her arms until she's sitting upright, staring at me. The drunken effort has caused her bangs to fall in front of her eyes, making her look a little like a furious terrier. "It seems like you never stop thinking about your problems," she says. "Never. Don't you get sick of that?"

"Hey," I say, but I'm too weary to protest properly.

"I'm drunk, so I can tell you what's what."

"Since when do you say, 'What's what'?"

"When I feel the need to preach to you, I turn into James Carville, okay?" Francesca holds up her wineglass and talks in this old-man Southern drawl. "I do declare, Charlotte Goodman, that you need to either get over yourself or get yourself a life. And Lord have mercy, I hope that you decide to do both, preferably in that order. Amen."

"You sound like Foghorn Leghorn."

"I think James Carville is hot," she says.

"You *must* be drunk."

"Hot," she says, pushing her sleeves up her arms. There's a nasty welt on her wrist, the kind of wound that compels something inside you to reach out and push it. So I do.

"What is going on with you?" I ask as I push. "Are you anemic?"

She yanks her sleeves down around her wrists. "It's nothing."

"Come on," I say. "I'm seriously concerned. What about that bruise on your ankle from earlier this week?" I reach down for the cuff of her jeans, but she's surprisingly fast and I miss her leg entirely, swiping the air.

"Stop," she says. "They hurt when you touch them, dumbass."

"Is something going on? Do we need to talk about Jacob?"

"No. He's out of town, remember? And even if he were in town, it's not him. He'd never do anything like that."

"Then why do you always look like you just survived a car accident?"

Francesca pulls her knees up to her chest, crossing her arms in front of her shins. As she hugs herself I am surprised at how small she can be. Ever since she exploded into my life, she's seemed much larger than this small-framed woman fetal on my floor.

She's staring at me, sizing me up. "Okay," she says, after another moment. She nods her head, licks her lips. She tucks the corner of her lower lip under a crooked tooth and sighs. "So you don't call the cops on me, I'll tell you what's been going on."

"Thank you," I say, relieved.

"But I want to be clear: I don't think you're ready for this. You didn't do Go Outside and you've failed miserably at Quit the Internet."

"This is part of the plan?"

"No, the plan was to get you ready for this. But I think I have to abandon the plan and just throw you in there."

"In where? Wait, are you in *Fight Club*?"

"Sort of." She chuckles as she scribbles an address on a piece of paper. "Go here tomorrow night," she says. "Don't dress up."

I'm standing in front of a warehouse in South Los Angeles. The billboards along this street are mostly in Spanish. I've never been to this neighborhood before. There are abandoned shopping carts tilted against the curbs. Puddles of trash line the street. A few transients have taken up temporary residence, organizing their belongings in possessive semicircles around their bodies. They're wearily propped between storefronts, resting beneath bold, multicolored blasts of territorial graffiti.

A white building with no discernible entrance looms over me. There's a parking attendant guarding the twenty or so cars in the lot. There isn't a vehicle less than five years old parked here, so it's unclear if his job is to keep people out or in.

"Do you know how I get in there?" I ask him, pointing at what I fear might be a sweatshop. I can just see Francesca forcing me to sew thousands of cheap T-shirts until I break down. *"Now will you leave your husband?"* she'll boom. And I'll wail, *"Yes! Anything! Please just let me go! My fingertips are bloody stumps!"*

The guard points around the corner, smiles at me, and winks. "Good luck in there," he says.

This morning, when I made today's plan, I told myself I had to go to this address, if only to be a good friend to Francesca, to find out why she looks like someone's throwing her against a wall when she's not at work. I'm sure whatever's inside is some kind of simple explanation. Maybe she's into kickboxing. Fencing. What do you do inside a warehouse?

I round the corner to find an open metal door. From inside the building I can hear squeaking, kind of like tennis shoes on a basketball court. Then there's this constant drone, a rumbling like something's coming, something's gaining speed.

I take a few steps forward, entering the building. Now I can hear women. They're shouting at each other, something urgent, but I can't quite make out what they are saying.

Inside the warehouse, it's gray and surprisingly bright. I zip my hoodie to ward off the chill in the air. It smells like someone turned an auto shop garage into a locker room. Like I'm getting my oil changed by a volleyball team.

Even though I can hear people, I still haven't seen anyone. There are benches in front of me; bags and shoes are scattered around, left unattended. Open suitcases are empty and abandoned, as if something went horribly wrong in an airport terminal.

I turn a corner to find a series of bleachers. The women are louder. I hear cheering.

There's a structure in front of me, about as high as my face, and at first I can't see what's inside it. It's got rails and posts, like an elongated wooden wrestling ring, but it's shaped more like a racetrack. A miniature racetrack, oval and tilted.

Standing in the middle of all of this, where it's flat and level, are about thirty women on roller skates. Not like the white roller rink skates with pink wheels that everybody had when we were kids. These look like leather tennis shoes with thick, chunky wheels in blue or green. Some are hot pink. The women are all in protective gear like skateboarders wear. Helmets, knee pads, elbow pads, and wrist guards. I see some of them chewing on mouth guards. Maybe they're all still learning to skate.

A group of the women peel off and stomp to the track together. Two other women wait a few feet behind them. A whistle blows, and the women in front all start skating. That's the word for what they're doing, but it doesn't describe what's happening. It's more like an attack, like an army on the move.

Wham-bam-bam-bam-bam-bam!

That squeaking I was hearing earlier, that strained squeal, was from the track. The wooden funnel is groaning and shaking under the pressure of these women like a roller coaster bracing the weight of a train out of control.

Another whistle, and the two women who were hanging back take off. Their speed makes me nervous as they propel themselves closer to the other women up ahead.

About ten of them swoop by, directly in front of where I'm standing. They slam into each other, pushing and leaning back and forth. It's chaotic, and I don't know where to keep my focus in this mob on wheels.

Sometimes they slam to the ground, tumbling on top of each other. It looks like it hurts, but they immediately get right back up and skate away. The protective gear they're wearing must be really effective.

They're talking to one another, too, yelling around their mouth guards. I watch one woman put her hand back, fingers wiggling. The girl behind her takes her hand, and then flings herself forward, rushing past the others. Someone yells in celebration. Another curses. I can't tell which girl is saying what because they're all so loud.

Bam!

A girl slams into the railing, right in front of my face. If the rail wasn't here, she would have flown right into me.

Bam! Another girl slams directly into her, into her back. The hit is so hard it makes my teeth hurt. My hands fly to my face and I hold myself like I'm in the audience at a horror movie. Before I can ask either of them if they're okay, they're gone, halfway around the track, rushing to join the others.

In the center, over where it's flat, the rest of the women are watching, shouting.

"Hit her, Killer! Hit her!"

"She's on your inside, Muffin! Don't let her get past you!"

"Call it off! Call it! Call it off!"

A whistle ends the action. The women skid to a halt, sliding to the center. Some bend forward, exhausted, hands on their knees, gasping for breath. Two women help each other up from where they've tumbled into a heap on the ground. One pats the other on the helmet.

"Woop woop!" I hear behind me. "You made it!" I turn around.

It takes a second to realize that the tough-looking bruiser in the black helmet and massive knee pads is Francesca. She's taller in her skates, and wearing not much more than tights, a T-shirt, and some booty shorts. I don't know what to say or think. I just start giggling.

"Yeah, yeah, laugh it up." She rolls a semicircle around me. "You're impressed, I know it."

"What is this?"

Francesca's eyes scan the track in front of us. "This," she says proudly, hands on her hips, "is roller derby."

17.

Francesca stands next to me as we watch the girls get into formation again. This time she explains what is happening.

"Roller derby is kind of like football," she says, her eyes never leaving the track. "Except a girl is the ball."

The group in front, that mob of girls, is called the pack. There are eight of them, four girls from each team, who are called Blockers. The two girls who are at the other line are called Jammers. They're the ones who score points.

When the whistle blows, the pack takes off. A few seconds later, the whistle blows again, signaling the Jammers to start skating.

The Jammers have to race each other through the pack. Once one girl has made it to the front, she's called the Lead Jammer.

"And then it's over?" I ask. "Like a race?"

"No, then she has to skate all the way around the track and go through the pack again. She scores one point for every opposing Blocker she passes."

But the other Jammer is still skating, and she's trying to take Lead Jammer position. The Blockers want to get their

Jammer ahead, while keeping the opposing team's Jammer behind. Usually by knocking her on her ass.

My brain can't compute what I'm watching. It still looks like madness on the track. The game seems to be over just as quickly as it started. A wheeled stampede.

"So when the whistle blows again, then it's over?"

"Yeah. That's called a jam, one round. Sixty seconds."

"What happens if the other Jammer gets all the way around?"

"Then she starts scoring, too. That's why the Lead Jammer should call it off before the other one makes a point."

I watch another jam. This time I notice the Blockers begin bumping into each other once the whistle is blown, knocking into each other's arms and thighs. One girl skids out, landing on her knee pads. But she jumps back to her skates so quickly it's like she's got rubber in her kneecaps.

A Jammer takes the lead. The girls watching from the center of the track are cheering, shouting at her to skate faster, skate harder, as she rounds the track alone. Within seconds she's breaking through the pack, angling herself between other girls, sliding through. A teammate reaches back, grabs her by the hand, and yanks her forward, shooting her past two other skaters.

"That's called a whip," Francesca tells me, pointing.

Once the Jammer gets through the pack, she pounds her hips with both fists. The whistle is blown.

"What happened?" I ask.

Francesca pats her pelvis. "That's how you call off the jam."

I cannot believe how hard these girls are skating, how fast they can go, and how brutal this sport it. In the next jam I see a girl slide pretty much on her face, narrowly missing getting her fingers run over. Another girl rams right into the wooden barricade. She bounces off, *turns in a circle*, and keeps skating. At one point two girls slam into each other and both fall down. Another girl quickly approaches from behind. Right when I'm about to shield myself from witnessing the pileup, the skater *jumps over them* and keeps going. Nothing seems to faze them.

These women are all different shapes and sizes, and they move like they were born with roller skates attached to their feet. You'd think they were in tennis shoes, the way they can maneuver themselves around. If I put on a pair of Rollerblades I look like an astronaut stumbling through an unknown gravitational pull.

"Do they get paid for this?" I ask. "Like, is this a job?"

Francesca just laughs.

The skaters take a break and move to the center of the track to start stretching. They take off their helmets, and I'm taken aback by the long hair that flows from their heads. After all that brutality, that aggression, their femininity makes them seem like superheroes.

Francesca turns to me, beaming. "What do you think?"

My heart is racing, and trying to imagine Francesca doing this makes me a bit nauseated. But, if I have to be completely honest, it looks like a lot of fun. Part of me wishes I were brave enough to try something like that, to be the kind of woman who could just strap on some skates, climb onto the track, and take off. It must feel pretty great to be able to go that fast, to slam into someone and not worry about the consequences. To be an athlete. To be strong and confident and fit. I get winded from climbing the stairs to my apartment.

"I don't know what to think," I tell her.

"It's the best thing I've ever done."

"It looks incredibly dangerous."

"Oh, it is. When I first started, I broke my collarbone." She points at her left clavicle, her tiny fingers sticking out from underneath her wrist guard. "That sucked."

"No, it sucks to lose your keys. You broke your *collarbone*."

"It got better. But I lost two months of practice. It took forever to get back in shape."

"How long have you been doing this?"

"About a year." She looks up, thinks. "Yeah, I can't believe it, but it's almost been a year. Wow, that went fast. I hope to get drafted to an official Hot Wheels team this year."

"And this is why you always look like someone just beat you up."

"Um-hmm. Because someone did." She points at a girl climbing off the track. "Usually, it's that one. She's a beast." I notice the girl's T-shirt. On the front it says HOT WHEELS DERBY DEVIL. The back has her name: KILLERIFIC.

"And you don't get paid for this?" I ask again. "At *all*?"

Francesca shakes her head, smiling. "In fact, it costs a whole lot of money to do this."

"Well, you're insane."

"And you're next. Come play with me. Meet me here after work and I'll put you in some skates."

I take a step back. "No way." Even if there's a small part of me that's curious, I couldn't possibly show up and do this. I'd look ridiculous. They'd send me home, laughing and pointing. "I don't even know if I remember how to skate."

"Don't worry. It's the rookie class. They call it Training Wheels."

"No thanks."

"You have to do it. It's the new rule."

"What rule?" I ask. "Kill Yourself?"

"No." I watch a bead of sweat roll from her forehead to her

chin as she breaks into a wide smile. "Do Something That Scares You."

A swell of laughter comes from the skaters as they chat with each other over their sport bottles.

"I think I'm better off trying to quit the Internet," I tell her.

"You'll never do that. But this you can do."

"I don't have knee pads. Or a helmet. I've never needed a helmet. In fact, I kind of don't want to ever need a helmet in my life."

She's grinning at me like the Cheshire Cat. "All you have to bring is a mouth guard. And I seem to recall you've got one of those. Don'tcha, Charlie?"

"Damn."

A girl calls from the track. "Pastor, get the fuck over here!"

Francesca jumps. "That's me."

"What'd she call you?"

But Francesca doesn't answer me. "Coming!" she shouts toward the track, as she hustles into her helmet and skates away. Over her shoulder she shouts back at me, "Tomorrow night! It's a rule!"

I'm gonna get killed.

18

I haven't been on roller skates since I was ten years old. This time, instead of a side ponytail and cute little terry-cloth shorts, I'm wearing two sports bras, an old T-shirt, and shorts that come to my knees. I wanted to look tough, like a girl who wasn't as scared as I am to be inside this warehouse, but I think I look like I'm ready to paint the garage.

Francesca skates over to where I'm sitting on a bench. Her giant black helmet makes her look like a carpenter ant. "You look great," she says. "Does everything fit okay?"

I feel like I'm wearing an exoskeleton. "The elbow pads aren't too annoying, but the wrist guards you gave me smell like they were pulled off a corpse."

"You're so hard-core. I love it. Ready?"

"I don't think I can get up."

She holds out a hand and helps me get to an incredibly tenuous standing position.

"Thanks, Francesca."

"No, I'm not Francesca," she says, shaking a finger at me. "Not here. Nobody knows who Francesca is."

"What?"

She rolls her eyes. "We have derby names." She points out

the other girls putting on their gear. "She's Bang-Up. She's Spank DaMonkey. That one's Sandra Day O'Killer."

"Wow."

"Shut up," Francesca says as she bumps into me with her shoulder. My skates roll out from under me and I immediately fall to the floor, smacking the concrete. A sharp pain shoots up my forearm.

"Yikes," Francesca says, helping me up. "Are you okay? That had to have hurt."

"It did."

As she helps me back to my feet, she instructs, "Try not to use your hands to break your fall. Fall toward your knee pads or your hips, where you have extra padding."

"You mean fall on my fat ass, not my skinny hands."

"Something like that."

"Why didn't you laugh when I fell? That's not like you."

"Well, I don't want you to quit yet."

There's the sound of wheels on the track picking up behind me as I watch the remaining few girls strap into gear. They look like action movie heroines prepping to battle fierce alien enemies.

I shake my head. "Derby names, huh?"

"Mock it now, but you've only got three months to come up with your own. And you'd better like it, because your real identity? It's gone."

I have to admit there's something intriguing about the concept of losing my real identity, about becoming someone else entirely. I could disappear under this helmet and just beat the crap out of people, become some kind of bruiser, a brawler. A take-no-shit, hot-shot lady. But it's absurd to think of myself that way. I'm sure I'll go home crying the second one of these women so much as gives me a glare.

"So, who are you, then?" I ask. "What's your derby name?"

She spins on her heels, revealing the back of her baby blue T-shirt. In hot-pink letters it reads, BLOWIN' PAST'ER. I have to say it out loud before I get the double entendre.

"Lord," I say.

She winks. "Exactly."

A voice booms through the warehouse. "Okay, Training Wheels, get on the track! Now! Now! Let's go, let's go!"

Francesca looks genuinely frightened as she says, "I'm sorry. I didn't know Trashy was teaching today."

"Trashy?"

"Trashcan Punch. She's kind of brutal."

"Brutal how?"

"Come on." Francesca skates away, hustling to the stairs that lead to the track. I grab my water bottle and follow, surprised at how quickly I've remembered how to skate. I thank ten-year-old me for all those endless loops around my neighborhood.

Climbing onto the track, I accidentally drop my water bottle. Before I can catch it, it goes rolling down the slope, straight to the center where it's flat.

I try to stand up, but immediately my feet slip out from under me and I fall. I don't know how to stand at an angle, and these rental skates they've got me in are missing toe stops. I try to stand, holding on to the railing, but I slip again. There's a line of women waiting to get on the track right where I'm standing in front of the steps, so I pull up onto my knees and slowly crawl over to my water bottle, real smooth-like.

The bottle is resting at the skate of a very tall woman. I guess it's possible that she's not all that tall. It could just be the effect of roller skates and a helmet on anybody who is standing directly above your head. But this muscular redhead is glaring at me with one eyebrow cocked and a grin smeared across her face like she's a giant who's just discovered the lost little villager soon to become her afternoon snack.

"You're the Super-Wheelie, right?" she asks. "Pastor's friend?" Her voice is low and sarcastic, like I amuse her no end simply by being here. I instantly feel a shaky combination of fear and humility. I want to apologize for entering what is clearly her lair.

"I'm with Pastor," I tell her, adding, "but I don't know what a Super-Wheelie is."

"It means you're new. Fresh Meat." She rubs her hands together gleefully. "We love fresh meat."

I can tell she's kidding, but she's not completely kidding, yet she's still kind of kidding while letting me know that she's about to be directly responsible for the kicking of my ass. My stomach feels like a swirling bathtub drain, emptying right down into my thighs, which have gone numb.

It takes a few seconds of pure determination, but I pull myself up and put out my hand.

"Charlotte."

She takes my fingertips between her thumb and forefinger and wiggles them, amused that I thought a handshake was somehow possible while wearing wrist guards. "I'm Trashcan Punch. Call me Trash. You ready, Super-Wheelie?" she asks.

"Of course," I lie.

"Good," she says, and then turns to the rest of the group. Her voice turns into a guttural growl. "Okay, Wheelies! Get on the track! Everybody on the track!"

Wait, that's it? Now I'm just doing this? What is this that I'm doing? How do I skate? How do I stop? What am I going to do?

I stumble-step over toward the track, my heart racing. I didn't tell anyone that this is new for me. Did Francesca? Does anybody here know that I've never done this before? Should I tell them, just so they know not to hurt me?

I feel a pull on the back of my T-shirt. I turn around to see Francesca, her grinning mouth puffed up from her mouth guard.

"You're going to be fine," she says, all muffled. She takes out her mouth guard before dropping her hand onto my shoulder. "Think of this as a skating lesson. But listen. Don't touch anyone, especially if you're falling. Don't grab onto anybody. Keep your mouth guard in your mouth all the time. But most importantly, if you fall, get right back up or roll to the flat part of the track and then get the fuck out of the way."

The cursing must be a part of the mind-set that comes with the level of insanity required to play this game.

Trash is now wearing a headset microphone. "Ladies! You have thirty seconds to get on the track, or I'm making everybody do thirty minutes of squats! Don't test me!"

"Have fun," Francesca says, and then totally abandons me.

I jam my mouth guard in between my teeth. I stand at the part of the track where it's flat the longest, before it curves around. Thirty or so women are skating along the track, some quickly, some at a more leisurely pace. A few seem to be going through drills, zigzagging up and down the slope of the track, racing each other. I watch one girl turn around in front of me and continue skating backward along the track just as quickly as she was skating forward, as if this is the most natural thing in the world.

Some of the girls are leaning forward as they skate, their hands clasped behind their backs. They look so serene, so peaceful. If I hadn't already seen what it looks like when an actual game is being played, I would think I was about to engage in some easy-breezy couples skate.

I was terrible at Double Dutch. I never knew when to jump in between the two swinging ropes in order to get to the center. I'd stand there rocking back and forth on my feet for an eternity, until some other girl would coach me, screaming, "Now! Now! Now!" Even then the ropes would hit me straight in the neck half the time.

I've got that Double Dutch feeling as I'm watching these women barreling toward me while I'm supposed to jump up on that track. *When do I go?*

"Get on the track!" shouts Trash. "This means you, Super-Wheelie! If you don't get up there, everybody else has to come down and do squats, and then everyone will hate you. Do you want everyone to hate you?"

I shake my head, feeling my helmet rattle. It feels like it's trying to jostle my brain into reality: *Get out of here while you still have all of your limbs!*

Trash yells at me like Godzilla finding speech: "Go! Now! Now! Now!"

I jump in with my eyes slammed shut, just like I did playing Double Dutch.

I'm on the track, pushing my feet, skating in what feels like the world's most important race. I wobble around the curve, trying to find the right way to position my weight at this angle. Girls are shooting past me. From either side, they call out: "Inside!" "Outside!" I try very hard to stay right in the center, right where I won't be in anybody's way.

"Behind you, sweetheart!"

"Watch your arms!"

My elbows are winged up near my ears, like I'm trying to figure out the chicken dance. As I drop my arms, I feel someone grab me gently by my hips, and she eases me to the right. It is surreal to have someone controlling my direction from behind, like I'm a toy car.

"Inside," she says, as she blows past me at a speed I cannot comprehend. Is she wearing special skates? And how can she be so fearless?

I look down at my skates and immediately start to pitch forward. My hands fly out in front of me. I'm terrified that when I go down everybody is going to fall on top of me and this is absolutely the last few seconds of my life because I can't control what is happening and I'm falling I'm falling I'm falling.

Wham.

I'm still alive, but I'm still on the track. And all I can hear are skates are coming closer. I open my eyes and see—

SKATES ARE COMING AT MY FACE.

This is where my brain disconnects from my body. In order to prepare for what will surely be intense pain and extreme physical trauma, I feel my mind detach from my nerves, float far away, and examine things like there's all the time in the world.

"Get up, get up, get up!" Someone shouts as she passes me, lifting a foot that barely clears my head.

And all I can think is: *Yes, I would love to. But see, skates are coming at my face. I am terrified.*

"Get up or get off the track!"

Don't you understand, skater girls? Skates are coming at my face. My face, where my teeth are. Where my eyes live. I never really thought about how many very important things are on my face.

"Get up!"

My nose is on my face. I need my nose.

"Help me get this girl up."

I feel myself getting lifted under the arms and spun around until I'm facing the right direction. I try to thank whoever it is, but I'm still confused, disoriented. I take a single step forward, and it's like I've forgotten that I'm on skates. My legs splay in two different directions and I fall to my ass, hard. It hurts so much that I fall onto my back, trying to catch my breath, my head resting on the track. I'm pissed off and disoriented. Have I even technically skated yet?

I hear skates coming at me again, and then . . . I hear nothing. But what I see is a girl jumping over my head, the bottoms of her skates a touchable distance from my face. I hear the slam of wood next to my ear, followed by the cheers of onlookers.

Now I can hear Trash on the overhead speakers. "Super-Wheelie, you must get up! Get up before you hurt somebody!"

Doesn't she get it? If I get up, I'm going to hurt *myself*. If I stay still people can just keep leaping over my body until it's time to stop doing this. I will spend the rest of my time here pretending to be an object in their reckless obstacle course. I would rather be a bump in the road than have to try to take another step.

"Get up, or get off the track and go home!"

Wait, *go home*? Like a quitter?

Trash can't know what she's just done, but she's said the secret words. *Go home*. What I've been struggling with all this time. If I can't make it, I have to go home. If I can't figure it out, go home. If I don't know what else to do, I might as well just go home. Go home and accept things the way they are, that nothing can change, that nothing is worth fighting for. If you can't hang here, then go home.

I'm not a quitter. Especially not when things are hard.

So I get up.

I get up and skate.

• • •

After what feels like a million attempts, I've almost been able to go an entire lap around the track without falling. But I am exhausted. My lungs are aching, my throat hurts. My lower back is clenched to the point where I might just snap right in half. I am panting around this hunk of plastic jammed between my teeth, and all I can think is *Oh, God, when are we going to stop skating? How long can this last?*

Trash's voice booms over the loudspeakers. "For the next sixty seconds, I want you to skate as fast as you can and see how many skaters you can pass. Go on my whistle. Get ready."

The whistle blows. It sounds like a thunderstorm is chasing me. For the next sixty seconds, I only have one goal: try not to get killed.

"Inside!"

"Outside!"

"Inside, baby girl!"

Aren't these supposed to be the new girls? These are the rookies in training? They are whizzing past me. I must look like a windup toy worn down, the slowest girl on the track. I am a spinning top, wobbly like a dreidel at the end of its rotation.

I can't focus on anything other than the pain. The muscles in my legs are yelling at me, calling me names. My stomach muscles are somehow all that's keeping me from doing a face plant. My feet have gone numb.

A whistle blows. Trash screams for us to come down off the

track. I've never been so happy to be yelled at in all my life. I thank the stars above that it's over. I made it. I did it. I am a warrior. A weary, weak, pathetic warrior.

I stumble to the infield in search of my water bottle, which I find and then suck like a hungry baby. As I look around I notice I'm possibly the only girl here who doesn't have a tattoo. The other women are fantastically multicolored, with dragons and symbols wrapped around their strong biceps, stars blazoned across the backs of their necks. I can see hints of tattoos peeking from underneath their fishnet stockings, streaks of color along their backs, their ankles, each girl marked uniquely but boldly. Where they don't have tattoos, they have piercings. Hoops and pins adorn their noses and eyebrows, chins and necks. They've had needles jammed into all kinds of body parts. I look down at my pasty body and think I might not be as equipped as these other girls to deal with this level of pain.

The girl next to me is on her knees, stretching out her lower back. Her shirt has ridden up to expose a tattoo of the handle of a gun, as if her butt is the holster. Watching her stretch makes my body ache, because I recognize her pain in my own pain, the feeling that I've destroyed all of the muscles that attach my ass to my body.

"How long was that?" I ask, noticing there aren't any clocks in the warehouse. "What, like an hour or something?"

She rolls her face toward me, sweat pouring down her cheeks. She laughs. "Dude, that was the ten-minute warm-up."

"What?"

"Hey, you've only got an hour and fifty minutes to go!"

"Are you serious?"

She eases herself to her knees, her hands on either side of her butt gun. "I am," she says. "Don't worry; it's not all on skates. Half an hour of it will be squats and crunches. Then some drills. And then, if you're lucky, maybe we will play some roller derby."

I groan, rolling forward to stretch out my back. It's awkward sitting in all this gear. I feel like the Michelin Man.

She stands up and raises her arms over her head, stretching her sides. I see streaks of pink hair curling down from the edges of her powder blue helmet. She's like an anime character, all taut muscle and neon coloring. "Good job getting up," she says. "My first month here, I was a total Bambi."

I shake my head, confused.

"Bambi. Like this." She breaks into a jittery scramble, hands flailing, eyes wide. "A baby deer on wheels."

I drop my head to my knees. For a moment I've forgotten about the gear, so I end up slamming my forehead into the hard plastic of my knee pads.

"Ow."

"Stick with it. You'll be surprised how fast you pick up everything."

"Uh-huh."

"I'm serious. What's your name?"

I don't know if I'm supposed to give my real name, but I don't have any other one. I'm not going to have these people call me "Char," and the only other nickname I've ever had is when my dad calls me "Bunny." So I tell her my real name.

"I'm Bruisey-Q," she says, patting my helmet. "Welcome to the Wheelhouse."

I spot Francesca on the other side of the track, laughing and joking with some of the other skaters. Her face is flushed, and her bangs are plastered across her forehead, heavy with sweat. She looks destroyed, but she also looks happier than I've ever seen her.

19

The next morning I wake up in agony. Every muscle I have feels swollen inside my skin. It's like I could grab my hamstrings and rip them from my femurs.

I hurt everywhere.

Today's plan: find the strength to kill Francesca.

I gramma-walk over to my cell phone and punch up her number.

"Morning, Charlie," she says, all sunshine and rainbows.

"You fucking bitch."

"Aspirin," she laughs. "And take a bath."

My wrist is purple, and there's a bruise streaking across my right thigh like I escaped a monster in my sleep. There's a blister on the inside of my left foot, right at the bunion. It's not just swollen—it's filled with blood. My shoulders ache, and there's a scrape across the inside of my right elbow.

"I'm so broken," I say. "Someone ripped out my arms and then shoved them back in again, but they didn't do it right."

"I'm really proud of you for hanging in there last night."

"I was too scared to go home. Those tough girls would have found me and beaten me up in the parking lot."

"That's not why you stayed. I think you might have loved it."

I try to flop back onto my bed, but my stomach muscles are so wrecked I actually see stars for a second. I ease myself back down instead. "What are you doing today?" I ask her. "Because I think we should immediately go to the spa, get massages, and sit in a Jacuzzi for about six hours."

"Can't," she says. "Jacob's flight gets here in an hour and I plan on spending the entire weekend in bed with him. Besides, don't you have to go buy your mom a birthday present?"

I have given up wondering how it is that Francesca can stay on top of so many people's schedules at once. It's one thing to know exactly where her boyfriend is at any point, but she often remembers not only what I'm supposed to do over a weekend, but exactly what I was doing this time a week ago. This is Francesca's weird superpower. She says she's been this way her whole life. When she thinks of people, a mental calendar appears around them, like they are surrounded by their own day planners. When I first marveled at how much this must come in handy, she told me it was more like an annoyance. Friends of hers over the years have accused her of being a creepy stalker, when in fact she can't help that she remembers how the last time you were at a sushi restaurant with her you ordered a rainbow roll, two spicy tuna hand rolls, and shishito peppers extra spicy.

"I would love to have that part of my brain used for something important," she once told me. "Or at the very least for my own personal memory storage, but I don't have a say in it. Do you want to know what my best friend in third grade was wearing the first day of school? A green jumper with big yellow buttons and two white bunnies embroidered on the front with a carrot between them. Why will I remember this forever? I don't know. But I will."

She might be tortured by her semiphotographic memory, but right now I'm thankful for it. Otherwise I probably would have wallowed in my pain all day until I gave in to a bottle of wine sometime around three, completely forgetting my mother's birthday. I'm aware that this makes me an even worse daughter than I've already admitted to being, but then again it's not every morning I wake up with my body completely stiffened with pain and regret.

"See, I still think your stalker memory is helpful," I tell her now.

"As long as someone thinks so. I'll see you at practice on Sunday?"

"No."

"Yes, I will! My stalker brain can already see you there."

"Well, then my blood type is B-negative. I feel like you should know that before I go there again. Seems like it's going to be important."

"Bye, Charlie."

I take a deep breath before gingerly going about getting out of my apartment to find my mother a card that reads, HAPPY BIRTHDAY. PLEASE DON'T ASK WHERE MY HUSBAND IS TONIGHT.

20

Charlotte Goodman is at her mother's fifty-fourth birthday dinner party with her best friend, Andy, who's filling in in the role of significant other for the evening. Charlotte's mother, who is well into her second vodka martini, has found Charlotte's choice of dinner companion to be, in fact, significant.

"I just don't like how you're making all these excuses for him," Elaine Goodman says, hands waving in the air like a dealer finishing out her shift at the blackjack table. "Your husband should want to be a part of your family." At this point she pauses in her lecture to swallow something that's suddenly demanding attention at the back of her throat. When she's sure that's been handled, she continues. "I don't know what you're doing that makes him want to stay away, but I hope you figure it out soon. I would hate for you to find out it was something easily fixable."

Charlotte Goodman doesn't think she looks like either of her parents, even though everybody comments that she has her father's dark, worried eyes and her mother's soft, too-small chin. She's always admired her mother's mouth, how she looks perfect in any shade of lipstick. Elaine Goodman has the ability to appear frail and powerful at the same time, like a French movie star. People always want to help her, to see gratitude in her round, glassy eyes, *but they are afraid to do anything she hasn't expressly requested, for Elaine's death glare can stop a person cold.*

Abe Goodman has more of a welcoming, friendly face. He looks like he's supposed to be giving directions, either in an emergency or on a forest trail. In fact, strangers often turn to him in amusement parks or malls, grabbing him by the crook of the elbow, saying, "Excuse me, but could you help me?" This is how he met his wife.

She was looking for her Biology 310 class, and he was lucky enough to have just stepped outside the science building when she actually needed someone. Since that moment, Abe has had his hands full helping his wife and therefore doesn't have time for all the lost strangers. He tends to keep his head down to avoid eye contact, for he cannot help how approachable he seems. Even in sunglasses, he looks like someone who knows how to locate an exit or turn you back onto the right path.

Charlotte wishes she could find an exit to this conversation, in which her mother is relentlessly tearing apart Matthew. Elaine has no idea how much her daughter would love to join in, but Charlotte knows if she says even one word, she will say the rest of them, and this dinner will turn into The Discussion.

This is still not the time to face the truth. Charlotte knows her parents will be disappointed in her, and she knows she isn't strong enough to hear what those words will be. If there has to be any kind of conversation about Matthew, at least right now it's about what's wrong with him.

"I mean, shouldn't a husband want to be with his wife?" Elaine Goodman asks, round dark eyes wide with disbelief. Her eyeliner has smudged a bit in the outer corner of her right eye. Charlotte is jealous of her mother's ability to look more beautiful the more damaged she seems. "Tell that Matthew his job can't be more important than his wife. Have you told him that? Have you

let him know that you need to come first, before the job? How are you supposed to make grandchildren for us if he's always at work?"

Under the safety of the table, Andy's hand finds Charlotte's and squeezes it. His other hand finds his mouth to rub his chin. Charlotte recognizes this action instantly; it is what Andy does when he gets excited, when he's about to mess with someone. Before Charlotte can stop him, he speaks.

"Elaine, I've been telling this one for months now that she should just divorce him," he says, using an overdramatic, sarcastic Mister-Man voice, invoking the kind of character who would refer to her as "the little lady."

Andy barks a fake chuckle, one that makes Charlotte's father look down at his plate, grinning and nodding. Andy always was good at entertaining her parents, and was a welcome addition at their Thanksgiving dinners when Andy's own fractured family stopped insisting on celebrating a holiday that ultimately created more drama and conflict for his relatives than they could handle.

"He has, actually," Charlotte says, finding her voice. She grips Andy's hand tight enough to make him wince. He kicks at her ankle and she kicks back.

"In fact," Andy says, emboldened by Charlotte's desire for him to stop with this half-kidding character, "I think a divorce is exactly what Matthew needs in order to be a better man to your daughter."

"Bite your tongue," Charlotte's mother says. "We don't talk about divorce in this house. Do we, Abe?" She reaches across the table to pat her husband's arm, as if reminding her daughter what a spouse looks like when he's doing his job.

"We aren't home," is all Abe says, but the look he gives his daughter from across the table jolts Charlotte to the base of her spine. It is the look that has seen through Charlotte her entire *life; that knew when she was out with a boy when she said she was at the mall, the look that forced her to come clean on stealing money from her mother's purse, to admit to throwing up a six-pack of Zima in the backyard behind the tulip mound on a Sunday morning. It's possible Abe Goodman immediately saw through Andy's jokes and knew the truth about his daughter, but also knew an Olive Garden was not the place to discuss such matters. For now, a look will suffice. A look that makes Charlotte feel about five years old.*

Andy must sense that something has transpired between father and daughter, because he finally changes the subject. "Elaine, what are you and those crazy women reading in your book club this month? Remember last time you said you all got together, drank wine, and tried to read the Bible, and I told you that's Drunk Church, not Book Club?"

"I stopped going," Elaine says. "People weren't taking it seriously enough. And I still think it's a good idea to read the Bible, even if you aren't religious."

"Amen," Andy says, reaching for a breadstick.

"THERE he is!"

Charlotte watches as a man engulfs her mother's head and shoulders from behind, leaning down into her hug. She cannot believe what she's seeing in front of her. Inverted and embraced in her mother's arms is Matthew Price.

Charlotte's husband is here.

From beside her, Charlotte hears Andy's quiet, rather irritated, "Hunh."

"Sorry I'm so late," Matthew says, disentangling himself from his mother-in-law's grip and easing himself into a chair that has been quickly placed between Charlotte's parents.

It has been more than a month since Charlotte has sat in the same room as her estranged husband, and she finds herself now having to remember that this is what he actually looks like. She recognizes his green eyes, his scars and moles, the way his hands stay moving, always moving. She recognizes the slope of his wide shoulders, the small patch of dark hair under the curve of his left jaw that he always misses with his razor. She knows that haircut, and if she could put her face to his scalp and inhale right now, she would know him molecularly, she could recognize him purely by the reaction in her own body. This is the man she fell in love with, whom she swore to spend her life with; this is the man she calls her husband.

This is also a man she does not recognize, who has a Facebook page and is too busy to return a text. This is a man who has been avoiding her, who walked out on her, who gets confused when she says she's lonely in his arms. This face has been absent from her reality but has remained the dominant figure in her mind. This man she tells herself might not be the one for her, who might be on the way out of her life forever, this person who has hurt her deeply and shattered her ability to even make it through a day without having to plan it out mentally before she gets up in the morning—this man has done what he always does, what he might continue to do, for as long as Charlotte wants it.

At the very last moment, when she is releasing her last fingertip grip of hope, this is when Matthew rushes in. He saves the day. He comes home. He shows up. He plays the hero. And indeed, right now, at her mother's birthday dinner, he has done it again. Despite the humble backdrop of the Olive Garden, despite what might be considered the rather tame audience of her parents and closest friend, despite the fact that he is too late for dinner and isn't going to even consider picking up the check as both an apology and a gift and is checking his cell phone even now, sending off a quick text as he listens to Elaine fill him in on the past few months of her life—despite all of this, the simple act of showing *up works on Charlotte. It always does. Her faith gets somewhat restored, enough to regain a firmer grip on hope, and her head rushes with images of possible happy endings. This could be the start of where everything gets better. Her happy ending only needs to find its beginning.*

And this is why later that night, even though Andy has her right hand under the table in his with a white-knuckled, nail-digging grip, when Matthew quietly asks Charlotte out to dinner, she says yes.

21

I sit across from Matthew and for a moment, it's forever ago. Nothing bad has ever happened between us. It's before. It's the past. We're just going out to dinner, like we've done a million times.

"Thanks again for coming to Mom's party," I say. "I never asked why you decided to go."

Matthew's attention is on the back of his collar, which he's pulling from underneath his sweater. "You wanted me to go," he says, and his eyes meet mine. The corners of his mouth twitch, almost grinning. "It seemed important to you."

"It was," I say. "I don't think I knew how much until you showed up."

"Well, then, I'm glad I did. And I'm glad you said yes to dinner."

It's the longest conversation we've had lately that hasn't turned into something spiteful. Anybody at this restaurant who might look at us would think, *"Well, there's a lovely couple. How nice to be in love."*

"I'm glad, too," I say.

"I was hoping it meant you'd made a decision."

"About?"

"About us."

The waiter interrupts us to hand out menus and discuss specials. I don't hear a word he says. Am I supposed to have an answer right now? Do I have to decide by the end of the meal? Did he come here expecting a decision about the rest of our lives over whatever soup special this guy standing between us is describing? Because I don't have one.

Is that why he really showed up at my mom's party? To get a decision out of me? To force me to choose?

The waiter leaves and Matthew turns his focus to the menu, his head shaking back and forth in a way that always makes me think he reads by keeping his eyes still while he somehow rotates the world around him. Right now he's planning his entire meal, computing and calculating each calorie, from the wine he'll have before the salad to the dessert he will finish with a cup of decaf. Matthew is a planner, and the second part of creating this plan involves the question he's about to ask me. I know it like my own heartbeat.

"What are you having?" he asks in a way that would make most people think he was talking to himself. Under the sweater, I see he's wearing the dark blue button-down shirt I got him for Christmas last year. He tugs at his cuffs as he leans over the menu, rocking his head.

Most people might take this moment to tease him about looking like Rain Man, but instead I quickly answer his question, deciding what I'll have as I tell him the words. "The salmon." It's important that I already know, because it eases his anxiety.

I watch his eyebrows settle. They shift like little caterpillars prepping for a nap. I know I've answered correctly for him, and the world is now safe. At least for another few minutes.

It took years for me to be able to navigate around the illogical logic of Matthew's obsessive-compulsive disorder. Some of it is absolutely insane.

That is why right now he's adjusting the position of the salt and pepper shakers. They must align with the left side of the table. If we get seated at a round table, the salt and pepper shakers need to be in the exact middle. I used to ask how one was supposed to eyeball such a thing, but something inside Matthew knows the answer, knows the placement. At some point I figured out the trick: the actual center is Matthew. For some reason he is convinced that the world only exists because he obeys these rules that only he knows. He also knows that this is impossible, but it doesn't mean he can stop these feelings from happening.

He tried to hide these thoughts from me at first. He made it through three months or so without my noticing the fact that after a red light his fingers had to tap the top of the steering wheel five times with one hand, twice with the other. He turned it into a little drumming beat so he seemed chipper rather than driven by compulsions. When he passed a car on the left, he had to reach over and touch my knee. He covered it by pretending to be a DJ, scratching my knee like a record on a turntable. It took a while for me to realize he wasn't just repeating his jokes; he was obeying mental orders. It wasn't that he wanted to touch my knee; he had no choice.

Eventually Matthew had to break down and tell me about his OCD because I was convinced his erratic behavior was due to his having decided he hated me.

Back when he had his own small apartment and I was first starting to spend the night, I'd wake up in the mornings earlier than he did. I'd tiptoe into the cramped living room/ kitchen, quietly make a pot of coffee, and pull a book I hadn't read from Matthew's overflowing bookshelves. In order to get the best light and make the least amount of noise, I'd drag the little wooden chair he had next to the front door over to the window. I'd perch with my mug of coffee resting on the windowsill and spend an hour or so alone, reading and listening to the hum of Matthew's wall clock. His neighborhood was quiet in the early morning, peppered with the occasional clamor of someone going through the trash bins for recyclables.

At first I thought Matthew just resented my early-morning nature. I used to be the kind of person who never got up before ten unless I was getting paid, so I understood the grumpiness that could ensue when someone had already had part of a day before you'd even brushed your teeth. But I could tell pretty quickly that Matthew wasn't even thinking about me when he was grumpy those mornings; he didn't always answer my questions the first time I asked, and sometimes he'd leave the room while I was talking. He was distracted, and I thought he was losing interest in me.

One morning I put down my book and went to the bathroom for a few minutes. When I returned, the chair was back by the front door.

I was apologetic. "Oh, I was going to move it back," I said. "You didn't have to do that."

"It's okay," he said, sitting cross-legged on his couch still in his pajamas, staring into his laptop screen. "I don't mind."

I moved the chair back by the window, explaining, "I wasn't done with it yet."

An hour later I got up to refill my coffee cup. When I returned, the chair was by the front door again. This time I didn't say anything as I moved it back to the window. I did, however, give him a really good glare that he might not have seen, as he was busy answering email.

It was when I'd left for fifteen minutes to grab us a couple of sandwiches, only to come back to find that the chair had been moved again, that I finally said something.

"Should I go home? Because I think I might be unwanted here."

Matthew's eyes widened and his mouth opened. Over time, I'd come to recognize that look as, *"I have no idea why this lady is tripping."*

"What—What's wrong?" he asked.

"The chair. You keep moving it."

He exhaled, a little too forcefully. "I'm sorry, but . . . it goes over there."

"Well, I was going to put it back. I like the light over here."

"I know." He began to choose his words carefully. "It's stupid but . . . but the chair goes over there."

"I was going to put it back, Matthew!"

"That's the thing! It goes there all the time!"

"All the time?"

"ALL THE TIME!"

And then it was quiet. I looked around the room, realizing everything had to be where it was, *all the time*. I put things out of order. I was unsettling. There was no place for me.

I stayed at my apartment for the rest of the week. When he called with his fifth apology for yelling at me, I made a decision. I was going to find a way to fit in, to work with his anxiety. I'd be something that fit in a certain place in his life, too.

I knew I'd succeeded the first time we vacationed together, driving up to a cabin in Big Bear. We stopped to take our picture next to a lake, right at sunset. There was snow on the ground. Matthew placed his camera on the hood of his car and set the timer. He ran to join me, posed, and then trotted back to the camera to check the shot. He hadn't gotten it the way he wanted it. He was mumbling to himself animatedly, like a scientist close to discovery. He tried pushing me gently this way and that, studying the light in front of me, the scenery behind me.

Back and forth, he ran and snapped, positioned and posed, studied and adjusted.

He must have taken thirty photos. Matthew kept taking our picture until there was no good light and our toes were burning from the cold. Not once did I ask if we could leave. Nor did I ask him why this was so important to him. I knew it wasn't just a picture. This image of the two of us had been elevated in his head as one of the things that kept the universe in order. I was happy to have become a part of his un-understandable madness.

I wasn't a saint about it, though. There were times when Matthew's need for order and the "right way" of doing things went against how I wanted to go through my day, and I would rebel. I'd leave a pile of folded laundry at the foot of the bed, knowing that Matthew was going to check on it several times a day until I put it away. Perhaps the laundry was at the foot of the bed because I was too busy buying groceries or at work. If it bothered him that much, I'd think, he could put it away himself.

Matthew's strict guidelines of how the world had to be arranged could include me, but I wouldn't allow them to govern me. An example: we have a few glasses that bother Matthew's fingerprints. When he holds one of the etched glasses in his hand, he feels like the grooves of the design are cutting into the swirls of his fingerprint. For him, it is the tactile equivalent of hearing nails on a chalkboard. He claims my fingerprints are tinier, and therefore that's why I'm not bothered when I hold the glass. I don't think it's so much that I have smaller skin patterns as that I'm more . . . let's go ahead and use the word . . . *normal*. When Matthew is one step away from needing a sippy cup, I don't toss out the offending glassware, or only drink from it when he's not home. I drink out of the etched glasses, and he uses something else. The world doesn't need me to stay away from the etched glassware. Only he has to beware. He's the one who needs to check the burners on the stove three times, even if it means going back into the house after he's left, just to make sure. The fate of the world rests on his shoulders. Check the burners three times: everything is okay. Check them only twice: destruction and chaos.

Nobody else is this well-versed in Matthewisms. Just me. I'm the one who knows why he does what he does when he does it. How will someone else ever learn all his weird little quirks? What if the next girl isn't as patient?

Maybe he already knows the answer to this. Maybe that's why he came back to me.

I say, "You look good."

"Thanks. You too. You changed your hair?"

No, I lost ten pounds. But close enough. "I guess I've just sort of changed in general," I say.

"Do you like the wine?" he asks. He's rubbing the stem of his glass with his thumb. I notice his fingers trembling.

"It's good."

Matthew instantly brightens. "It's great, right? When I saw it on the menu I got excited, because I didn't think I'd see it here."

I'm confused. "Here, like this restaurant?" We'd never eaten here before. Matthew, in a completely un-Matthew move, had suggested this cozy place closer to my apartment than the house. *His* house.

"No, here, like Los Angeles. I was looking when I got back, but I could only find it online."

"Back from where?"

Matthew is reaching for a piece of bread, but he stops. And I mean he stops everything. I might have to check his pulse. Then he says what he always says when he's found himself in a situation where he's caught and needs more time: "*Hmm?*"

I know he knows what I just asked him, and I know he knows I know he knows what I just asked him. So instead of answering, I wait.

"I went somewhere," he says, his robot voice having returned, talking to me like I'm a tiger about to pounce.

I don't want him to feel like I'm testing him, or trying to trick him. I try to sound normal. Casual. "You can go places, Matthew. You're a grown-up." I try joking. "I mean, it's not like you went to Hookerville, right?"

Matthew laughs, his eyes still focused on his plate, his head nodding, but more relaxed. "No, I did not go to Hookerville."

"I didn't think so."

"I went to Italy."

A muscle somewhere near my diaphragm, or perhaps it is my diaphragm, immediately forms a fist and tries to punch through my stomach right into Matthew's face. My knees jolt. My fingers clench. All at once. My heart, my head, my lungs, my skin, all at once, all of it wants to destroy.

"Italy?"

He sighs. "I had a feeling you'd react like this."

I don't answer right away. I keep my face in my water glass, taking carefully measured gulps. I'm upset that he went, but I'm also upset he's making it sound like I failed some big test of his by being upset.

"You can understand why that might hurt my feelings, Matthew," I say finally.

"I wasn't even going to tell you."

"Well, thanks."

"What I *mean* is," he starts, but takes a breath when he realizes he's starting to yell. Then he gets much, much quieter, dropping in pitch to almost a monotone. "If I was going there to hurt you, wouldn't I have told you I went? Or told you before I went? Or told you when I was there? Sent you a postcard?"

The logic isn't quite working on me. "There are lots of other places in the world. If you wanted to travel, why not try any one of them?"

"Oh, so I guess even if we don't work out, I never get to go to Italy? Is that it?"

"I would say any time you ever went to Italy *without me* means you were going to make sure that you went there. Without me."

He rubs the back of his neck while he looks around the restaurant, like he's looking for backup, like everybody else should be staring at him with total empathy. He raises a cocky eyebrow and says, "It's probably not just Italy. Maybe you should give me a list of all the places where I'm not allowed to go. Or maybe you could just keep my passport."

"I didn't get to go to Italy," I say. "I stayed here, working on this decision that apparently you think I'm supposed to make before dessert."

Matthew stretches his arms out like he's trying to hug the room. "Do these people get to go to Italy? Or is Italy completely blocked off from all people forever? What if you met someone new and *he* wanted to take you to Italy? Would you say, 'Oh, I'm so sorry. But my ex-husband and I had plans to go there *a million years ago*, so that entire country is just off-limits.' Bullshit."

He called himself my ex-husband. And he used this *voice*, this mocking shrill sound that I certainly do not make. His cheeks are flushed and his forehead is dotted with sweat. Consequently, he's rearranging and organizing the table. He unfolds and folds his napkin. He switches the positioning of his fork and his knife and then edges the candle closer to him.

I see him thinking: *"If the napkin stays this way something bad will happen, so I will move it. Maybe if I move it, she will stop being mad at me. Regardless, I must move this fork closer to me, so that I have a weapon. And if all else fails, I will set her on fire."*

As I struggle with what to say in response, my jaw sets. I force myself to release it, thinking of my mouth guard, remembering the pain in my head I used to have upon waking a few weeks ago. I take a deep breath, but with that comes the familiar swell of tears from somewhere in my throat. I choke them down, determined not to cry. I've cried in more restaurants than a two-year-old.

It's like we're constantly on the edge of a major decision. We're always about to irreparably change our lives. Funny how we planned on spending the rest of our lives together, but now we can't even make it through a dinner without wondering whether or not this should be the last time we ever speak.

"I'm sorry," he says, as I watch him let something inside drop.

"I'm sorry, too," I say. "It's none of my business. I shouldn't get mad at you. I didn't mean to—"

Matthew raises his hand, gently, easing me to stop. I do.

We both say no to dessert.

22

Y ou should go to London. Or Mexico. Or the cold place you were talking about."

"Iceland?"

"Yeah. I have no idea why you'd want to go there, but you should go there."

"I can't just go somewhere. I have to work."

Francesca is trying to pace my office, which means she's pretty much turning in circles on her heels. "If you were that blond lady with the book, you could go all over the place. You'd meditate, have sex, and then have Julia Roberts play you in a movie."

I crumple another piece of wastepaper and toss it into the open desk drawer by my side. I'm storing up reserves for the next time I'm engaged in a paper-wad battle with Jonathan. I never know when the next missile will strike, and I'm determined to be ready with a stockpile he never saw coming.

"I'm not rich enough to go flitting around the world," I tell Francesca, as if this is not obvious. "I can't have a fancy-lady breakdown. Also, didn't she go to Italy? Italy is closed!"

"Okay, fine," she pouts. "Then let's go to Australia."

"Sorry. After I left my lawyer husband, I spent my savings

repurchasing an entire life's worth of supplies. Therefore I rarely eat, I don't pray, and I'm done with love."

Francesca drops back to the wall and flops down on the floor in front of me, tossing herself like a rag doll. *Bang, whap!* "You're officially no fun," she says. "If I were you, I'd be in Paris right now."

I point over her head at the closed door behind her. "When Jonathan comes back in here, you're going to get hit."

"I don't care."

The cuff of her pant leg has risen up on her shin, and I see a dark bruise peeking out from under her sock.

"Ow. Who did that?" I ask.

She pulls her pant leg down over her shin and rubs the fabric just over the contusion. "You did," she says. "At practice yesterday when you wouldn't tell me what was wrong, and you just kept slamming into me."

I surprised myself by going back to the warehouse yesterday, but when I woke up angry about Matthew, I needed a place to go where I not only wouldn't talk about him, but couldn't. I spent an hour exhausting myself learning to stay upright while skating the track before the trainer taught us how to throw hits and take hits. By the end of practice I'd learned something important; I can hit someone pretty hard if I want to.

"Well, sorry about the bruise," I say to Francesca.

"Make it up to me by taking me on a trip around the world." She pulls up her pants to rub the bruise, mashing it with her thumbs. It looks like torture.

"Yikes, don't do that," I tell her. "You'll make it worse."

"It's a hematoma. I have to break it up or I'll get a welt for six months."

"Frannie," I say, intentionally using the nickname she hates so I have her attention.

She looks up from the floor, where she's crouched in a ball. "Yeah, Charlie?"

"Did that count as Going Outside?"

"A date with your husband? No."

The door opens, smacking Francesca in the back of the head.

"Ow! Jesus, Jonathan, can't you see I'm lying here?"

He casually steps over her head and walks to his desk, as if girls are always strewn about the floor of his office. "You don't do any actual work, do you?"

Francesca fakes a wail, crawling petulantly to Jonathan's ankles. "Don't be mad at me, Johnny. I'm sorry I'm taking up all your precious time with your girlfriend here."

Jonathan gives me a quick glance. "Whatever. I see her every day," he says.

"Admit it," she says. "You're jealous."

Jonathan sniffs, and pretends to wipe a tear. "It would be nice to be included, that's all."

"Aw, Johnny." Francesca pulls herself up and perches in his lap. "We're sorry. Aren't we sorry, Charlie?"

Jonathan looks at me. I nod. Francesca reaches forward, grabs my wrist, and pulls me to her. Now we're both sitting on Jonathan's lap, each on a leg.

"Please forgive us, Johnny!" Francesca wails, clutching Jonathan.

"Get off me," he says. "Both of you."

"Not until you say everything's okay!"

"If HR sees this I am going to be sued!"

"Say everything's okay!"

As Jonathan and Francesca continue bickering, I try to make it seem like I'm an active participant, but all I notice is Jonathan's hand on my hip, how his fingers have curled around me. His fingertips are resting at the top of my thigh. I stand up and go back to my desk before either of them can see that I'm blushing.

It's not that Jonathan is touching me, it's that I'm being touched. My body wants to come back to the land of the living, but I know my head isn't ready. Where and with whom could I ever feel safe?

23

I'm having a hard time with transitions.

Yes: *ha, ha, ha, that's quite the understatement, Charlotte.* But transitions mean something different in roller derby.

A transition is when you turn around and skate backward. You can't do it like you normally would skating for fun, coasting in an arc until you've circled around to face the other direction. That's dangerous, and maybe even impossible when you're skating at high speed on the banked track. If you even managed to do anything other than spin right onto your ass, you'd definitely slam into someone in the process, or have someone roll right into you.

To execute a transition, you have to lift your foot and turn around. That means you're skating forward, pick your foot up into the air, drop it behind you facing the other direction, and then have your other foot follow suit. Sounds simple, but it's terrifying.

I've been coming here for three weeks now. I've probably put in a good fifteen or twenty hours on this track. Still, I can only land a transition when I'm standing still. Trash told me to pretend my body is a door. You "open the door," or lift one leg and rotate your body toward the direction in which you want to go. For about a second you're skating sideways, like a flattened frog. Then you lift the other foot and "close the door," bringing the other half of your body to join the rest of you. When it's over, you're still skating in the same direction but you're facing the other way. You're going forward, facing backward. A transition.

It sounds so easy, but my brain doesn't want this to happen to my body. Clearly it's thinking, *Why on earth would I want to turn around while I'm barreling forward?*

The really good girls, the ones who know what they're doing, their transitions look like hip-hop moves. *Boom-Boom!* And they're suddenly backward, booties up in the air, wiggling their hips to pick up speed. They make it look so easy.

It's not.

God, it's not. I've fallen 6,315 times. Not that I'm counting. I feel it in my body. In my muscles, in my bones, there are little reminders that I'm not good at this. The aches and pains yell at me: *Please don't try this again! You are making a huge mistake! Falling hurts! YOU ARE THIRTY.*

Last practice I was working on a hitting drill, partnered with a girl named Muffin Top. We were practicing hip blocks—using the better part of your ass to knock a girl aside, or even better, over. Getting knocked to the ground is tough enough, but getting up quickly over and over again is exhausting.

We'd been doing the drill for about five minutes, which in derby time means it felt like an hour and a half. Muffin Top was tired; I was wishing I could shut off my pain sensors.

That was when one of the coaches shouted from the infield, "Broken! I know you can hit harder than that! Get her!"

That's what they call me. Broken. It's short for Hard Broken. It started when I got frustrated at myself one practice and pulled too quickly on my shoelace, snapping it. "I can't skate with no lace!" I wailed to Francesca. "I'm heartbroken!"

As Bruisey-Q handed me an extra lace from her skate gear, she smiled. "I think you just found your derby name, Hard Broken."

"Thanks, but that's not what I said."

"Sounds good to me," Francesca said, grinning wildly. They bumped wrist guards, and thus I was christened.

Sometimes they call me the cutesy Broke-Broke, and occasionally, Brokey. But for the most part, I'm known, somewhat affectionately, as Broken. I've come to appreciate it.

Back to last practice's drill. After I gathered up all the strength I had remaining in my body, crouched low, and pushed all of my might into Muffin Top's left side, something terrible happened.

Instead of falling over, Muffin lost her balance. She stood straight up, arms flailing backward, and to stop herself from falling over, she somehow spun herself around. She actually did a transition, I guess accidentally, and was suddenly facing me with this look of confusion and fear on her face. Unsure of what to do next, she shot her arm straight out and grabbed me with one hand.

On my right breast.

Confused about the fact that she was holding my boob in her hand, she looked down at her hand, lost her skates completely, and went toppling to the infield.

But when she fell, she did not let go. I went flying with her, breast-first, skates over helmet, into the infield. A mess of girl parts rolling and slamming to the concrete.

I stayed there for a little while, holding myself, yelping.

"I'm so sorry," Muffin immediately said. She didn't know what to do, so she patted my arm ineffectively.

"It's okay," I moaned.

"Are you okay?"

"No." I rolled onto my side and went fetal, an arm protectively curled around my chest, hoping I wouldn't lose a nipple.

"I was falling and I panicked. I didn't mean to grab you *there*."

I eased myself up, still rubbing my chest. "You gave me an actual titty twister."

Muffin sat on her knees, scooting over to me. Then she arched back, sticking her chest out. Her pink T-shirt rode up until I could see her belly button, which was encircled with star tattoos. "Do it back," she said. "Twist my tit."

I laughed. "No, thank you."

"You have to do something. I feel terrible. Punch me in the face."

"What? No, Muffin, I am not going to punch you in the face."

Suddenly from behind us, we heard Trash's deep, deadpan order. "Broken, either punch that girl in the face or get your asses back on the track."

That was a few days ago. Right now I'm staring straight ahead, skating at a pretty good speed, dreading that I have to turn around. This upcoming transition fills me with such anxiety that I no longer know what I'm supposed to do, even though I know exactly what I'm supposed to do.

Technically.

I open the door; I close the door. But it's not that easy when I think about lifting my foot. Lifting my foot means I lose my balance, which means I'm supposed to be off balance.

Then I'll fall, which means it is going to hurt. It will hurt because I will have broken my wrist. Simple cause-and-effect at work.

Bang-Up, the trainer with the giant green eyes and the leopard-print helmet, is trying her best to be patient with me, skating easily alongside my jerky body. "This time, you can do it," she says. "How are you feeling?"

"Don't ask," I grumble.

I am reminded of the time I visited my grandfather in the hospital and went with him on a walk through the halls. He'd just had a bad bout of pneumonia, but he was determined as he shuffled along, pushing his IV, struggling to catch his breath every few minutes. I'd walk and stop, walk and stop, but he wouldn't let me ask how he was doing.

"I only want to know about the fifth grade," he'd say between gasps. "Just fifth grade."

So I talked about fractions and kickball and the mean girls in my class who all had better denim miniskirts than I did as Grampa kept his eyes focused and his feet moving forward. When we'd finished our walk and gotten him back into bed, he'd patted my hand, called me a good girl, and given me his Jell-O.

I remember my mom telling me she was proud of me that day. "It's not easy to sit by and do exactly what's asked of you, when you want to do everything," she'd said. That was the first time I ever saw my mother cry. My dad took me out of the hospital room right after, and I still can't stand the taste of Jell-O. It tastes like my mom is hurt.

"Don't look at your feet," Bang-Up's saying to me now. "You know where your feet are."

I might know that my feet are at the ends of my exhausted legs, but I don't know what they're going to do next. Will they stay under me, or will they shoot out in alternate directions, causing me to slam down onto my coccyx? Even Bang-Up can't accurately predict where my limbs are going to be in the next five seconds. Nobody can.

"Look where you are," she says, "and then, don't think about it. Just turn around."

My mind tries to make me do what she says, but my feet make me fall. A girl trips on my legs and flies over me, landing on her face. She gets right back up and skates off, but not before she gives me the stink eye.

"Sorry!" I shout.

"Don't say 'sorry,'" Bang-Up says. "The girls here are all new, too. They need to practice not tripping over you." I like that somehow my falling is helping them be better skaters. *You're welcome, everybody.* "But fall small," Bang-Up adds.

"Fall what?" I'm back on my feet again, skating with her, but my ankles are wobbly and my back is screaming in pain. I want to get down but don't want to just as much.

"Fall small," she says, pulling her elbows to her sides, crouching. "Don't flail yourself everywhere when you fall. That makes it harder for you to control yourself, and you end up taking up more space on the ground, so someone's more likely to trip over you, or run over your finger or something. People can get hurt in these pileups. We've had broken ribs, bruised kidneys. One girl got a skate to her nose. That was a lot of blood."

I can't believe she can say all of this to me while we're skating, while she's wearing a mouth guard. When I talk I sound like Eliza Doolittle, her mouth filled with marbles.

I try another transition, but I fall and end up facing the oncoming skaters. One sees me, panics, and instantly drops to the ground. This causes the girl behind her to fall. I pull in my limbs and stand up.

Bang-Up is waiting for me on the high side of the track. She rolls back over and continues, as if I hadn't just given her a perfect example of what she was asking me not to do.

"Fall small. You curl up and either spring back onto your feet or roll into the infield as quickly as possible. Just don't be a splat on the track. You're no good to anyone."

In roller derby, even falling has rules.

"Okay, try another transition."

I try, but nothing's happening. "I can't lift my feet," I say. It's true. They feel weighted and numb, like the laces have cut my feet from below the ankle. I'm covered in sweat. It has dripped into one eye, and I'm squinting like a pirate.

Bang-Up screams at me: "Now!"

Terrified, I lift my foot, turn at the hip, and drop it. My other foot drags behind me, and I begin to spin out, falling forward, my hands outstretched in front of me like a toddler going down.

I fall, but I jump right back up, my legs somehow finding their balance.

My secret? This time when I fell, I imagined that girl with the busted nose. I fell, thought *Skate to the face!*, and then jumped right back up. I want to tell all of the other skaters my secret. Just imagine your face destroyed; your legs will do whatever it takes to keep that from happening.

"I fell small!" I cheer, even though the mouth guard makes it so I really said, "I fawll schmell!"

"Good," Bang-Up says. "That's right, you get right back up. That's good. Keep practicing. Open the door, close the door."

I fall. I get up. I fall. I get up. I fall. I fall before I even get up. Fear keeps me motivated. I drop to the ground and instantly think *Get up, get up, get up*.

And while it's good that I'm getting right back up, there's another part of me that realizes that I'm a girl who has fallen about six times in a row without taking a single step in between.

Bang-Up watches this whole spectacle. I can see her searching for the right words of encouragement, as a trainer, as a skater, and as a human being who doesn't want to mock the feeble. She finally settles on: "Who's a winner?"

I laugh so hard I end up drooling around my mouth guard.

She skates away to help the girl who's got this look on her face that says she's realized she's made the worst decision in her life by entering this track. Her hands are constantly fluttering up by her shoulders, elbows out, her legs stiff straight like she's got stilts under her hips. Looking at her makes me nervous, and I wish there was some way she could wear an extra helmet.

But through her I can see how far I've come in these past few weeks. I feel stronger when I'm here, and the best part about it is the rest of my life goes away. When I'm on the track it's just me and whatever seemingly impossible physical activity I'm trying to master, over and over again. There's no room for anything but the work. My real life is forgotten, inconsequential. I don't even have the mental space to let the voice of John Goodman narrate a few laps. It's me, my skates, and this thing that it turns out I'm not completely horrible at. I do wish my learning curve wasn't so sluggish. But I'm happily no longer the greenest girl of the Training Wheels.

"Look out, Broke-Broke!" I hear next to me. I recognize Trash's voice. "Coming through!" I can hear her skates, and they're very close. I move. It's only then I see that I turned around. I did it. I made a transition.

I give a shocked huff around my mouth guard, so proud of myself. I look to see if Bang-Up caught it. She did, and gives me a thumbs-up.

"I'm a winner!" I shout. I start to skate off, but another skater falls spectacularly un-small-ly in front of me, and I topple right onto her.

The victories here—while hard-earned—are unfortunately quite brief.

24

Charlotte!"

I sit up quickly, wiping my mouth. "No, I'm up, I'm up."

Francesca's brought me a triple-shot latte. "You have a deadline," she says. "Finish that copy."

"I know. I know. Damn." I just need some more sleep to let my muscles and tendons and quite possibly my blood heal. Every time I move I can feel the last few practices up my spine, down my legs, pulsing through my brain. I need a vacation from my flesh. Just for about a week or two, until I no longer look like I just escaped a gang fight.

"This is all your fault," Jonathan says, wagging his finger in Francesca's face. "You are both too old to be playing these lesbian sports."

"You should see how good your girlfriend Charlie is out there."

I'm shaking my head before I even find the words to say, "I'm just trying not to embarrass you, at this point."

She hops up onto the one clear area on my desk, still knocking over a stack of unread memos in the process. I don't know where she finds all this energy. She's like an overactive bird, always twitching and moving, bobbing through space like she's got to keep life bouncing in the air around her. She inches the paper cup of coffee closer to my wrist, then points at it. "You're getting so much better so quickly. I can't wait for the Rookie Rumble. We are going to kick ass."

Rookie Rumble is the yearly event where girls in Training Wheels compete against other girls in Training Wheels like they would if they were placed on a team. It's in front of a crowd, with the lights and music, all the spectacle of a real roller derby bout. I haven't seen an actual bout yet. We're doing that this weekend. Francesca assures me that once I see the real thing, I will get over any hesitation I have about playing in the Rookie Rumble. I think once I see what I'm really in for, I'm going to panic and flee.

"I still don't think I'm good enough for the Rumble," I tell her.

"Whatever. You're already better than Missy Eater, and she's been skating five months longer than you have. And I saw how you knocked Tara Hymen right on her ass last practice. She's a big girl!"

"Oh, my God!" Jonathan shouts.

Francesca looks over at him with impatience. "What now?"

"All you two ever talk about now is roller derby. Do you even listen to yourselves? 'Hey, Pastor, did you see Vagina Knees hit Knuckle Sandwich into the rail?'"

Both Francesca and I fail at our attempts to hide our amusement. I cock my head, jutting out my lower lip. "Aw, Jonathan," I say. "You said 'rail.'"

Francesca laughs, her feet kicking out in front of her. "I know! He's been paying attention!"

"But listen," I tell him. "I'd never skate with a girl named Knuckle Sandwich."

"Vagina Knees is really good, though," Francesca says.

"Man, I know. She's amazing."

"The girl has vaginas for knees, and she still skates circles around us."

"She's badass."

Jonathan attempts to execute a double-fisted, simultaneous paper-wad toss, but he misses both of us.

"Have you checked your email lately?" Francesca asks, leaning close to my monitor.

"No. I'm working on Quit the Internet," I say. "Your rule, remember?"

"You're never going to do that one. So check it now."

A quick click and I find I have something from Francesca, something with an attachment. I open it to find a certificate, one made using a Word template with art and cheesy graphics. There's a cartoon dog jumping in celebration, a cheeseburger, some fireworks, and—for some reason—a giraffe wearing a superhero cape.

CERTIFICATE OF MERIT FOR: CHARLOTTE GOODMAN it says. FOR THE COMPLETION OF: DO SOMETHING THAT SCARES YOU.

"I love it," I tell her. "I really do. What's with the cheeseburger?"

"I was hungry when I made it. Now don't forget the rules you haven't done yet. They're important, too." Francesca points at the untouched cup of coffee. "In the meantime, drink this," she says. "You've got to get that copy turned in before lunch or Petra's going to shit herself."

I shake my head, getting rid of the last of the lingering sleepiness. She's right; I am way past deadline. It just doesn't seem to really matter right now. Not much does, other than when I get to skate again.

Jonathan moans. "Seriously, you guys. Just admit you're

completely in love with each other. Then you can both be happy. Francesca can toss her cell phone in the ocean, and Charlotte can finally be with someone just as crazy as she is."

"You aren't funny," Francesca says, suddenly yanking her phone from her pocket to check the screen again. She frowns.

"Let me guess. He's not calling again?" Jonathan asks her.

She shakes her head. We don't talk about how Jacob's been absent lately; Francesca says she doesn't want to make a big deal of it.

Jonathan leans back and clutches his chest. He groans with a terrible accent, "*Amor de lejos, amor de pendejos.*"

I find the wad of paper Jonathan threw at me earlier and flick it back toward his head. It lands perfectly, with a very satisfying *swip!*

"Stop trying to impress us with the Spanish you learn from your housekeeper," I tell him.

"She's a very wise woman," Jonathan intones. "Look it up, Francesca. It'll give you something to do before you break up with that *pendejo.*"

"I don't want to break up with the *pendejo,*" she says. "I hate when Jacob does this, but I'm trying to not be crazy."

Jonathan snorts. "Right. I bet that comes easy to you."

She jams her phone into her pocket. "I would rather he not tell me he was going to call me and surprise me with a phone call than say he's going to call me and then never call. It's like holding my breath for forever."

"Which is why you should dump him and make out with Charlotte," Jonathan says. "This guy sucks. I've been telling you this for weeks."

Francesca carefully tucks her hair behind her ears and gets quiet. "He doesn't. He's just busy."

"You're busy. I'm busy. We're all busy. We still make time

for each other, if we care about each other. He used to really be into you, but now it doesn't seem like he is. This guy's not worth your time. Dump him and move on."

Sometimes the dude in the room breaks it down to something too simple to ignore, but too hard to accept.

I take a long gulp from my coffee and try to change the subject. "Thanks for this, Francesca."

"Just being a good derby wife," she says, brightening.

"A what?" I ask, having to compete over the sound of Jonathan clapping.

"This gets even better!" he cheers.

"You're my derby wife," Francesca says, crossing her arms like this is the end of the discussion. "You know, you're my best friend on the track. Everybody has one. We keep each other motivated. We're a team. You're my wife. My derby wife!"

"I will be your best friend, but I will not be your derby wife."

"Oh, come on! Everybody else has one. They all were married off before I got there."

"Married?"

Jonathan is laughing so hard he's no longer making sounds. He has resorted to rapidly patting his knees like he's trying to make a drumroll. I grab my entire arsenal of paper wads and toss them at him. He doesn't even flinch as he's showered in crumpled scraps.

Francesca's insistent. "Not *married,* married. Obviously. You're already married. Kind of. Technically."

"And you see how well that's going," I say. "I've been separated in my marriage longer than I was married."

"Whatever, you're my derby wife."

"No, I'm not."

Jonathan has found his voice, but it's still trembling from trying to hold in his laughter. "I will be the bigger man here," he says, adding, "No offense, Francesca. I know you're probably the guy in this relationship." He stands and takes a bow, one arm dramatically waved in front of him. "So I offer up this office for any hot girl-on-girl action. Feel free to start immediately. And although I cannot leave, because my work is important to me, I promise I won't make any noise while I'm watching you."

I turn back to my monitor and continue to work, ignoring both of them.

Francesca pouts. "Look. I embarrassed her, and now she's mad at me."

"Don't take it personally," Jonathan replies. "She hates everyone she's married to. She's a complicated woman, our Charlotte."

25

My therapist is wearing pink socks today. I cannot stop staring at them.

They are vibrantly pink. One is practically yelling at me from beneath the gray of his pant leg. "CHARLOTTE! I AM A PINK SOCK! NICE TO MEET YOU!"

The clock on the wall behind me hums, the only sound in the room until Dr. Hemphill asks, "So, what's been going on?"

The question makes me smirk. "You asked to see *me*," I remind him.

He wiggles his foot, and I'm captivated yet again by the pink sock. How did this pair of pink socks enter Dr. Hemphill's life? Did a Mrs. Hemphill buy them? Another Mr. Hemphill? Is there a man who holds my therapist and calls him Gary, just like he's always wanted?

"I felt we needed at least a follow-up," he says, consulting his notebook. "Since your insurance carrier approved you for ten more sessions, you might as well use them."

I like that somewhere, some person deemed me Ten Hours Crazy. I hope there's a stamp for that, all bold at the top of my case file. "Wacko x 10." Officially in need of consultation: that's me.

What I'd like to happen, though, is that by the end of this session, once I catch Dr. Hemphill up with my life since I last saw him, he'll realize how much better I'm doing. I'm nothing like that mess who cried on his couch and complained about her marriage for an hour. And once he sees I'm doing better, he'll tell me I don't need to come in after all. I'll have graduated from therapy, nine sessions early. Perhaps he'll want to write up a case study or use me as the inspiration for one of those self-help books. *You* Can *Do This Alone—The Charlotte Goodman Story*.

"So, what has been going on?" he asks again. And I tell him.

I tell him all about the past few months, from meeting Francesca at Petra's party to joining roller derby, and how challenging it's been.

"And you like it?" he asks, unable to mask an eyebrow raised in titillation. Like he's imagining me in roller skates and a miniskirt. Maybe there isn't a Mr. Hemphill after all.

"I can't believe how much I love it."

I tell him about going to the bout with Francesca last weekend. How once I sat in the bleachers watching this spectacle, I lost my breath and didn't find it again until the last skater left the track.

It wasn't just the crowd screaming, the flashing lights, the way everybody looked larger than life up there in their uniforms and makeup. Those women were tremendous athletes, playing hard and fast while having fun, and I loved every second I got to cheer for them, especially when I saw Trashcan Punch take a Jammer to the rail, causing her own Jammer to score five points, taking her team to the lead. What was so fantastic about it all was being a part of it, not just a spectator. I skate that track. I play that game. And I get better at it every day, and one day, if I work hard enough, I might get to be on one of those teams. It might be my name the crowd is chanting.

Until then, I'll keep working on my transitions.

Dr. Hemphill takes a moment to write a few thoughts. Probably about how the patient has exceeded his wildest expectations.

He shifts in his seat, tucking one pink-clad foot underneath his thigh. "And what has happened lately with Matthew?" he asks.

I tell him about Mom's party and how horribly our dinner went a few nights later.

"I guess I haven't talked to him since," I say. "But he hasn't tried to call me, either."

"How do you feel about that?"

"I don't know."

"How is the Lexapro working?"

Now it's my turn to shift in my seat. I grab a pillow and hold it in my lap. "I haven't taken it. I don't know if I need it."

"Charlotte, it's good that you've found an outlet with this derby thing, but you know, distractions have a way of deceiving you."

"It's not a distraction." It comes out harsher than I intended, but I don't regret what I've just said.

"Even so. Sometimes things can come crashing back down. You shouldn't be afraid to get some help. With me, or with the Lexapro. These are tools for your recovery."

"Recovery from what?"

He holds up a hand, not really in apology, more like he's trying to slow me down. "I just mean the grieving process."

"Can't skating be a tool? Why is it a distraction?"

"Have you told your parents about the separation?"

"No. But that—"

"Have you come closer to making a decision about Matthew?"

"There's nothing that says I have to know right now."

"It seems like he wanted to know when you went to dinner." Dr. Hemphill puts his notebook aside and leans back in his chair, as if he wants to see me from a greater distance.

"Last time I asked you what would happen if you were to make a mistake, and you said your world would end," he says, squinting. "Do you still feel that way? That you would rather keep your life frozen than make a decision you might regret?"

It feels like he's pulling me backward, back through all the questions that used to spin through my head all of the time, keeping me awake through the night, keeping me in tears during the day. Why would I want to go back to feeling that way all the time? Isn't it okay that I took a break from the anxiety of the unknown?

I don't have the answer, so I let the silence sit between us for a while.

Charlotte Goodman is weary from all the questioning, all the wondering. She is tired of trying to figure everything out. When she thinks about being with her husband again she remembers how he left her, and it feels like it's happening for the first time. She remembers the times he was angry with her, how scared she could be. How there are ways they just don't fit together. She sees their relationship in new ways now. Charlotte is a little different now.

But conversely, when she imagines going through a divorce, severing her life from Matthew's, Charlotte is even more terrified, certain that she would lose her place on this planet, that gravity would stop recognizing her and she would float away. The world would let her go because she wasn't strong enough, because she had wasted so much of everyone's time.

All she knows for sure is that she was married, finally getting her happy ending, but somehow wound up pushing past it into a brand new story, one that is messy and has no end in sight.

Charlotte Goodman is starting over at the finish line. She got through a marathon only to find out she still has another ten miles or maybe even ten marathons to go before she gets to stop running. She's trapped in one of those seemingly endless races where they hand out crappy refreshments at the break tables, like orange slices and pretzels, where all the other runners appear to be having a blast, laughing, cheering. Some don't even seem to be taking it seriously, dressed like penguins or wearing giant foam fingers. And yet, they're running faster, they're getting that medal, they're doing a better job. It might be the same road, but it certainly doesn't feel like the same race.

Charlotte's wondering if it's okay to slow down until she's standing still. She wants to know if she does indeed do that, how long it would take for someone to come pick her up.

"Charlotte, am I upsetting you?"

I clear my throat, but my voice still comes out in a rasp. "All these questions. All this judgment. You're like hanging out with my husband and my mother at the same time."

A sharp bell pierces the air between us. Dr. Hemphill jumps in place, his hand flying to the pocket of his trousers. It's his cell phone. A text.

"I'm so sorry," he stammers, blushing. "Let me—"

"No, it's okay," I say, getting to my feet. "I believe our time is up."

26

I moved out one year ago today. I am standing in the ladies' restroom of my office building, staring at myself in the mirror, trying to see if I look any different, if I look any less married.

Jesus Christ, what am I supposed to do with my wedding gown? Do I take it back to my apartment? Leave it for him to deal with? The thought of Matthew tossing my wedding dress into the garbage is just unbearable.

It wasn't supposed to go on for this long.

Petra walks in and I see it written all over her face. She knows what day it is, too.

"Charlotte." She fills my name with such emotion I can tell she's enjoying walking into this moment. When she tells all her friends about this later, I'm sure she will embellish this situation, saying I was inconsolable, hiding in a stall, thanking her profusely for being such a caring friend. The truth is she doesn't talk to me anymore. If we're in the same hallway at the same time she darts into an office. When she needs me to do something, she sends a memo, or an email. "Don't hide in here," she says to me now. The crease between her eyes deepens, reaching practically to her hairline.

"I'm not hiding."

She rests a hand on my shoulder before stroking a lock of my hair. "I think it's good that you're sad today, don't you?" She nods at me, waiting for me to nod back.

"No, I would prefer not being sad."

"That's not true. Your sadness means you care. This is a good thing. Pain makes us better people."

"So does charity work. I'd rather go volunteer at an animal shelter."

Petra sighs exactly like my mother does when I tell her TiVo didn't erase something on purpose in order to upset her. "It means you're ready to work things out with Matthew," she says. "That it's time to go back to him."

"I don't see how that makes any sense."

"Every couple has problems. That's what you signed up for. For better or worse. Maybe this is the worse, and it just breaks my heart to watch you give up."

I wonder just how much trouble I would get into for shoulder-blocking Petra into the mirror until it smashes into a million glittering pieces.

Before I can say anything, there's the sound of a snarf from inside one of the stalls. The door blasts open to reveal blindingly pretty Suzanne. She busts through, her face puffed up and streaked in hot-pink blotches. She wipes her face until the tears and snot mingle together, pushes past both of us, and leaves the room.

Petra turns back to me, and even though we are the only two people now in the bathroom, she still whispers, not wanting to diffuse a second of this drama. "Her wedding got called off. She said it was mutual, but look at her. Either he got cold feet or she caught him cheating. You see, Charlotte?

That's when you make that kind of a decision. *Before* you get married."

I turn to leave, but Petra reaches out and grabs my left hand. She's so excited about this show she's putting on, she's practically panting. She holds my hand in front of my face, forcing my wedding ring to eye level. My engagement diamond sparkles even in that crappy fluorescent lighting. "This was your decision," she says. "Remember that."

Petra turns on her heels and starts to leave, and for some reason I cannot let her leave this room first. Before I even know what I'm doing, I am practically sprinting to be in front of her. I get around her hips easily, and she stops, having no choice but to bump into my back. *Ha!* I've beaten her.

Charlotte Goodman has just booty-blocked her boss. This cannot be a good sign. Most likely this will be mentioned on her next progress report.

27

N o, thank you," I say, looking through a box of helmets to find one I like.

"Come on, Charlotte," Francesca says from behind a hockey mask. "This one's easy. Don't you want to pass 'Something New'? Another certificate!"

"When do I graduate?"

"When I say so."

We're at a sports store because it's time for me to get my own gear. I'm tired of smelling like some other girl's armpit when I finish practice. Last week I spotted a skater wearing a helmet in this shiny gunmetal color, and I've been coveting it ever since.

"I'm not going on a date," I say to Francesca, for what has to be the fifteenth time. "I'm not interested, I don't want it, and I don't need it. Put that on your certificate."

"He's a model," she says to me, yanking the mask off her head. "So, if you want my opinion—"

"I don't, actually."

"It's that you need to go on a date."

I can't find the helmet I want. Frustrated, I shove the box of equipment back to where it was, garnering a disapproving glare from the shop owner. I shrug at him. It's equipment; it's supposed to take a beating.

"Frannie, I think the last thing I need right now is another man to fret about all day long."

"You're not supposed to fall in love with him, Charlie. You're supposed to have sex with him and then move on."

"Uh-huh. Have you ever done that?"

She hides coyly behind a hockey jersey, pulling a sleeve over the bridge of her nose. "Wouldn't you like to know?"

"I know," I say, heading over to the shin guards. "You haven't."

Francesca mumbles, but I hear her. "Sounds like someone needs to get laid."

"Or you miss your boyfriend, and you're trying to live vicariously through me."

"Yes, and probably. But don't bring up Jacob. I'm mad at him right now."

I spot what I'm really looking for. A pair of black speed skates with white racing stripes down the sides sits on a shelf behind the counter. They are calling to me with their beautiful blue wheels and super-clean white laces. I point and say, "Mine."

"The skates?"

The shop owner smiles. He's wearing a Dodgers T-shirt and baggy cargo shorts. He leans forward on his elbows; his red arm hair splays against the glass counter like hundreds of squished spiders. "Derby girls? Cool."

I ignore him. "It's 'Something New,' Frannie. And it makes me really happy."

She sighs. "Fine. I'll print up the certificate. But only because you're my derby wife."

"Nope."

"Dammit! Just for that, your next new rule is going to piss you off."

"I'm not having sex with someone."

Francesca pats my back. "I want you to tell your parents the truth."

"You're evil."

"No, ma'am. I'm the best thing that's ever happened to you."

28

A wad of paper smacks my monitor. Seconds later, another one strikes me in the back of the head.

"Quit it, Jonathan." I close Matthew's Facebook page. Today he wrote that he's "In a long meeting." Does he really think people want to know that? Then again, here I am still checking his profile, so I might as well shut up.

Another paper assault. It lands next to my wrist. I pick it up, intending to hurl it back.

"I know you're not working through lunch," he says. "What are you still doing here?"

I turn around just in time to catch another missile to the face. "Francesca was supposed to meet me, but she's ten minutes late," I explain.

"Why don't you go find out why? You can go to her office, too. This isn't the center of the universe."

I throw a paper wad at him, but he catches it. "Thanks for the advice," I say.

Jonathan's cell phone rings. As he's adjusting his Bluetooth earpiece, I take my opportunity to toss a handful of paper wads at his head.

"Hey, honey," he says to the caller as he's dodging. "What did the baby doctor say?"

It stops me right as I'm about to walk out the door. I whisper, "She's pregnant?" but Jonathan just waves me away.

As I walk the hall to Francesca's office, I do that thing only single people can do, which is letting someone else's life crisis completely throw you into one of your own. Jonathan's having a kid. I never thought of him being a dad. Not that he won't be a great one, that's not what's weird to me. It's that I don't see him outside this office, and I forget about this whole other life he has going on.

Francesca's office door is closed. I knock while I'm opening it.

She keeps her office dark, sometimes only candlelit, which is against office policy, and this time she's got one candle next to her monitor. As my eyes adjust to the darkness, I hear a man's voice.

"Hey! Hey, are you Charlotte?"

It's coming from a video chat box on the monitor. There's a man in the box, staring at me. He's too far away for me to make out much more than a head of dark curls and sideburns that don't fit his baby face. This must be Jacob.

"Um," I say, starting to turn around. "I was just . . . Sorry."

"No, wait!" he says. "Don't go. Francesca's there, isn't she? I know she is."

My eyes have adjusted, and now I can see Francesca standing just off to the side of her computer, her back to the desk like she's hiding around the corner. She stares at me, shaking her head like a warning.

Dear Lord, I've walked into the middle of a Skype Fight. Honestly, this entire office would run more smoothly if we banned all technology, including the technology we manufacture and sell.

I stammer, "Um . . . she's . . ." I flip the light switch on, just to have something to do.

"I know she's there," Jacob says. "I would have seen her leave the room. Will you tell her to sit down again?"

Francesca grabs a notepad from her desk and scribbles something. She holds it up: TELL HIM I'M MAD AT HIM.

"I think he knows that, Frannie," I say, causing her to smack her notebook against her thighs.

"What'd she say? What did she say?" He keeps leaning closer to his computer's camera, like he can somehow push himself through the lens.

"She said she's mad."

"Francesca," says Jacob. "Please. Just sit down and talk to me. I'm sorry. I mean it, I'm sorry. Charlotte, what's she doing now?"

"She's shaking her head. What did you do?"

"I missed our last date."

"Last *two* dates!" Francesca shouts.

"Okay, okay, last two dates. But one of them you were late so I thought—"

Francesca hurls her notebook against the camera on the computer monitor. Jacob jumps back.

"I'm going to go," I say, turning to leave.

"No!" they both shout.

"Charlotte, tell her I'm sorry. She'll listen to you. You're her best friend."

She sneers at me, tongue between her teeth. She scribbles: NOT ANYMORE.

"Jesus, this is stupid." I take a seat in Francesca's chair. "Okay, Jacob. What happened?"

"The first time, I got busy at work, and I didn't have my phone with me. So I couldn't text her that I was going to miss our date."

"What happened when you texted her later?"

"I don't know. She was pissed."

Francesca gasps, and I place my hand on her leg to quiet her. "Okay, well, what happened the second time?"

Jacob looks off-camera, says, "Just a minute, Jim." He looks back at me. "Sorry, I'm at work. What did you ask?"

"I asked where you were the second time you were supposed to chat."

"I fell asleep. I guess she was late coming home from practice, so it's not completely my fault . . ." He looks away, grabs something. "I DID text you back!" he shouts at me. I look up to see Francesca typing furiously on her cell phone.

I stand up, grab her by the shoulders, and shove her into her chair. "Work it out, you two," I say.

Jacob's face crumples in desperation. "I didn't mean to fall asleep."

"I wasn't late because of practice," Francesca says. "It was because I got dressed up for our Skype date. We were going to pretend we were in Paris, but I couldn't find anything to wear and I tore my closet apart. That's the pathetic excuse we had for a date, and you stood me up."

"I know, I'm sorry." He reaches out for the monitor, like he's trying to touch her face. "I was stuck in a meeting."

"They don't let you go to the bathroom? What kind of prison do you work in?"

"I didn't think of that. I should have done that. I'm sorry."

"I'm so stupid. I got dressed up. In a *dress*."

He smiles. "The green one?"

Francesca runs her finger down the keyboard, and I watch

as she softens. "Maybe," she says. "I can't believe you remember my green dress."

Why can't I forgive this easily?

"I bet you looked really pretty, Francesca."

"Yeah, maybe."

"I know you did."

I'm probably not supposed to be watching this. I lean back on the desk, in Francesca's hiding place, and hope to disappear.

"You'll never know, you jerk," Francesca says.

"I am a jerk. Can we talk later tonight?"

"You know what else we could do tonight?" Francesca flirts.

"Pause!" I shout, sheltering my eyes as I leave the room. "Pause! Pause!"

• • •

I'm pacing the parking lot, waiting for Francesca, when I see Jonathan sitting in his car. I knock on his window.

"You okay?"

He pushes a button and the doors unlock. I go to the other side and climb in.

"I know you love your sports car, Jonathan, but this is kind of crazy. I didn't know you went to visit it on breaks."

He bought this thing a few months ago, after having pictures of it taped to his wall for the previous six months. I remember telling him he was way too young to be having a midlife crisis, and he told me I was just jealous that I didn't have enough money to get one for myself.

Jonathan has his hands on the steering wheel as he stares straight ahead at his name on the sign above his spot. His hair is shoved everywhere and I can tell he's been crying.

"Jesus. You look like shit. What's wrong?"

"I don't want to be a dad," he says.

"Oh. Of course you do. Everybody does." It comes out like a reflex, and I realize I sound just like those people who used to tell me that everything would work out with my marriage. I'm now the one saying stupid things to someone who's scared.

"No. This wasn't planned. We didn't want kids; we said that when we got married. And Cassandra's freaking out even more than I am, so I've got to act like everything's okay, or everything will not be okay. I know we're both not talking about how miserable we both are, and I can't believe we're going to bring a kid into a world where two people don't really want him."

"Him? It's a boy?"

He rolls his eyes as he turns to look at me. "I don't know. It's five weeks old. It still has gills."

He slams his head into the steering wheel. "Oh, God. We're going to have a baby. This is the worst thing ever!"

"Maybe not. Maybe you'll have a really cute kid who will hate everything almost as much as you do." I reach out and take his hand. "And you can teach it all the things that suck in life, like laughing and rainbows. You can make sure he hates unicorns. Or if it's a girl, you can tell her how she's genetically crazy and will never make a man happy, and she's destined to live a life alone except for her cats. You always know what to say to people, Jonathan."

"Stop trying to make me laugh," he says, his words muffled from underneath his sleeve, his head buried in one arm. His wedding ring glints in the sunlight coming through the windshield. It makes me fiddle with my own rings, twirling the diamond so it's in the palm of my hand. I hold it, feeling the sharpness against my skin, thinking of Petra shoving it in my face earlier, thinking about what day it is and the baby I'm not having with Matthew. Then I push those thoughts aside, because Jonathan looks like he's in complete agony.

"It's going to be okay, Jonathan," I say. "Lots of people have kids. Even incompetent people like you."

He turns toward me, both arms outstretched. I move in and hug him.

"Okay," I say, patting him on the back. "There you go. Everything's fine. You're going to be a great dad. And you've got like, eight months to figure it all out."

"That's not enough time. You've had like eighteen months, and look at you. You're a mess."

"Is this really what you want to say to the woman trying to make you feel better? I mean, we're hugging and everything."

He holds me tighter as he laughs. His neck brushes against my face as he moves, and I can feel my skin warming. It's too much contact, and as I try to untangle myself from my friend, he slides his cheek across mine. He kisses me, right on the corner of my mouth. Not on my lips, but close.

I yank back, pushing him with both hands. "Don't!"

"I didn't!"

"You did."

"I didn't."

But his eyes are wide and I see him trembling just as much as I am. "You did," I say again.

"I didn't mean to."

"Don't you ever do that again."

"I wasn't trying to do anything. I'm just messed up, and—"

"I don't care."

He smacks his leg. "Oh, come on, Charlotte. I didn't mean anything. I wasn't going to really kiss you. I don't want you that way. It was just a friendly kiss on the cheek, but you moved and my aim was weird. You moved!"

"Yeah, this is my fault." I put my hand on the door.

"Okay, you are blowing this way out of proportion." He reaches out, but before he can touch any of me I open the car door.

"Don't try to pin this on me," I say as I climb out.

"I'm sorry, I'm sorry. I'm sorry." He's staring forward again, looking like I've slapped him. "We've been friends for a long time. I've kissed you on the cheek before. It was just a mistake. Don't be so upset."

I slam the door and head back to the office. My face is hot, not from desire but from anger. My hands are still clenched into fists as I jam them into my pockets. I know he wasn't trying anything. I know him too well to think that he would ever cheat on Cassandra. It was just a mistake, he's right. It wasn't because he touched me that I freaked out. The truth was he could have been anybody at that moment. I freaked out because *someone* touched me. And I don't know what that means.

I try to calm down but my chest is only getting tighter and my head is pounding and I suddenly can't hear so well and I'm going into the first panic attack I've had in forever and I just want this to stop and I'm crying and I lower myself to the ground because my legs won't hold me anymore and Jesus, God, what is broken inside of me, and why can't I just get over it?

29

Charlotte Goodman does not feel well.

She's pissed off at herself, furious for this giant leap backward, unable to answer her own question: "When will I feel normal again?"

She's standing now in her bathroom, a showdown at her medicine cabinet. She knows what nobody else does. Hidden behind a box of tampons, jammed underneath the hot rollers she never uses, is a white paper bag from Sav-On. Inside the bag is an unopened prescription bottle of Lexapro. Her name is printed on the label. It is suggested she take one daily.

One day at a time.

Charlotte pulls the bottle of pills from the bag with the hope of a kid reaching into a cookie jar. Perhaps this is her answer.

The plastic container rattles in her hand, reminding Charlotte of visiting relatives in hospitals; of being in bed in the early-morning hours, her mother's lips pressed against her forehead to determine if her fever is worth staying home from school; of her recent dependence on ibuprofen for the hours after practice.

Charlotte carries the container of pills with her down the hallway, her hand clutched tightly, her mind racing with wonder—will this change everything for her?

She stops in place and stands still in the dark of her hallway, listening to the sounds of the night as it surrounds her apartment. She can hear dogs barking, the constant drone of her downstairs neighbor's television. Somewhere distant a car alarm is announcing itself—insistent and ignored.

Charlotte reaches her free hand to the wall switch to flood her path with light. A click, but no reward. Charlotte has forgotten again:

The hallway light has blown out.

It happened a couple of weeks ago, on one of those mornings when Charlotte was sure everything had conspired against her. She'd heard a crash from the other room, jumped up with deep conviction that the Big Earthquake had finally arrived, and run from her room like it was her job to frighten this natural disaster from her apartment as if it was an intruder.

In her half-asleep confusion she misjudged the distance from her bed to the invisible assailant, and ended up slamming her toe into the door frame. She then hopped to the hallway, howling and growing ever more sad for herself. Then she flipped the switch, heard the pop of a lightbulb losing its filament, and flailed herself to the ground in resignation.

It was there she learned the crash was from a fallen picture frame, one she hadn't hung very well in her haste to make it look like she'd truly moved into this temporary shelter. The frame, just like Charlotte, had given up its tentative cling to the ruse.

It isn't laziness that has prevented Charlotte from replacing the lightbulb, although there is some apathy. The real reason is that she knows she'd have to stand on something sturdy to be tall enough to change it. Charlotte knows that as a single woman living alone, if she stood on a chair all alone in this apartment, that is when the Big Earthquake really would happen, or the chair would slide on the newly varnished floors. There is *no way around the fact that Charlotte would fall, cracking her skull, leaving her to a lonely, isolated death in a pile of lightbulb shards.*

So Charlotte will wait until there is someone else beside her as she changes that bulb, someone to watch her, to hold the chair steady. Charlotte is willing to wait until that companion is male, someone who will offer to stand on the chair for her to keep her even safer.

And then there's that part of Charlotte, that part with hope, that clings to the happy ending. It says, "Leave this. Leave it for Matthew."

She can imagine him coming over to her apartment one day, finally seeing where she lives, and acknowledging how strong she must have been to create this place for herself. She can picture her husband looking around her space, saying, "I can't believe you did all of this by yourself."

This is when Charlotte would say, "There's still one thing left."

She'd show him the useless light switch. Matthew would laugh, grab a chair from the kitchen, and replace the bulb in the overhead fixture.

"Don't want you to get lost in the dark," *he'd say.*

After he climbed down from the chair, Charlotte would hug him. A thank-you.

But then Matthew would refuse to let go. She'd cling tighter. He'd move his face close to hers, and then they'd kiss—slowly at first, with all the hesitation that was appropriate, until they broke apart to watch each other's reactions.

Then, without another word, both would start the process of packing up Charlotte's apartment, so that she could return home.

Every night Charlotte forgets that this has not happened, and that she hasn't replaced the lightbulb. So at some point every night she flips that switch to find herself still standing in the dark.

Every night Charlotte stands there wondering, "Where is he?"

This is the last thought Charlotte Goodman has before she takes her first Lexapro.

• • •

Three days later, Charlotte Goodman does not feel like Charlotte Goodman. It is hard to think, to have thoughts that have thinking in them. To make the person in her head who's supposed to sound kind of like Roseanne's husband . . . what's his name . . . what's his . . . Mister Goodman . . .

She's looking for Mister Goodman. But not her dad. The other one. But her dad's a good man.

Lexapro is wow.

Things are slow. Things don't move like they did, and when Charlotte sits she hears Philip Glass songs and watches people walk but she doesn't want to walk with them.

Charlotte remembers things, like being called the Sleep Zombie by the girl with the dark bangs who has two names. Frannie Frannie Bo-Banny. She seems confused by this Lexapro, but hey-ho, it's better to just be sleepy and numb numb numb, that's what this has done done done.

People are so far away, it's funny. Even Charlotte is far away. Hi, Charlotte! Way over there, sitting on your tuffet, that little pain ball, that little wad of hate.

Day three. Day four. Day five. Day six.

Six, six, hooray!

There's lots of sleep. Nothing much else. No need. No need.

There's that girl with the dark hair, and she is holding the pills of shh. Charlotte likes her quiet pills; why is that girl holding them?

The dark-haired girl holds Charlotte's face and says, "No more pills. I am calling your doctor after I throw these away."

She gives Charlotte juice. Juice and her lap. Charlotte remembers watching the Fuck You Television where Muppets are singing. She hears Francesca fighting with Jacob on her phone and the last thing she can recall from this time of fog is learning what it feels like to have her eyes crying at the same time her body feels nothing.

30

Now that I've detoxed from the medication, I don't care what anyone thinks, what anyone says. I just want to skate. I need to skate. On the track I'm good. I'm great, actually. I'm Hard Broken, and nobody gives a shit about what's going on in my life, including—and most importantly—me.

Right now we're learning a strategy called Passing the Star.

This isn't easy. It's a bait-and-switch strategy that works by confusing the other team. In every jam, the Jammer wears something called a "panty." This is a stretchy fabric cover for her helmet that sets her apart from the rest of the pack so that everybody knows she's the Jammer. The panty has a star printed on both sides. Both Jammers wear star panties in their team colors. The only other players who wear panties over their helmets are the girls playing Pivots. The Pivot is like the team leader of the pack. It's her job to devise the strategy, to call out plays during the jam, and to make sure every girl is doing exactly what she should be doing. She's like the mother hen.

I am a lousy Pivot. I get up there and even if in my head I know what we're supposed to be doing, the words don't come out of my mouth. I can yell and bark orders just fine if I'm not in charge. I call out to my Jammer or a fellow Blocker all the time, but if that Pivot panty is on my head, I fall silent. It's frustrating.

In Passing the Star, the Jammer pulls the star panty off her head during the jam, passing it to the Pivot. The Pivot then pulls the panty over her helmet and takes off, making her the Jammer.

If the panty falls to the ground during this transaction, both skaters have to go all the way around the track to pick it up, effectively taking the Jammer out of play for the rest of the jam. But if it's passed the right way the Blocker has become the Jammer, and before the other team knows what's happening, that Jammer is halfway around the track, about to score some points.

We're practicing this strategy right now. Francesca is the Jammer, and she's supposed to pass me the helmet panty. Bruisey-Q is assisting her, helping her get through the pack by knocking the formidable ass of ThunderSmack out of the way.

She's getting closer, so I put my left hand out, low but visible enough that she can find me, but not obvious enough that the other team will know we're about to Pass the Star.

But Francesca blows right past me. Just like her derby name. She tap-dances through the pack, right to the front, and takes off. I'm trying to figure out why she avoided the play when I get slammed from the right and go flying into the infield, right on my face. I get back up and jump into the pack, but I forget I am still the Pivot, and now I'm way at the back of the pack, too far away to do any good. The other team's Jammer whips past me—I've just become a point for the other team. I watch her breeze past my Blockers, who all seem to have become scattered lost lambs along the track. The whistle blows, and the jam is over. Five points for the other team, nothing for us.

Francesca skates up behind me.

"Dude, that sucked," she groans, pulling the star panty from her helmet. She bends over, hands on her knees, trying to catch her breath.

I yank my mouth guard out and smack her helmet. "What the hell? You were supposed to pass it."

"Yeah, that didn't happen."

"Why not? It was the plan. We had a plan."

Francesca looks up at me, her face scrunched with incredulity. "Jesus, Broke-Broke. Sometimes you ditch the plan, you know?"

"No, I don't know. Why make a plan if you aren't going to keep it?"

"I was busy getting my ass handed to me by Volvic Nightmare, so I didn't have time to pass you the stupid panty," she shouts. Other girls are starting to stare.

"No way, you had a clear path right for me. I was open. You just wanted to make some points and be the rock star. Admit it!"

"Ladies!" Trash shouts from the infield. "Is there a problem?"

"No, ma'am!" I shout back. As I pull the Pivot panty from my helmet I tell Francesca, "I was open."

"Whatever," Francesca says, and skates away.

I let it go during the next drill. We're skating in a pack, and on the whistle a Jammer tries to break through. We are to put ourselves in front of her, surround her, push her up toward the rail, or slam her down toward the infield. Whatever happens, we are not to let her pass us by.

We've been skating for almost two hours now, and my legs are feeling like wiggly pieces of string. The pain in my lower back has me bent forward, and I'm starting to swim through the air with my arms. I don't want to grab any other players, as it's against the rules. But sometimes it's tempting to reach out and jungle-climb across the skaters, flipping through them like I'm frantically searching for something in my wardrobe closet.

I shove my hands between my thighs as I skate. Bang-Up told me to do this to keep them to myself. Someone needs to tell this tip to Muffin before she rips off another nipple.

Boys are practicing with us today. They are referees, which is the only role a man can play in the sport, and sometimes they skate with the Training Wheels to get better acquainted with the rules, to build up their own stamina, and probably— just a hunch—skate with a bunch of scantily clad badass ladies.

One in particular, known as Maker Moan, currently has his hand angled back toward me, his head turned over his shoulder to catch my eye. He's offering me a whip. I'm supposed to take his arm with both of my hands and let him swing me past him. He may be right in front of me, but he might as well be a million miles away. I can't reach him, no matter how much I want to. And I really want to. I've never taken a whip before, and I could really use the help right now.

"Come on, Broke-Broke!" he shouts. "Take it. Take it!"

"I'm sorry," I shout.

Beside me ThunderSmack growls in frustration. Not because I'm falling behind but because I've accidentally broken a rule I know damn well, even though it's not on the books. I know it because I break it all the time.

"Don't say 'sorry!'" she shouts as she steps right in front of me and skates away. I wobble from the near impact. I know not to apologize. I know not to get weak. I'm supposed to just keep going.

Hands find my rump, and I'm suddenly going much faster. I've been grabbed by Bang-Up, and I hear her behind me. "Just keep skating," she coaches, keeping her hands on my hips as she steers me. "Keep moving your feet. Don't stop skating. You stop skating, and you're more likely to fall." Then she gives me a forceful push as she lets go.

The push helps, and I'm back with the pack. But now I can't see anything because my helmet has fallen forward from all the sweat on my forehead.

Whap!

For a brief second, I am flying, actually tumbling, my feet back, arching higher than my head. My shoulders are locked and my brain seems to understand I'm about to feel impact seconds before my body takes an incredible jolt. My head slams against the track, just above my right temple.

I can't move, and I can't see. Everything is black, and for a second I'm convinced I've just become a paraplegic.

Sounds fade in, like someone's turning up the volume in my head. I hear people ask if I'm okay, but I don't know how to talk. I'm counting my limbs. Can I still feel them? Hands, two. Feet, two.

My head, oh, my head.

It's oddly quiet when I'm finally able to open my eyes. Bang-Up is standing in front of me, tall and beautiful, like a warrior come to my rescue. "Are you okay?" she asks.

"Yeah." I hear myself say it, but I don't feel like I'm saying it. It's like I'm watching this from up above. That's it; I'm dead. I'm floating away, watching my own stupid roller derby death. My parents will never recover. They will write in the obituary that I died of sudden, unnatural causes but will refuse to tell anyone what idiocy their daughter was engaged in when she severed her spine from her brain stem.

My helmet comes off. I see Bang-Up holding it, her eyes wide with concern. Someone hands her an ice pack. "Where do you need this?" she asks me.

"Everywhere."

I ease myself to the infield, holding the ice pack to my neck, which is currently winning the battle for Worst Pain, as I try to get my bearings. This is when I see that everybody else is on one knee, watching me. The entire track has come to a halt, a rare moment when all eyes are focused on me and whether or not I'm okay.

"Oh, I'm sorry," I shout. "Thanks, but I'm okay, thanks."

"So polite," Bang-Up says with a smirk. "We gotta change your name to Nice-N-Easy."

I laugh, but I still feel woozy, and I wonder where Francesca has gone. She must have left the track, because even if we were just having our first fight, I know she would have checked on me after that wipeout. Maybe she went to find ice or painkillers or a doctor.

Bang-Up has started practice again, and the sound of wheels on wood makes my ears hum.

"What happened?" I ask the two girls still by my side.

Sweetheart Wreckline, a girl with enormous thighs and two flame-red pigtails, says, "Holden Wood slammed into you when you weren't looking. This is why I don't like playing with the boys. They're too rough."

"It was a legal hit," bone-thin Stick-N-Stoned says. "I've been hit by Skate Beckinsale harder than that. The girls playing on the Hot Wheels teams hit harder than any boy on this track."

"Broke-Broke's still a Super-Wheelie," says Sweetheart.

"She chose to be here," Holden's defender says, shrugging. "That's roller derby." She skates back to the track.

Sweetheart pats me on the shoulder. "Glad you're not dead," she says as she takes off to join the others.

Practice has resumed, and I'm the only one sitting in the infield holding an ice pack to my head. The class has split into two packs and they are working on keeping an equal distance between them as they skate, rotating within their formations. I scan the bodies, looking for Francesca's pink helmet, but I still don't see her.

Even though I'm in pain, I feel left out. I want to be back up there. I'm a little wobbly when I stand, and my neck would prefer it if I just went home and fell into a hot bath, but we've only got fifteen minutes left of practice, and I know I can do it. I hop-step into a stride, joining a pack as it whizzes past.

"Up here, Broken!"

This time, when I see Bang-Up's outstretched hand, I reach out and take it. I whip past a skater, increasing my stride, and then I'm in the pack, I'm with the others. I hear Stick-N-Stoned call out that she's on my left. I reach back my hand and feel a grip on my wrist guard. I swing my arm, swooping her around and past me.

"Awesome!" she shouts as she disappears in front of another skater.

There's grunting and panting and the pounding of skates as we move as one machine. Bodies push into each other, striding in and out of the formation. I look back and notice we're falling behind. I call out to the girl behind me, "Pick it up, pick it up!" and as I'm saying it, I'm doing it, too. I don't feel the pain right now; right now I am so freaking proud of myself for getting back in here and doing it.

When the whistle blows, I'm almost a little sad that it's over.

Almost. I'm still not *that* crazy.

• • •

I stumble off the track, mouth guard between my teeth, my arms too tired to hold my water bottle in any other way than in the crook of my pit. I am drenched in sweat, my elbow pads slipping down my arms from the slickness of my skin.

I find Francesca sitting by my bag, huddled over her cell phone. She's in full gear aside from one wrist guard, which she seems to have flung away in frustration. Her phone balances atop her knee pad as she tries to type with one hand.

"What are you doing?" I ask her. "Is this where you've been?"

She ignores me and keeps typing.

"Pastor," I say, which still sounds foreign to me, like we're undercover when we're in the Wheelhouse. "Pastor! What the fuck?"

She's still not answering, so I start ripping the Velcro straps off my wrist guards, dropping my gear in front of me. I ease myself down to the bench so I can take off my skates. I am mad that she skipped out on practice. There's a 90 percent chance I have a concussion and I still hung in there. What could Jacob want that's so important?

By the time I finish getting out of my gear and packing my things, she still hasn't said a word to me. "Bye," I tell her as I loop my skates over my shoulder by their laces.

"He's not writing back," she says.

I turn back around. "What?"

"It's been three days. I keep texting him, saying I just want to know if he's still alive. But I'm getting nothing."

"Do you think he's dead?"

"He will be when I kill him."

My legs are trembling and I really want to get home. I want that bath. I have earned that bath. "Maybe you're bothering him."

"I haven't done anything wrong."

"Some people don't like to get one hundred texts in a row."

She looks up from her cell phone and stares me down. Her eyes are burning with anger. "I don't give up, Charlotte."

A girl skating past me pats me on the ass. "I never took you to be a Charlotte, Broke-Broke," she says, chuckling. "Nice work out there."

"Thanks," I tell her over my shoulder. When I turn back to Francesca, she's sending another text. "Frannie, leave him alone." I reach for her phone, but she pulls it away.

"No!" she shouts. "What he's doing is rude."

"Maybe you should break up with him, if he's not treating you the way you want."

"Is that it?" she asks, standing up. I forget how tall she seems in her skates, so tough and scary in all that gear. "You just quit on someone because they aren't making you happy all the damn time? If you want something, you fight for it." Then she looks me over, like head to toe. "Not that you'd understand that."

"I don't? What do you think I've been doing all this time?"

"Waiting! Waiting for someone else to make this decision for you."

I'm too tired for this argument. "Forget it," I say. "I'm going home."

"Nice. I have to hear about Matthew every second of the day, literally nurse you back to the world of the living when your therapist puts you on medication that practically gives you a lobotomy—"

"I had a bad reaction! I wasn't trying to—"

"And now you don't have any time for me when it's my turn to be sad? You kind of suck right now."

Trash skates in between us with the swiftness of a boxing referee. "Okay, you two bitches need to get to couples counseling," she scolds. "No more fighting at my practices or it's toilet detail for both of you. You can yell it out while you scrub the bowls clean. Understood?"

"Yes, ma'am," Francesca says, her eyes still fixed on her cell phone.

As Trash skates off I take a moment, trying to get us both to calm down. "You're going to hear from him in the morning and then everything will be fine," I say. "It always is. Why should we go through hours of anxiety for nothing?"

"Because that's what friends do, you asshole." Then she skates past me, bumping my shoulder. She keeps going, skating out of the warehouse, into the parking lot.

"She okay?"

It's Bang-Up asking. She's sitting across from me, shoving gear into a rolling suitcase slapped with a sticker that reads, MY DERBY WIFE CAN BEAT UP YOUR DERBY WIFE.

"She will be," I say.

"Take care of your head," she says. "You probably shouldn't have gotten back up there, but it's pretty badass that you did. And get a new helmet. Your old one's useless now."

Francesca's car is gone when I get to the parking lot. But

someone's standing next to my car. It takes a few seconds for me to realize it's Holden.

"I know I'm not supposed to say it," he says, "but I'm sorry. I didn't mean to hit you that hard."

"I just wasn't expecting it, that's all. I was looking the other way. I'm fine. But I am getting a mother of a headache."

"I would imagine."

It always takes me a second to relearn what someone looks like without a helmet or gear. Holden is all right angles, a thick forehead, angled chin, ears that seem pinned into the sides of his head like afterthoughts. He's got dark, short hair that's jagged and wild, sticky spiked from sweat. His black T-shirt is sagging across his chest, damp and worn. His arms are crossed in front of him, and I notice a bird tattoo on his biceps, near the crook of his elbow. He catches me staring and rubs at it. He lowers his head to catch my eyes, and I am suddenly aware of how close we're standing. I take a step back.

"So, I'm going to get in the bath," I say. "And try not to slip into a coma tonight."

"Right. Listen, Broken, I don't know if this is okay to ask, but are you—"

"No."

He pauses, thinking. His eyebrows knit together in confusion. "No, it's not okay to ask, or no to whatever I didn't get a chance to ask?"

I'm aware of how ridiculous I sound, as my mouth goes dry. "I don't know," I say quietly. "Both, I guess."

"Sorry," he says. "For asking. And for not asking."

"Not your fault," I say, trying to ease the tension. "I'm the one with the head injury."

"Right," he says, pointing at me. "Or maybe you're just smarter than I thought."

He puts out his hand and I shake it. He slides his hand across my palm and grips my fingers with his. I pull away like he's hit me with a joke buzzer. I don't want to bring on another panic attack, and I don't know how to tell Holden it's not his fault that I can't seem to handle a man touching me.

"Okay, then," he says, and heads to his car. A red Honda, covered in bumper stickers, including one for Obama and another for the Hot Wheels. As he drives away, he ducks his head and raises his hand, one more apology for the road.

There's a breeze on the back of my neck as I toss my gear into my trunk. My head aches and I just want to go home and hide.

I'm not waiting, I tell myself. *Francesca's wrong. I'm just not ready.*

But then I have to wonder: *Ready for what?*

31

So, call me today, tonight, whenever. I'll be up. Okay, bye."

It has been two days since we fought, and I can't get Francesca on the phone. She even called in sick to work. I kind of have to admire her dedication to avoiding someone. I used her office while she was gone so that I didn't have to be near Jonathan. It's awkward between us right now, and I know he wants things to go back to the way they were, but he'll just have to wait. He's not my first priority.

I open my laptop to check Matthew's Facebook page, but stop myself. I actually don't want to know any more. I just don't care. It's not a decision that requires any further thought. Right now there seem to be more important things than trying to figure out what Matthew is doing with his time without me. I have to figure out what to do with my time without him.

Charlotte Goodman realizes she's just repeated to herself something her friend Francesca has told her a million times. If Francesca were in charge of the narrator in Charlotte's head, right now she'd be telling him to say: Suck on that, Charlotte Good-

*man. Now watch your tiny friend dance around your apartment
with the freedom that comes from the satisfaction of being right.*

I delete my fake profile, which removes my access to Facebook. It feels like I've made an executive decision, one that
should come with . . .

A certificate.

I text Francesca: I QUIT THE INTERNET. WILL THAT MAKE
YOU FORGIVE ME?

No reply.

This leaves me with just the couch and the Fuck You Television. How easily I can just stay here again, like I used to,
falling asleep to Jon Stewart, only to wake up disoriented and
depressed. The couch is calling to me, asking me to curl up
around a cushion and give up. Give in and stay there until
everybody has forgotten about me, until I've forgotten about
everything.

But I can't do that. I've come too far.

I call Andy.

Two hours later we are at a dark Chinese-themed bar,
crammed into a wooden booth, mashed against a brick wall
from elbow to shoulder. The truth is we are grateful for the
structural support, as the drinks in this place are superstrong.
We haven't come here in years, and I had forgotten how much
I love this place. Having to squint through the dark to see each
other, the jukebox that plays every song so loudly you have to
lean in to understand each other, the red bulbs everywhere
making everyone look mysterious and foreign. I find it to be
incredibly romantic, and just what I want as I sip my martini.

That said, I don't think I should have a second one.

"Too late. I've already ordered it," Andy says, as he pushes
the drink in front of me.

"I owe you one."

"You owe me nothing." Andy steals my skewer of olives and pops one into his mouth before returning it to my drink. "Except maybe some of your time. I was going to pretend to be mad at you, but you look so pitiful I just don't have the strength to go through with it."

"Sorry."

"Do you ever wonder how many times a day you apologize? Because you do it a lot."

He scratches at his wrist, a habit he's had as long as I've known him, which means he is uncomfortable.

"What's wrong?"

He fiddles with his glass of Scotch. "I don't know, Charlotte. It feels like there's too much to cover, really. You kind of dropped out of my life."

"So you weren't going to pretend to be mad at me. You *are* mad at me."

"I'm not mad," he says, still scratching at his wrist as he searches for the words. "I'm surprised how quickly I got dropped."

"I didn't drop you. Derby's been kind of hectic, and—"

"I lost my job."

This shuts me up.

"I got another job, so it's fine. But you never even knew that I was unemployed."

"I'm sor—"

"At first I thought you ditched me because I reminded you of all the shit you've gone through, but then I figured that couldn't be it, because I never even liked Matthew to begin with. No offense."

"Okay."

"But it sucks, Charlotte, because at a certain point you're

supposed to ask me how I'm doing. That's what friends do. The problems go both ways." Andy turns in his seat to lean his head against the brick wall. "I hate it when you make me talk like a girl."

"Well, I'm not sorry about that," I say, trying to make him laugh. But he's got his focus far away, his face bathed in the red light, softening his features. It makes his skin flawless, and he looks exactly like he did the day I met him. It makes me yearn for the past, our past, and wish I could go back and do some things differently, enjoy the times I was truly happy but didn't stop to notice.

"I know things have been difficult for you, but you make them worse," he says, now turning his gaze toward me. "You go into this bubble of pain and act like nobody can understand. Guess what, Charlotte? Everybody understands. We aren't idiots. We've all been through pain. And you have been missing out on things because you seem incapable of moving on."

The martini is making my brain fuzzy, and I'm worried I will talk uncensored. "Everybody wants to make sure I know how much I suck lately."

"It was tough watching you spin yourself into depression, but I was there. And then when you spun yourself hard enough, you just forgot about everything and everyone. Including me. You don't call. You don't ask how I'm doing. And when I do get a call from you it's to play Matthew at your mother's birthday party. It's all you, all the time. It's exhausting."

"I'm sorry."

He smacks the table. "No! Don't be sorry. Fix it."

"Okay! How do I fix it?"

Andy reaches over and pulls down my lower lip with his

thumb as he talks. "'Hi, Andy. It's me, Charlotte. Your shitty friend. You got a new job? What's that like?'"

I pull back. "Get your finger out of my mouth." I wipe my lips with my wrist. "What's your new job?"

"I don't want to talk about it."

"Andy!"

"I'm working post-production at a reality show about babies, okay? The job is fine, but I spend almost my entire day hearing whiny women talk about their problems. And it's made me really fat, which is why I'm lonely and miserable, and I'm taking it out on you. I'm volatile when I'm fat."

This makes me smile. "Are you done?"

"No. Then you called and brought me here to this black hole of Chinese sadness to scream all your problems at me over the jukebox, which reminded me that no matter how bad I might think my life is, you believe yours is worse, and therefore you're still a more miserable human being than I could ever be."

It takes a certain kind of lifelong friend to have not only the courage but the right to talk that way. Andy is such a friend.

"I'm sorry, Andy."

"That's all you have to say?"

"What do you want me to say? I'm *really* sorry. I'll be a better friend. I'll stop talking about my problems all the time. I'll ask you about your life. No more being selfish. Okay?"

Andy drains his drink. "Do you really think *that's* what I wanted to hear from you?"

Then it hits me. "You're not fat."

His grin is a relief. "Thank you."

I'm bent over my skates, untying and retying them, hoping to make it look like I'm experiencing an equipment malfunction when really I'm just trying to catch my breath long enough to stop being nauseated. I'm guessing my little trick is no longer working, because Bang-Up skates right up to me.

"Broke-Broke, are you going to sign up for the Rookie Rumble?"

"I don't think so."

"Why not? You should." She isn't wearing a helmet today, and her long brown hair is flowing over her shoulders, making her look like a roller-skating pinup from the seventies. I heard that Bang-Up is a kindergarten teacher by day. Every time I see her, I think of her making kids get ready for nap time, breaking up fights, and snuggling weepy children. I hope she doesn't make her little ones do push-ups when they spill their juice.

I was supposed to have signed up by now, but I don't want to without Francesca. She's skipped the last two practices. She still won't return my calls. If Andy was sick of how I was treating him, I can only imagine how furious Francesca is with me. It's kind of ironic how she's ignoring me the way Jacob's been ignoring her. Or maybe she learned it from him, how to ice someone out until they're going crazy. Either way, it's working. I thought for sure I'd see her here tonight at the track. She's never missed a practice for as long as I've been coming here, and now she's on her third.

"I'll think about it, Bang-Up," I say.

"Don't think." She points at a clipboard on the nearby bench. "Go sign up. The rumble's in three months. I want to cheer for you."

Trash calls me from the track. "Broke-Broke! Come up here and do this drill."

I shrug at Bang-Up. "Gotta go!" I say, skating away.

It's a jamming drill where I'm the Jammer, and I've got to break across two Blockers. There are just the three of us on the track, so they have time to plan a formation before I get to them. I skate hard, but they surround me, taking me up to the rail, effectively getting me to a standstill. No matter how much I try to dance around them, one or both of them find a way to stay in front of me. I can't get past this wall of ladies.

Bruisey-Q is one of the girls I'm trying to pass. Her warm smile does not match the fact that she's got a shoulder block so severe I've had a bruise on my upper arm for the past week. It's gotten to where I've asked her to sign it, just so I can show it off properly.

"Come on, Brokey," she says. "You can get past us. Find the hole."

I slow down and let the two girls get some distance in front of me so I can figure this out. I just have to find a hole, a space they aren't guarding. I decide to come at them like I'm going to go high, and then shoot down low, hoping I can pass them on "the pink," the pink line at the very edge of the track, the last edge of fair space just before the infield.

I try to bolt in that direction, running on my wheels, but I still feel clumpy in my skates. I'm as graceful as an elephant on a beach ball. With all the work I put into moving, you'd think I'd go much faster.

The Blockers are slowing down, their heads cranked back to watch me, to anticipate what I'm going to do next.

Now.

I make it look like I'm going high, pumping my elbows, stomping my skates. It works, and the Blocker on the inside takes a stride toward the rail. I turn and arch down to the infield, lifting one foot so I don't step out of bounds as the other Blocker throws herself toward me, but she's too late; I've already passed her. I saw the hole and I got through. I can hear the girls in the infield cheering, and I pump a fist in the air because everything went just as it was supposed to.

Who's a winner?

I look back, fist still in the air, to see my adoring crowd.

And that's when I lose my balance. I'm falling forward, but I don't want to land on my face again, so I yank my body back, arms flailing. I tuck my feet under me, but I don't just land on my knees. I somehow fall even harder, slamming my butt right into the metal underside of my skates.

When they say you can hurt yourself badly enough to see stars? You really do. Everything's sparkly and white and dotted and your tongue swells and your throat tries to close up and kill you so that you don't experience any more of the shooting pain that's taking over your spine. My hands wiggle, making me appear to be finishing an elaborate dance number.

I know my fall looked absolutely hilarious. So I'm even

more impressed when Bruisey-Q and Trash rush over to me with comforting words, and wonderful ice packs.

"Shit, Broken. That must have hurt," Bruisey-Q says.

I'm not crying, but tears are streaming down my face. My body has completely abandoned my head and is operating on its own now. "I think I broke my tailbone," I say.

Trash nods, the corners of her mouth turned down. "I'm positive you did. Way to earn your name, Hard Broken."

Bruisey-Q is shoving an ice pack down the back of my tights. "I did the same thing when I first started. You bent your knees too far, so instead of your knee pads taking the impact, your ass did. Into your skate."

I couldn't possibly care any less *why* I just broke my ass. I only want it to not have happened.

"You might want to see a doctor," Trash says as she unlaces my skates for me.

It takes half an hour for me to get out of the rest of my gear and ease myself into my car. When I sit down, my body screams in pain. It hurts so much I can't even see. I don't care if I'm still technically at practice because I'm still in the parking lot. I lean my head against my steering wheel and break down in sobs. I don't want to not be able to skate.

There's a knocking on my window. I see Bruisey-Q waving at me, her face flushed and sweaty, her black Hot Wheels hoodie wrapped around her shoulders like a cape. She's biting her lower lip, concerned.

Instead of lowering the window, I open the door. Bruisey-Q stands in the crook of it, leaning an elbow onto my roof as she observes me.

"I know," I say, wiping my face. "There's no crying in roller derby."

"Dude, you broke your *ass*. You get to cry. And take lots of drugs. I mean it."

"Every time I think I'm doing well at this, I immediately hurt myself. Maybe I don't belong here."

"Yes, you do."

"But I hurt all the time."

"Yeah, welcome to roller derby. We all hurt all the time. Look, I can't even extend this arm anymore because I jacked up my elbow so badly." She extends both her arms, and indeed one is curled slightly at the joint, sending her forearm in the wrong direction.

I shake my head, letting tears roll under my chin, down my neck.

"Come on, you know it's fun," she continues. "You go fast, you hit hard, and you do something most people are way too chickenshit to do."

"Well, maybe those other people are the smart ones."

"They're pussies. Open your hand."

She drops five Vicodin into my palm.

"That's just a starter pack," she says. "But take them. Do yourself a favor."

"Thanks."

"No need to thank me. Put your booty on ice and rest. Call a doctor, but he'll probably tell you the same. Just promise you'll come back when you're all better. And listen. Pastor will be back. Give her some time."

I must have looked shocked, because she laughed and added, "Oh, yeah. We all talk. You think we don't know anything about you? We know everything."

"Good to know."

"Word on the street is people think you're pretty cool.

And if you want to know the truth, I already have kind of a girl-crush on you. Drive safely." She turns around, her skates strung over her shoulder, banging against her back. As she walks away, I hear, "And I'm really sorry about your divorce. That sucks."

They may not know my name, but they know my secrets.

After she's gone it takes a few minutes for me to figure out that I can drive if I roll over onto my hip. I'm pretty much sitting sideways, but it works.

After I get home, I leave Francesca a miserable message filled with self-pity, begging her to be my friend again. I tell her I don't want to skate without her, and that I miss her more than she can imagine. I hang up and learn it hurts to do anything other than breathe.

I may not have any more Lexapro to numb me from my body, but I have Bruisey-Q's Vicodin. I pop one and shuffle over to the couch. When I can't find a good way to watch the Fuck You Television on my stomach, I give up on this mistake of a day and fall asleep with an ice pack stuffed in my underwear.

33

Here's something you can't do when your tailbone is broken: sneeze.

Unfortunately, you also can't *not* sneeze, because holding it back means your body sneezes internally, forcing you to take it through your spine. That sneeze will travel all the way to where your tailbone is currently a boiling hot welt of fury.

One sneeze. Just one sneeze and you are done. It brings on such a massive, body-wide spasm of pain that everything else in the world stops. It's like in cartoons when a guy gets his head smashed between two cymbals, and he rises into the air, a quivering mess. That's what a sneeze does. You just sneeze and then cry.

A broken tailbone never stops hurting. Before I had no idea just how much *sitting* I do in an average day. I've now missed three days of work because if I go anywhere near a bucket seat or a hardwood chair, I will start whimpering. I can't drive, not just because it's unsafe to drive on one hip, but because potholes and speed bumps are evil. I refuse to buy one of those doughnut hemorrhoid things, as I'm still clinging to some false sense of dignity, but I'll admit there have been times when I've fashioned a fake doughnut out of a jacket or a few pillows just so I could sit down. About the only place to sit that doesn't overwhelm me with pain is the toilet, and I find that to be the saddest fact in the world.

Crueler still, it's even harder to stand up. I find myself grabbing for anything I can use to yank myself upright. I can't take a bath, I can't sit on the floor to put on my socks, I can't take a quick break to watch television. Sometimes I forget and drop to the couch, tucking my foot under me in the process, thinking, "*Tra-la-la I'm normal*," only to immediately scream with regret.

It hurts to sleep, it hurts to wake up, and it hurts to live. It hurts to put something down, move something over, or push something aside. It hurts to laugh. Not that I'm finding things to be all that funny these days.

But really, more than anything, I cannot stress this enough: it hurts to sneeze.

Having a broken tailbone takes over your thought process so that every decision boils down to whether or not the action you're about to take will make you hurt worse.

This is how I ended up saying yes to Matthew asking to meet me at a coffee shop. It's been a long time since we've talked, so I'm guessing whatever it is he has to say at a place as ubiquitous yet ominous as a coffee shop is going to have some weight.

But the thing is, anything he's going to throw at me won't make me hurt any worse than I already do.

• • •

There's no way I'm going to be able to fake feeling completely healthy, so as I wince into my seat across from Matthew, I tell him the truth.

"My tailbone's broken," I say.

He shakes his head, confused. His hair has gotten longer, and he has sideburns that seem way more renegade and aloof than Matthew would normally allow for his appearance. Like at any minute he might decide to become a sheriff. "Does it hurt?"

"Yes. Because my tailbone is broken."

He's crinkling his nose and tilting his head, his eyes so filled with concern they're watery. I haven't seen him look at me like that in so long. With compassion. Right there, that's the Matthew I remember.

After all this time, I still can't believe we're living so separately that I can be injured and he doesn't even know about it.

Matthew had to take me to the hospital once, a few months before we got married. I'm never lucky enough to get one of those sexy afflictions, the kind of illness where you suffer beautifully, resting in a hospital room with your hair flowing all around you, your lips even more crimson against the paleness of your skin, your body rendered vulnerable due to both the IV drip and your enviably solemn determination.

No, I got some kind of cyst on my face that could spread to my brain and kill me immediately if someone didn't lance it open and drain it.

That sentence contains a lot of the words you hope never to say to someone you love. "Lance." "Drain." "Cyst." Things related to your face that you'd rather not have to share with someone you want kissing said face in the future. But there I was, with this gigantic pus-filled welt on the underside of my chin. If Matthew didn't get me to a hospital quickly, so that a doctor could squeeze infected body fluids out of my head, he'd have a dead fiancée on his hands. I remember joking that he had to at least get to the "widower" part before I died or it wouldn't be fair to him. A widower can get sympathy sex, but a guy who loses his fiancée is technically just an unlucky bachelor.

Matthew insisted on staying with me in the doctor's office while they cut open my face, so I made him close his eyes. I went so far as to make him promise he'd always have his eyes closed for any medical procedure he might share with me, including any and all possible births. He could be in the room to be a dad, so long as he didn't look anywhere near me. As far as I was concerned, he was allowed to see all the parts that were visible from outside of me, but anything that came from inside of me was off-limits.

The lancing and draining was a success, and I went home with my chin a giant cream puff of a bandage. But the next night, I had a hard time sleeping. My pain medication wasn't working, and I couldn't find a way to rest my head on the pillow that didn't make me want to rip my lower jaw from my head and toss it into the trash.

At one point I turned to my right and noticed Matthew was flat on his back, eyes wide, staring at the ceiling. Our bedroom window was a few feet from a streetlight. Consequently, the room never got that dark.

"You're still up," I said.

"Yeah."

"You okay?"

"I have to tell you something," he said, swallowing hard. "But I don't want you to get mad."

I gently eased myself up onto my elbow, trying to look like I wasn't nervous. "What's wrong?"

"I watched them drain your cyst."

Instinctively, I covered my chin with my hand. "What? No! Why?"

"I was curious! It was a mistake!"

"Yes, it was!"

Matthew turned to me, his eyes wide with shock. "Charlotte, it wasn't blood. Not at first. First it was green and then it was purple with this yellow and . . . and it was coming out of your head and . . . oh, the purple was just . . ."

That's when Matthew pushed himself out of the bed, ran to the bathroom, and threw up.

This time he doesn't have to deal with what I'm going through. The ice packs, the skate-shaped bruise across my ass, the hematoma on my inner right thigh I will eventually have to break apart with my fingertips.

"How did you do this?" Matthew asks me now, as he leans over the table to sip his iced mocha. I tell him it's from roller derby, and his mouth drops, the straw momentarily clinging to his lower lip.

"You mean like girls on skates?" he asks. "Beating each other up?"

"Something like that."

I tell him how I got into it, about Francesca, and about how much fun I'm having. I show him my arm muscles and make fun of my bruises.

He fiddles with the edge of his T-shirt and I notice his hair is starting to thin at the top of his scalp. It makes him look vulnerable and nerdy. I want to touch it, to see if it feels different, wondering if I will feel different when I touch him.

Matthew looks back up at me, cocking his head. He is clearly amused. "Did you get a tattoo yet?"

"No. And I'm not getting one."

He scoffs. "But you're done with roller derby now, right?"

"Why would I be?"

His incredulous smirk is so wide it threatens to jump off his face. "Because your tailbone is broken!" he shouts.

I'm immediately defensive. There's no need for him to act like I'm an idiot. "Everybody gets hurt," I tell him. "This is a pretty common injury, actually."

He reaches across the table and gives me a patronizing pat on the wrist. "Look, Charlotte, you know I love you, but you're not exactly the most coordinated person I know."

I push his hand off me. I haven't heard him say those words in so long, and I wasn't prepared to hear them used in such a casual manner.

"Come on," he continues. "You know this. Don't be stupid. You're going to break your arm. Or your face." He reaches over and touches a bruise on my forearm. "Derby, too?"

I nod.

"This from the woman who wouldn't go skiing because she said it was like playing Russian roulette on a mountain."

"It is."

"I still think you should stop while most of your body is still unbroken."

It's a little shocking how outraged Matthew is, like I've just told him I've taken up bum-punching.

"Have you even seen roller derby, Matthew?"

"I don't have to. I wouldn't want to watch that anyway. I don't want to watch women intentionally hurting each other. I thought you were a feminist. I can't believe you want to participate in this."

"I'm *completely* participating in it," I tell him. "In fact, I have a bout in a couple of months with all my feminist teammates."

I hadn't known I was going to say that, but I know I have

to be in that Rookie Rumble now. If Matthew thinks I can't or shouldn't do this, I have to do it over and over, proving to him just how badly he can underestimate me. I will kick ass all over the place, whether he likes it or not.

"Brilliant," he says, shaking his head. "Have fun living the rest of your life in a wheelchair."

"What do you care, anyway?"

He slams his plastic cup onto the table. He opens his mouth to say something, but then stops himself. He laughs in the back of his throat as he straightens the empty sweetener packets in front of him.

With all of the terrible things we've said to each other over the past year, I wonder, how much worse are the ones we choose not to say? Especially the words we stop at the last second, the ones we have to swallow before we give them breath.

"I care, Charlotte," he says slowly, carefully. "Because I care about whether or not you are hurt. You know that. I would think."

"Are you seeing someone?" I ask.

Charlotte Goodman wishes she could take that question back. She didn't mean to ask it, but she knows she has to know. She only pretends she doesn't care, but now that she cannot look at Matthew's Facebook profile, she knows she's losing her closest connection to him, even if it's one-sided. She needs more evidence that their time is coming to an end, hoping that with every fact she learns, the pain inside her will lessen and shrink, until these two people who used to love each other with both fists clenched finally let go.

Matthew stops rearranging, but he doesn't look up. "Not exactly," he says. He taps the tabletop with his index finger.

Then he taps again. Two more taps, then one. I see his shoulders drop, the tension lessened.

I rub my face, frustrated that this conversation doesn't feel like normal people talking. There must have been some sugar or something on my palm, because the second I stop rubbing, I can feel the worst coming: I'm about to sneeze.

I lift my chin, staring at the ceiling, which makes Matthew think I'm being dramatic, but I'm so busy concentrating on not sneezing that I don't have the ability to explain. I just put up one finger, open my mouth, and try to wiggle my nose out of this potential hell.

It doesn't work. Too late. I sneeze my pain-yelp: "*ACH-AAAAAAAHHHHHOOOOWWW!*"

"You okay?" Matthew asks, looking appropriately frightened at what he just witnessed.

"I have to go," I say, knowing that getting up from this plastic chair is going to make for the opposite of a dramatic exit. I end up executing a half-roll, heaving into a standing position.

"Why are you leaving?" Matthew asks.

"Because you have no idea how much I love you."

"Charlotte." My purse knocks over my chair as I yank it to my shoulder. Everyone turns to look but I don't care. I push through the glass doors and keep walking.

I don't know what I'm going to do next, but I think I know where I have to start.

34

The drive to my parents' house would probably be much more painful if my blood weren't pumped full of adrenaline. I have no idea how I'm going to tell them the truth, but I know I have to do it. It's the first step in making a decision, in having to deal with not just trying to get back to what was "before" with Matthew but what will happen when I finally reach my "after."

I'm also doing this for Francesca, to prove to her that I listen, that I take her advice seriously. I know there's a good chance I'll get a certificate at the end of this, which I'm hoping for, because it would mean Francesca was talking to me again. I miss her in that way where it can feel like you're stuck in a dream; how that's the only logical explanation for why the most important person in your life is missing.

I try to picture what I'm going to say when I walk in the door.

"Hi, Mom. Dad. I'm separated from Matthew. Let's eat."

"Hey, guys. Yeah, I have lost weight. And my marriage."

"I am now a spinster. Let's go see a movie!"

My parents live about an hour's drive away in an area that's made for people who technically should live in Los Angeles because they work there, but they want to pretend they don't have anything to do with that city. When you go out to Lancaster, it's easy to forget you're even in California. I like getting out of the city every once in a while, but once I moved inside the metropolitan area, I could no longer imagine doing the kind of commute my father does every day.

The city's skyline withers away in my rearview mirror as I continue to mentally prepare myself, knowing that there's no way I can predict what my mother's going to say when I break her heart.

• • •

"Charlotte, don't you dare get a divorce. Go back to that man and apologize for whatever you did."

I might have been able to predict that one, if I'd given it a few minutes' more thought.

Charlotte Goodman would love for her narrator to take over here, but she knows it's best to stay in the present, to truly be in one place, both body and mind. Besides, her mother might lash out or something. Remember: hair on fire. Better to be on guard.

"Mom, it's not that simple," I say, watching her storm away from the kitchen table. I can't get up to follow her because it took everything I had to ease myself into this chair without her noticing I was wincing.

"Yes, it is that simple," she says. "I don't believe in divorce. You shouldn't, either."

Her anxiety has driven her to clean her already spotless sink, apparently worried that whatever disease I'm carrying that caused me to be a woman on the brink of divorce might contaminate her immaculate home. She pushes the sleeves of her pink, puffy robe until they are up to her elbows and gets to scrubbing. I don't know how she can be comfortable wearing what looks like a gigantic, quilted Peep costume.

"How can you not believe in divorce?" I ask her. "Lots of people get divorces. Are you saying you don't recognize them? What happens if they remarry, are they polygamists?"

"Don't get smart with me," she says. I can't see her face, so I watch her swaddled backside wiggle as she furiously scours the drain. Her hips are shaking in frustration, as if they're trying to shimmy some motherly advice up to her head. "Abe!" she shouts, staring straight up at the ceiling as if my father is in Heaven instead of in the living room. "Come and yell at your daughter!"

My father shuffles into the room, empty coffee cup in hand. He runs a hand over the back of his head where the last soldiers of his scalp stand guard. "What's wrong?"

Mom turns around to lean against the sink, devastated in a most dramatic way. "Your daughter is trying to get a divorce," she practically wails. She's tattling on me like I just got caught sneaking the car out of the garage. "Tell her she can't," she says, staring me down with disappointment.

Dad's face softens as he looks to me for confirmation. The disappointment in his eyes is crippling. "Is that true, Bunny?"

I start to defend myself. "I'm not trying to *do* anything," I say, choking on the words.

"She moved out!" Mom says, her hands outstretched. "She already left him. Tell her to go home."

Mom's so loud I worry the entire neighborhood has suddenly gone on pause, waiting to find out the details. I bet every single one of them is thinking, *"That Goodman girl is a disaster."*

Dad joins me at the table. I like how he drinks coffee at night. I still associate that smell with the end of the day, with getting into my nightgown and dragging a pillow into my parents' bedroom. I'd climb up onto the bed, snuggle beside my father, and have him pet my head as he read me a bedtime story. It makes me want to crawl back to the time when he was the only man who mattered. I didn't know how great I had it back then, to be blessed with someone who would never make me wonder if he loved me.

"Jeez, Bunny," my father says to me now. "I knew something was up, but I didn't think it'd be this. You guys just got married."

Dad almost didn't walk me down the aisle. Seconds before the music started, he grabbed my arm, clutching so hard I had to gently pry his fingers loose.

"I don't think I can do this," he said, trembling. "It's too much."

"Everybody looking?"

"No. It's too sad. I'm giving away my baby girl. You'll be someone else's now."

As I held him to me, feeling him shaking from head to toe trying to keep from shedding even a single tear, I whispered, "It's going to be okay." Just like he used to soothe me when I woke up from a bad dream, I was now holding my father, assuring him there was nothing to be afraid of.

"Let's do this," he whispered back.

We walked down the aisle together, surrounded by people on their feet, smiling at me in that way that's reserved just for brides—a combination of awe and heartbreak over this one moment, knowing that if it ever gets to come at all, it only comes once in your life (or at least, that's the plan), and it's so heartbreakingly brief. Everything is frozen in perfect potential, and then over in seconds.

I remember in that moment how I squeezed my father's hand and asked, "Not so bad, right?"

"Not anymore," he said. "Your Aunt June gave me a pill earlier and it just kicked in."

My father is looking at me now with that same reserved confusion. "You think splitting up is for the best?"

"I don't know. I don't know what to do."

Mom shouts from the pantry, "You go back to your husband is what you do."

"Elaine, cool it," Dad says as he takes my hand. "If you want to yell at someone, go check the dining room table. I'm sure I set it all wrong."

My mother heads straight for the dining room, because while she knows he's being sarcastic, she also knows he probably did set it all wrong, most likely on purpose, just so she'd have something to fuss over while he sneaked off to play a round of online poker. This might be exactly what marriage is, finding ways to keep someone right on the line between adoration and insanity. And if that's the case, then perhaps I've been too hasty with Matthew. I should be thanking him right now for keeping me teetering on the edge.

I tell my father the truth. "A few months after the wedding, Matthew had some doubts. He took some time, moved out."

"Your mother said you moved out."

"I did. Once he came back."

"Because he left you, and you thought he might do it again."

I nod, wiping my nose on the inside of my wrist. Dad hands me the handkerchief he keeps in his robe pocket. I bring it to my face, not to use it but to inhale the scent of his aftershave on the fabric.

"Did he ever hurt you?" he asks.

I stare at the fabric of my jeans, wiping my free hand up and down my thigh, making the color change from light blue to dark and back. I quickly shake my head. I've turned into a little girl, unable to answer questions with more than a shake or a sniff.

"What about this?" Dad turns over my palm and points at my wrist. There's a purple and green streak circling from my thumb down to where my pulse is thumping.

"That's from . . . working out." As much as I could use the distraction, now isn't the time to explain roller derby to my father. I'm not sure if he'd get it, and he might freak out if he knew I was intentionally slamming myself into other people in my free time.

He whistles through his teeth. "That is some gym you go to."

"Mom is so mad, but I didn't mean for this to happen. With Matthew, I mean."

"These things sometimes happen, Charlotte. But you never know. It might work itself out." My father leans back in his chair, bending his knees until he slides into a slump. "Don't be too hard on yourself," he adds. "Just try and make it through today. There's nothing you can do right now, right? Whatever is supposed to happen will happen. That's life. Life is unpredictable, and we just hang on for the ride. Hopefully, with a seat belt. And if you're not wearing a seat belt, maybe because you're on a motorcycle, at least you should be wearing a helmet. Although that doesn't protect your heart, does it?"

"Dad. What are you doing?"

"I don't know."

"You sound crazy."

Dad shakes his head, bringing his thumb to the bridge of his nose. "I know. I'm sorry. I don't know what to say, and you're not talking, so I'm saying a bunch of bullshit."

I lean into his shoulder. "Well, I appreciate the bullshit."

"You do what you have to, Bunny. And I'm here if you want to talk. Now go to your room and hide out until dinner's ready. I'm going to tell your mother I grounded you."

It's not really my room at all anymore. Not that it should be; I haven't lived here in almost ten years. But I'm not sure what kind of room it's supposed to be. Mom keeps a few pieces of antique furniture in here, as well as a bookshelf filled with cookbooks and encyclopedias, none of which she's ever opened. I'm their only potential overnight guest, yet they haven't found the time to get a spare bed.

I open the closet in search of the air mattress and the electric pump. Instead, I find my old art box. My beloved Caboodle from when I was a little. It's shoved behind Mom's abandoned macramé projects and a box I choose to ignore that she's labeled For When I'm Dead.

The Caboodle is purple and covered in My Little Pony stickers. I'm rather shocked at how girly it is, because I don't really remember myself being that kind of kid.

I open the box to find everything I need to make a miniature. It's been a long time since I've held even the simplest materials. I haven't had the slightest desire to start a new project. But right now, perhaps only because I'm trying to avoid my mother, my fingers are itching to see what I can come up with in an hour.

I grab a few pieces of wood and an X-acto knife. I stack a few cookbooks and my cutting board into a makeshift table and get to work.

The day my mom first let me use this knife was a big deal. It meant she trusted me not to cut off my own fingers, and I remember thinking at the time it made me very grown up, using the same tools real artists used. Dad called my miniatures my Occam's razor. "You take the big things and make them smaller. The simplest solution is the best."

It's funny that I can do that in my miniatures, harness something large into something you can hold in your hands and inspect from all angles. I can break something down to the bare minimum, if I need to. Hint at detail where there is none, make one stroke of paint represent something hundreds of times its size.

Why can't I do that with the rest of my life? Make all the questions go away, and find the simplest, tiniest way to illustrate the enormity I feel?

The door whips open, startling me out of my world. "There you are," my mother says, as if she's been searching for me, which I know she most certainly has not. "I figured you'd run away from home."

"Dad sent me to my room," I say. "For not finishing all my marriage."

Mom sighs. "I'm not cleaning that up," she says, pointing at the work in front of me.

"I know. I'll do it. I'm sorry."

"What is that you made? A wooden doughnut?"

"It's nothing. Just playing around." I miss the days when she would crouch beside me and ask all kinds of questions about what I'd just done and what made me so creative. She'd smooth my hair and kiss my face and call me her little artist. Something came between us as I got older. My life gained speed as hers slowed down and I guess we sort of passed each other. The distance between us hurts, but only when I allow myself to stop and think about it.

"Dinner's ready," she says. "Go wash your hands. They're covered in glue." She shuts the door behind her with too much emphasis. I take a second to admire my little wooden derby track. It's not bad, considering I didn't have much more than some balsa wood and a few Popsicle sticks. I know I can do a better version, but this one's a start.

• • •

We get through almost our entire meal in silence. To stave off complete boredom, I've started to count how many times I'm chewing each bite. With my last hunk of chicken I managed to chomp sixteen times before there wasn't anything in my mouth but a soup of liquefied meat—that almost made me get sick at the table. So now I'm seeing how quickly I can swallow each bite.

One, two, three, four—gulp.

Got it. Next bite.

One, two, three—gulp.

Awesome.

One, two—

A piece of chicken lodges in the back of my throat. My hands fly up to my mouth and I immediately start trying to cough. The lurching and retching makes my tailbone scream in pain, which makes *me* want to scream in pain, but I can't do anything other than hack and try to breathe.

My mother's on her feet, hurling the pink Peeps coat to the floor. "Abe! She's choking!" she screams.

I'm in so much pain I'm making an actual chicken noise, squawking and choking as my father rushes behind me, puts his hands under my sternum, and gives me the Heimlich maneuver.

One, two, three—

The chicken lump flies out of my throat and onto the table. My parents stare at it expectantly. I guess they figure with such a dramatic entrance, it should continue with a soliloquy.

"Oh, God!" I wail, one hand on my throat, the other on my butt. I'm rocking back and forth, hurting from end to end. "Thanks, Dad," I manage to scratch.

"No problem, Bunny," he whispers, and I can tell he's shaken.

"Jesus, Charlotte," my mother says, rubbing the crease between her eyes. "Don't kill yourself before you meet your *next* husband."

In the shocked silence, her eyes meet mine. We both break into laughter. True, good, honest laughter that says all the things words can't. It's as real as the tears of grief we're soon wiping from our faces as she walks over to me, leans down, and embraces me. I nuzzle my forehead into her warm neck and breathe in her lemony perfume.

"I'm sorry, Mommy."

She pushes my hair aside and kisses the bridge of my nose. "Me too, baby. We'll get through this. We're strong."

My father dramatically lowers a napkin over my hacked-up chicken wad. He glances at his watch before he solemnly intones, "Time of death: 9:27."

As I sign the form for the Rookie Rumble, I don't even recognize my signature. I'm trying to work this pen, but it's difficult while wearing a wrist guard. It's like a monster scrawled, "BROKE-BROKE." Maybe the other girls will think Frankenstein is skating the Rookie Rumble and will be too scared to sign up.

But I did it. I signed up. Now that I'm committed, everything has a new perspective. I'm here for a reason. I'm in training. I've got a competition coming up, and now every skill I learn, every hour I log on my skates, is getting me prepared. Just over a month left. I've got a lot of work to do to be an asset to my team.

Teams! I still can't believe I'm going to be on a team. I think of all the years my mother wouldn't let me near anything even slightly athletic, and I wish I'd gotten to experience just a taste of this earlier.

Still, this isn't right without Francesca. She's the one I want to be stretching with, discussing the bout. I need her strength, her determination. And I need her pep talks. I wouldn't even mind fighting with her again, just so I could hear her voice.

"Broken!" I hear from the other side of the track. "What the fuck are you doing?"

It's Bang-Up. She's wearing little pink shorts with silver stars on each butt cheek. Her tank-top says, EAT SLEEP DERBY. I skate over to her.

"Hey. I signed up for the Rumble."

"Great. Now go home."

"What?"

"Or go sit in the bleachers, but get off the track." She smacks me on the helmet. "You've got a broken tailbone, dumbass. You can't skate. Technically you can't train again until you're cleared by a doctor, but if you get out of here before anybody else notices you, I'll let you come back in two weeks."

My heart sinks. "Two weeks! But I need to practice for the Rumble!"

"Even if you weren't an insurance lawsuit waiting to happen, you can't scrimmage. You can't do crunches. You are useless to me. Get out of here."

"But—"

"What are you, Old Yeller? Go away, stupid yellow dog!"

I gather my things and clump up the track to the steps, hoping someone will notice and demand I get to stay. It doesn't work, as they're all busy on the track. As I head toward the benches, Bang-Up shouts at me, "And tell your derby wife to get her ass back to practice!"

* * *

It has now been two weeks since Francesca has spoken to me. Between the work she missed and the work I missed, the practices and the phone calls avoided, I have no idea where she is or what she's doing. She can't just quit her job to avoid me, but I wouldn't put it past her. And I'm afraid if we don't make up soon, she will really let me go. Forever.

The Buddhists talk about the danger of attachment, how nothing is permanent and the key to ending suffering is to learn how to let go, to focus on only now. Frankly, I find that to be terrifying. If you let everything go, if you decide there's truly nothing real to hold on to in this world, what keeps you from floating away past the atmosphere?·

In my dreams, that's how I fly. I don't just take off and soar, like with wings. I start by walking, and then I skip. A few steps later I can jump, and as I continue jumping, I get higher. Soon I'm leaving the ground for gaps of time before I come back to the earth, only to jump again. Higher and higher, longer and longer, I'm leaping across the land, until inevitably I jump high enough that I break past something, something important that keeps us tethered to the planet. And at that point I have to reach out and grab onto a fixed object. It can be anything. Usually a lamppost or a tree branch. I'm like a helium-filled balloon, and if I don't find something to wrap around I will leave this planet and never come back.

It happens every time I try to fly in my dreams. At a certain point I've gone too far, and there's nothing holding me back. If I let go, I will be gone.

People have to stay attached to something. Those who are unattached are the ones who run out into the wilderness only to get eaten by bears, or alternately, they fill their homes with everything they've ever encountered, surrounding themselves with fixed objects that can't leave. Until one day they get buried under their things.

If we don't stay attached to someone in this world, how do we have any proof that we exist?

Even scarier than that, just like in my dreams, if we soar high enough in life, we could end up alone.

I call Andy.

"I know I'm supposed to be focused on you right now," I say, "but do you think you could help me with something?"

"Of course," he says. "Rome wasn't built in a day, and Charlotte Goodman won't become unselfish that easily, either."

"Just get over here."

It is not without a considerable amount of pain that I make my way to the hall closet. I'm not sure which box holds what I'm looking for, but I can't do what I want to do for Francesca without it.

The first box I open is filled with books. I pull a few out and stack them to the side, just to make sure there are only books in there. The next box, more books. I stack those aside, too, and break down both boxes.

I pull open a double-taped box and find my wedding pictures. Obviously I was trying to save this future version of me from this moment, but it doesn't hurt to see them as much as I'd feared. I can see how happy I looked, how handsome Matthew was. I'd forgotten about this great picture of Andy and me goofing around with my bouquet, pretending he was catching it, pretending to knock bridesmaid Petra to the ground with a punch.

I find boxes of papers, family photographs, linens and matchbooks from restaurants I'd gone to with Matthew. Little memories that I'd stuffed away, hidden from me to protect myself. There's the tiny owl figurine I won in the third grade. There's the necklace Dad gave me for my sweet sixteen. I didn't realize just how haphazardly I'd thrown my things together when I left the house. As I sort through the chaos, something inside me finds order.

At the back of the closet, in a suitcase, I find what I'm looking for: Halloween costumes from a few years ago. Matthew and I went as Pepe Le Pew and a black kitten who'd had an unfortunate run-in with a freshly painted white bench. A picture of us from that night's party sits atop the clothes. I'm squirming in Matthew's grip as he's posing seductively for the camera.

Andy strolls right into my apartment, like we're still roommates. As he takes in the complete mess I've made, scanning the piles of books and papers and mountains of clothes, his smile is huge.

"Now *this*," he says, "is what I call progress."

"Me too. Help me carry this stuff into the kitchen."

I hand him a roll of butcher paper and my art supplies, snag a bottle of wine I'd been saving for the perfect moment, and get to work.

36

I'm not leaving until you open up," I say into my cell phone. "So unless you want your neighbors to think you've got a heartbroken lesbian lover camped out in your creepy hallway on the dirty green carpeting, I suggest you let me in. Also, I know you can hear me in there. I'm talking to voice mail, not an answering machine, so I'm just going to take up all the free time on your phone. And all of my minutes, so if you think about it, I'm making the sacrifice here."

The door opens. Francesca's in a pair of green Paul Frank monkey pajamas, holding a cup of coffee. "What do you want?" she asks.

"I'm sorry."

"Yeah, I know. You said that a million times on my voice mail. And all the little Post-It notes on my office door. And the carrier pigeon you sent over."

"But no email! See? Still staying away from Internet."

"If you're here for a certificate, you can fuck right off."

"No certificate," I say. "I'm here to kidnap you a little."

"I don't think that's physically possible. Kidnapping just a little."

I check the time on my phone. "Just get in my car. I'll explain later. Please."

She sighs as she starts shuffling back into her apartment. "Let me put on some clothes."

"No!" I say, leaning forward to grab her arm. "No time. You can change later!" She snatches her keys as I grab her, coffee cup, bare feet, and all.

• • •

As we enter my place, I tell Francesca I can't believe she kept her eyes closed the entire time.

"Unlike you, I believe in promises," she says. "Plus, if you're taking me somewhere to kill me, I don't want to see it coming."

I push her into my bathroom, hand her the black dress from my hostage kitten costume, and tell her to change. I start the kitchen timer I have sitting on the sink. "When that bell rings, open your eyes and come out here," I say.

I run over to the kitchen, turn on the Christmas lights I have strung from end to end across my ceiling, straighten the backdrop I have covering the windows that I've painted to look like the interior of a Parisian café, and start the *Amélie* soundtrack on my iPod player. I run over to the table, open the laptop, press a few keys, and pour a glass of wine while I wait.

A few seconds later, Jacob's face appears in the chat window. "Is she there?" he says, his excited face filling the screen. He's dressed in a red-and-white striped shirt, a beret on his head. He's painted a silly skinny mustache over his upper lip.

I quickly shush him and hold up two fingers. "Soon," I mouth. I point at him and shake my head, letting him know he looks ridiculous.

He shrugs, chuckling, and I can see how excited he is. He gives me a thumbs-up. "Thank you," he mouths. Then he whispers, "It looks awesome. *Très magnifique!*"

I check the time. I've got sixty seconds to get out of that apartment.

"*Au revoir!*" I whisper into the microphone. I quickly put the plate of cheese and bread next to the glass of wine, grab my keys, and run out through the apartment.

I hear the kitchen timer go off just as I shut the door.

• • •

An hour later, Francesca finds me at the coffee shop, where I'd told Jacob to send her when they were done with their date.

"What you did is about 60 percent stalker and 100 percent awesome."

I put my book aside. "I didn't know how else to get your attention."

"So you got me a date. With my boyfriend. In fake Paris. In your kitchen."

"I couldn't afford to do the real thing."

She wrinkles up her nose, and for the first time I notice she has a sprinkling of freckles. "Did you see what he was wearing?" she asks. "He looked like a candy cane."

"Don't let him wear that if he ever takes you to the real Paris."

"I can't believe you orchestrated all of that. He told me you found his number in your cell phone."

"You borrowed mine once when yours died."

"I remember. While I was busy hating you, I kept remembering other nice things you've done for me. Like when I was sick that night you made me soup. Or when you broke up my shin hematoma with your thumbs when I was too grossed out to do it."

"About that," I say. "I've got one on my thigh I might need you to do for me."

"Not until you say you're my derby wife." She passes a fresh cup of coffee across the table. "Anyway, all those thoughts pissed me off, because it made it so much harder to stay mad at you. I missed you."

"I missed you, too. Things with Jacob are better?"

She nods. "I told him that things had to end if he couldn't find a way to fit me into his life. I said—and don't take this the wrong way—that I didn't want to be like you, always in limbo."

I understand, but I don't know what to say to that. So I nod.

She goes into her purse. "This came for you."

She unfolds a new certificate. It says: CHARLOTTE GOOD-MAN HAS SUCCESSFULLY COMPLETED: FIX SOMETHING YOU DID WHEN YOU WERE BEING A TOTAL DOUCHE BAG. HAS ACHIEVED LEVEL: LIEUTENANT BADASS.

"I particularly like the drawing of the douche bag."

"I'm pretty proud of that myself."

"I didn't know this was one of the rules."

"I had to make it up after you turned into such a douche bag. But I obviously forgave you when I let you kidnap me." She leans forward, resting her chin on her fists. "So," she says, her tongue darting briefly to her front teeth as she poses. "What's new?" she coos.

"I signed up for the Rookie Rumble."

"I know. Bruisey-Q told me."

"She did? When?"

"When I signed up." She kicks me under the table, not lightly.

"Ow."

"Would you rather I kicked your ass?"

I shift uncomfortably, reminded of the pain that I've oddly become accustomed to over the past couple of weeks. "You'll be doing it soon enough, once we're on the track."

Her face turns to worry. "Oh, no! What if we don't end up on the same team?"

"Either way, we're going to die."

"I know." She reaches over and takes my hand. "But it'll be fun getting killed with you."

37

Finally, I'm cleared for light practice. While I'm itching to get back on my skates so that I don't end up being the worst one on my team, a slight problem has developed. I'm scared to get back on the track.

This is why Francesca and I have come to the Wheelhouse an hour before practice to skate alone for a little while, until I don't feel like throwing up at the thought of skating next to someone. She's also brought me a present: crash pads.

They're shorts that are padded around the hips, with extra protection around the tailbone.

"These things always existed?" I ask, incredulous. "Why don't they make you skate with these all the time?"

"I don't like wearing them. They feel like diapers to me. But for you, they will be your Confidence Pants."

"How do I look?" I twirl on my skates, feeling three feet wider around my ass.

"Like a dinosaur. Charlottosaurus. A C. rex."

"Okay," I say, as I skate to the track. "Now what?"

She runs at full speed, slamming into me. I fall immediately, right on my ass. "Hey! It didn't hurt!"

"I know! Confidence pants!"

I chase after her. "*Grr!* C. rex angry!"

After we're warmed up, Francesca suggests working on hitting. "You're probably going to be a Blocker since you're good at slowing people down, so you should get used to knocking people over."

I tell her something I haven't told anyone before. "Sometimes I feel bad when I knock into a girl."

"But that's the game."

"Do you know Sandy has four kids?"

"Who's Sandy?" Francesca asks, scrunching her face.

"Oh, um. Bloodfist. I saw her driver's license when she was paying dues at the front, and now I can only think of her as Sandy."

"Bloodfist has four kids?"

"*Sandy* has four kids. Four! One of whom is a newborn. What if I hit her and she falls on her arm and then can't breast-feed? I can't hit a baby mama."

"You hit me. I'm smaller than you are."

"Right, and I don't want to hurt you, either."

"Why not?"

I sigh. "Because you're my *friend,* Francesca."

"No. I'm Blowin' Past'er. Why do you think we all have these other names? That's why on the track Sandy-with-the-four-kids is known as Bloodfist. And you're supposed to knock Bloodfist down before she does exactly that to you. Her baby-popping vagina's not the only thing that's mighty. That girl can hip-check you right onto your face."

Francesca bumps into me. "Hit me as hard as you can," she says.

"I don't know."

"Do it, Broke-Broke! You have to hit me. Everybody on

this track knows the risks. Including you. Are you mad at the girl who broke your tailbone?"

"No. Nobody did it. I fell when I was celebrating."

"Well, that is hilarious. Now hit me."

I bump into her. Not a hit. A bump.

"Are you kidding me?" She jams her mouth guard in and growls around it. "Hit me like you mean it. Like I called you fat. Like I called you ugly."

I go at her, but she sidesteps around me. I miss, and fall.

"Get up," she says.

I get my feet under me and push toward her. I skate up the incline so that I can use the momentum down the track to plow harder into her arm. I go at her, but she picks up her pace. I miss, sliding right into the infield, crashing on my knees.

I hear her from the other side of the oval, taunting me. "Are you mad yet, Broke-Broke? Get mad. Get mean!" She rounds the bend, coming toward me. She points at herself. "I'm not your friend up here. I'm Petra. I'm Matthew. I'm the dick who cut in front of you at the grocery store. I'm—"

I sidestep into her, hitting her hip with mine. She goes down quickly, her chatter quickly halted. She looks up at me with surprise. "Whoa."

"You okay?"

"Broke-Broke. That hurt!"

"I'm sorry!"

"Don't say 'sorry!'" she yells. Then a huge smile breaks out on her face. "I'm so glad you're on my team! We're *so* going to win!"

We spend the rest of the hour chasing each other around the track, slamming into each other. Each time we call out another thing we're hitting instead of each other. Whatever it is that gets us furious.

"I'm not hitting you, I'm hitting my mother!"

"This time you're the babysitter I had when I was ten!"

"Hit me, I'm Elmo!"

"Take *that,* soy milk!"

We are in hysterics by the time the other girls show up for practice.

During the last jam of the last scrimmage, Francesca plays Jammer for the opposite team. As she tries to pass me, I step in and slam her, not just her shoulder, but as if I were hitting her *through* her shoulder. She leaves the ground, shooting up and spinning as she falls backward. Terrified that I've just killed her, I turn around and skate back to her.

"Jesus, are you okay?"

She's flat on her back, eyes closed. Her tongue pushes out her mouth guard and it bounces onto the track near her neck as she whispers, "Holy fuck, Broke-Broke. You're a killer. That was awesome."

That night I buy the beer, and Francesca makes me a certificate of completion on a cocktail napkin. My favorite one so far: CHARLOTTE GOODMAN GOT ANGRY.

38

When Petra calls my name from the door of my office, it makes both Jonathan and me jump right out of our chairs.

"Jesus, Petra," Jonathan says. "When it's quiet because we are working, I would think you'd like that."

It's also that quiet because Jonathan and I don't talk to each other much anymore, and I'm starting to miss his company. He's on the phone with Cassandra half the day now, her pregnancy having taken over both of their lives. I like listening to his half of the conversation, though, to hear how concerned he is for her comfort, for the safety of the baby. He thinks it's going to be a girl, but Cassandra is hoping for a boy. One day when Jonathan thought I had music playing through my headphones, I heard him tell Cassandra to put her cell phone to her stomach. He sang the baby an impromptu song about how fetuses shouldn't make their mommies want to puke every day. Then he freaked out when he realized how dangerous it might be for his wife to press a cell phone against her womb.

"I need to talk to you," Petra says to me. "Conference room?"

As I walk down the hall, I quickly go over the past few weeks in my head, trying to determine what I've done wrong. I can't think of anything, but whatever it is, it can't be that bad. This job is just a job, nothing more. The more I've started to enjoy my real life, the less of a hold this place has on me. It's no longer my solace but once again a place I feel like I just have to endure.

On nights off from the track, I've been playing around with making miniatures. At first I was just seeing what came out of fiddling with a few pieces of wood, but I had all these empty boxes from my closet, and an idea started to take shape.

I'm making a series that re-creates the places I've lived in over the years. Each box is transformed into a diorama of the layout. My childhood home, my dorm apartment, my first tiny studio all by myself, and lastly, my house with Matthew. That one has been more difficult, and I find I get stalled around the bedroom, the front porch where I was once carried over the threshold, the bathroom where I shared a shower with my husband, the back porch where I planted lilies . . . Even in tiny form they are still filled with powerful memories. Going back to places where I lived in high school and college was much easier. The thoughts that emerged during that time were mostly warm ones, filled with silly nights amped up on too much caffeine when Andy and our friends and I laughed way more than we studied.

Even though it's been a long time since I've worked on anything, I'm impressed with the changed direction my art has taken. There's a mood in my miniatures now that I think was missing before. I'm not so worried about getting the re-creations exactly right, but more concerned that they carry an emotion in them. The rooms feel like they've been lived in. They aren't just dioramas or models; they are snapshots of my life.

Petra is already seated at the table when I enter the conference room; it seems like she'd have to have teleported herself there for that to be possible.

"Sit down, Charlotte," she says, because apparently she assumes I might choose to drop to the floor or crawl up onto the overhead projector and perch like a monkey.

I take the chair across from her, opting to place as much table between us as possible.

"Is something wrong?" I ask, trying to smile.

She's changed her hair. It's red, and she's attempting to pull off a headband, but her forehead is too exposed, her skin dry and flaking around her eyebrows. She must have just applied lipstick, but she did it hastily and it doesn't cover her upper lip. In the harsh lighting of the conference room, it glares orange. She says, "This is awkward, but I'm wondering if you've decided what you're going to do about Matthew."

"Is this why you called me in here? Is this the meeting?"

"You know, he's seeing someone. Someone he . . . well, I'm not supposed to tell you these things."

"Then don't."

"Look, I've watched you destroy yourself over the past year—"

"I'm doing better now," I say, hoping she will take the hint and start minding her own business.

"Really?" she asks. "Because fun time with Goth Girl seems to be taking away a lot of time from work. You had to take time off because you hurt yourself roller-skating? Aren't you thirty?"

"Petra."

"Do you know Matthew spends most of his time at our place? Neither of you want that house. It's making it so that my life is affected now. Not just yours. Pete and I aren't on the plan anymore."

"The plan?"

"We were going to buy a house, start a family. But ever since you and Matthew split up, Pete's worried that we're not going to make it, and all he talks about is whether or not we'll ever get a divorce. And if this keeps up, we will get one, and I don't really want to end up like you and Matthew."

Now that I hear someone else talk about how frustrating it is to deviate from a personal plan, I realize what Francesca's been trying to tell me all this time; my daily plan wasn't just ridiculous, it was futile. That's what sets people up for disappointment. It's not the promises that let you down; it's the plans. You can't predict your day any more than you can predict the next thing a person's going to say.

"I quit."

Like that. That's what I've said, and I couldn't have predicted it.

Petra taps her pen on her bottom teeth. "What does that mean, exactly?"

"I quit this job." My brain is racing through my bank account. If I don't spend any money on anything I don't truly need, that doesn't feed or house me, I can make it for a few months.

"That's not necessary."

"I think it is." I stand up. "By the way, you've been an incredibly shitty friend."

I practically float back to my office.

"Hey, guess what, I just quit," I tell Jonathan as I head

straight to my desk and open a drawer. I drop pens and Post-It notes into my purse.

Jonathan's quickly on his feet. "What? No! If this is about me and the car, I promise it's never going to—"

"Don't. It's okay." I open the filing cabinet and hand him all my untossed paper wads. "I can't stay here anymore. I hate the job, Petra hates me, and all this personal stuff is wrapped up in my private stuff. Things with you got weird and sad. I just need something else."

Jonathan looks devastated. "What made you do this?"

I toss one last wad of paper at Jonathan's head. He doesn't even flinch as it bounces off his forehead.

"I got angry," I say. "Keep in touch."

Francesca meets me in the hall, breathless. "I just heard. We have to celebrate."

"We sure do. Where do you want to go?"

She smiles. "Do you have a passport?"

39

It's rather remarkable how quickly you can be on a flight to Mexico.

"God damn," Francesca says as she kicks off her shoes. I've never seen someone so happy sitting in the middle seat. "I knew we'd run away together someday." She beams.

It's not a long flight, and it's not for a very long time. I'm unemployed, so theoretically I could stay in Mexico for as long as I wanted, but Francesca only had four vacation days left. We used our combined miles to buy our tickets, and the resort is some kind of hookup through Jacob. Basically, we're only paying for food and suntan lotion, which means we can afford about three days total. Besides, we both have Rumble practice next week that we can't miss. This is just an escape, not a solution.

Francesca hands me a piece of paper. "This is your next certificate," she says. "But to earn this one, there's a time limit."

It says: MAKE A DECISION.

"I just did that," I say.

"Not that one. *The* decision. You have from now until we leave Mexico."

As the plane takes off, I think about how she's right. This

needs to be done, and it can't wait any longer. It's going to hurt if I decide right now, and I know it'll still hurt whether I decide in ten minutes or ten years.

But for now I'm going to stare out the window and watch the world from a safe distance as it continues to shrink behind me.

● ● ●

By the afternoon we are both flattened on our lawn chairs, having been silent for hours. Francesca stretches her arms up high. Through the space between her bony wrists, the sun is piercing. It gives her a glow, like she's all-powerful, summoning the spirit of the sun. She looks like an angel, a hero.

She turns to me, glowing in a fuzzy ring of sun, and declares, "We need more margaritas."

My hero.

During our stay in Cabo San Lucas, Francesca's in charge of the important things, like ordering food, reapplying sunscreen, and buying more magazines. Any questions asked by the staff are directed toward her. I am simply here to be as small as possible, a human in hibernation. I am to sleep, drink, eat, and reset my internal clock.

A funny thing has happened. Since setting foot on this land, taking my first sip of ice-cold beer that cost roughly the change in my pocket, and feeling the warmth of the sun on my eyelids—I haven't felt like moping. I can still feel the sting of a million teardrops just under my skin, but I can't seem to get this smile off my face.

The margaritas arrive. Francesca pulls herself over onto her elbows to sip from her oversize green straw. Her sunglasses are almost as big as her face, and I see myself reflected in them.

I'm distorted in her lenses—all giant knees and tiny head. But I can still make out my little smile.

"*Hola, señorita,*" Francesca says, almost a whisper. "You were asleep there for a while. You might want to smear on some more sunscreen."

I drop white goop along my shins as I look out toward the endless blue water before me. I can hear music piped in from somewhere near the swim-up bar. Harmless adult contemporary. Back home this music would be irritating, but here it's the perfect melody to accompany the show just to my left: a small group of sunburned and smiling guests engaging in water aerobics. They bob and smile, bob and smile, far away from their own problems, enjoying the easiest exercise on the planet.

"Francesca, guess what?"

"What?"

I hold up the bottle. "Sunscreen. Petra's party. My wish collage came true."

She nods, pursing her lips. "And my heart and lungs appear to still be doing their jobs. Maybe we shouldn't have been such jerks. Let's call Petra and apologize."

"We should wish-collage a bag of money."

Later we wander down to the shore, walking past the remnants of a Zen garden in the sand. There's an empty bed on the beach, the white sheets of its canopy flapping in the wind. Every vision is like a dream. I hear nothing but the surf, the breeze, and the occasional strains of adult contemporary, which is quickly becoming my favorite sound in the world.

Francesca fiddles with her tiny digital camera. "Stand in the water," she says. "You look like you're on the edge of the earth."

I pose, one hip jutted to the side, like a pinup model. I know I'm covered in bruises and abrasions, but I've never felt so comfortable in a bikini. I cannot seem to get anxious about the things that normally get me neurotic. I just am. Right here. Everything is perfect. The Buddhists would be so proud.

"*Señoritas! Peligroso! Peligroso!*"

A man is running toward us from the resort. He is shouting, waving his arms madly. I know very little Spanish, but this word—*peligroso*—I recognize.

Danger.

I jump forward, out of the water, toward the sand, grabbing Francesca by the arm to drag her with me.

The man catches up to us, his neck bulging against the stiff collar of his white uniform. "*Peligroso,*" he says again, pointing at the water, at the shore, then back at us. "No-no, *señoritas.* No-no!"

He points at a nearby sign, one that we somehow had breezed right past in our excitement to plant our feet firmly in the waves. It tells us that the undertow where we're standing is dangerous, and the surf is extremely unpredictable. Another minute or so and we could have been dragged into the Sea of Cortez.

"*Gracias, señor.*"

I wonder how many times a day that man has to save giggling white women from accidentally drowning themselves while trying to snap a photo.

We're walking quietly back to the resort when Francesca bumps into my arm. "I barely recognize you," she says. "This smile on your face."

"I know it's hard to believe," I tell her, "because you've never known me to be this way. But before you met me, I was a really happy person. This is more like who I really am."

She puts out her hand. "Well, then, it's nice to meet you."

That night, the world around us somehow turned even quieter, Francesca and I sit on the porch, staring at the stars. My skin feels tight from a day's worth of sun baking, and the breeze rushing along my shoulders soothes me into a deep calm.

"Thank you for doing this for me."

"No thanks necessary. I'd been planning this for a while." I see her catch herself, then turn her focus to her drink.

"A while?"

I hear the slight clink of her empty beer bottle finding the cement of the porch. "I don't understand why you always let him have so much power over you." She chews on her thumbnail, looking me over. "I'm going to ask you something I've been wanting to ask for a while. I'm not asking to be nosy, and I don't want to piss you off."

"What is it?"

"What did he do to you?"

"Nothing."

Her thumb pops out of her mouth with a wet smack. "You don't have to tell me. But know that I know that's bullshit."

It's so quiet for so long after that I'm surprised to hear my voice finally cutting through the space between us, almost in a whisper. "If I tell you, it becomes real."

She looks at me, eyes filled with tears. "Hey," she says. "If you don't tell me, I'm afraid it's going to kill you."

40

I've never told anyone this, and I honestly never thought I would. I thought it could be my secret, that I could remove it from the story of Matthew and me.

One night after we'd been married, I was working on my miniatures, everything spread out on the kitchen table. Matthew was out drinking with friends. He was later than he'd said he'd be, but I had gone past the point of being upset. Fully thrown into my work, I was in that zone where everything else disappears, and I live inside the place I'm creating. Things aren't small in my hands; they are becoming what I see around me. I am sitting in the chair I'm making. I'm leaning against the wall I'm painting. Not that the small stuff is big. Rather, I'm small. I'm so tiny nobody could find me.

I was working late because I'd had a showing coming up. My first big showing had been the month before, where I'd been a part of a "New Faces" exhibit. I'd brought three of my pieces—the Laundromat, my mother's dining room, and the Disneyland strip club. (It's Donald Duck spinning on the pole, since he doesn't wear pants.) Despite my nerves, the pieces were received exceptionally well. So well, in fact, that they caught the eye of the owner of a gallery down on

Wilshire where I really wanted to show my things. There was something about that gallery, its location near the museums, its tiny, inviting white cube of a room. Whenever I saw it, all I wanted was to see my name painted there, right at the entrance. I had always assumed it was nothing more than a pipe dream. But now it was possible. The owner had come right up to me at the showing, handed me his card, and said he'd like to see the rest of my pieces.

He also slid his hand around my waist and said I was gorgeous. In front of my husband. My brand new husband who was still getting used to all the changes in our lives—the house, the marriage, my career.

Even before he saw this man's arm around my waist, Matthew hated everything about him, from his faux-hawk to the way the guy's jeans were frayed around the ankles. Honestly, it was enough for Matthew that the guy's name was Book. "That's not a real name, Charlotte," Matthew kept saying as we had gotten ready for the showing that night. "Maybe his name is Bookman or Booker or something, but not 'Book.' No way."

I think the real reason Matthew got hung up on the name was because Book got Matthew's wrong.

We were standing there, the three of us, this stranger's arm snaked around my waist, when Book said to Matthew, "And you must be the husband."

"I am," Matthew said, bristling. I was silently hoping Matthew could understand that it wasn't like I wanted someone named Book to be touching me, but he was a gallery owner so sometimes I might have to do things like that.

Book never stopped smiling, which was when I noticed one of his teeth was capped in gold. He tilted his head back to look down at Matthew as he said, "You must be so proud, Mr. Goodman."

Matthew rolled one of his shoulders, as if he was physically clicking himself past the first few things he wanted to say. "My last name is Price. Goodman is her name," Matthew said, pointing at me. "She kept it." And then added, "For now."

For now? He said it like he was the one in charge of it, like he was in charge of me. Now I was the one clicking a shoulder, lowering my head. But Matthew didn't see that.

Book's penciled eyebrows rose to the very fringe of his fauxhawk. "Well," he said as he started pulling my arm, dragging me away. "*For now* I just need to tell your wife something over here," Book said. "It's very important, and will just take a second. I promise not to ruin this honeymoon."

I looked back at Matthew, who raised a hand in acquiescence.

As I followed this man with an object for a name, he shouted over his shoulder, "Thanks for releasing her."

"That wasn't funny," I said to Book as soon as he stopped pulling me.

"Yes, it was. He got all *manly* with you. It's very Promise Keeper, 1998. It's cute."

By the time I rejoined Matthew's side, the damage had already been done. I knew he wanted his wife to have looked Book right in the face and said, "I am married to this man. Now take your hand off my ass and apologize to my husband."

And I knew, partially, that he was right. I shouldn't have been so casual in front of Matthew. But I hoped we had an understanding that dealing with certain types of people means sometimes dealing with uncomfortable, inappropriate situations.

I'd certainly sat through a hundred catatonically boring functions for his law firm where one drunk woman after another thought she was being supercasual as she flirted with him.

"I bet you're suuuuch a good husband," she'd slur, before turning to me to ask: *"He is, isn't he? He's a good husband, I just know it."*

After the showing, back at home and in my pajamas after Matthew had finished his crossword and gone to bed, I flipped through the guest book people had signed. Friends wrote about how proud they were, how exciting it was to go to an art opening and see my name on the wall. My parents wrote that they loved me, and my mother said she was so glad I wore lipstick because it made me even prettier.

I wondered if Matthew had written something. What would he say to his brand-new wife at her first showing? I flipped through the few pages, giddy with anticipation, until I saw his familiar handwriting.

MATTHEW WAS HERE,

It broke my heart. He had tagged my guest book like a kid with a can of spray paint. Had he written that for others to see, or had it been for himself? Regardless, it had nothing to do with me. It wasn't for me. He wanted to see his own name.

Soon after that, I found myself having to interact more and more with Book. First it was phone calls and emails, but after he said it was impossible for him to communicate with written words (which made his moniker even more baffling), I met him for lunches. Sometimes dinners. Matthew was working all kinds of long hours at the time, and then would stay out with his friends anyway, so I wasn't missing anything by spending time with Book.

But then we sometimes went across the street to the Contemporary Museum, or down the street to a bar. I wasn't attracted to Book in a romantic way—I mean, the dude's name was Book, after all—but it was nice to have someone to talk to about the things Matthew didn't care about.

I tried talking to Matthew about it, but he would get uncomfortable, huffing and puffing, rearranging any object within arm's reach.

"Maybe you should keep it all separate from me," he said. "That's probably for the best. It's your little hobby and I'm glad you have something to do that makes you happy, but I don't want to hear stories about all these assholes. It really drives me nuts. I don't know how you can stand it."

We stopped talking about it, and because of that Matthew never told me how he truly felt about everything, until that night he came home late and drunk.

First, he forbade me to see Book ever again. He said there were plenty of other galleries out there, and I didn't need this one. That he'd buy me a gallery, if it meant that much to me to have my things shown. That I was making a fool out of him, that I was making him feel like a cuckold. That was the word he used. *Cuckold.* As if I were having a *ye olde affaire*.

I accused him of feeling threatened that I might find success, that I might become more than just his wife, that I might have my own world, my own identity. That made him angry, and he said I was just making excuses for my behavior.

"I would never be that kind of person, Charlotte. And fuck you for trying to make me one. You just want to be a victim, but the truth is you're selfish."

I didn't recognize the people fighting. We didn't sound like us. These weren't our problems.

I think too much changed for both of us too quickly. We didn't know how to handle all of it. We didn't try to figure out how to be homeowners and a married couple. I didn't adjust well to the pressures of balancing a day job and my artistic one. Matthew didn't want to communicate, but would rather have had things somehow just fix themselves with time. Instead of either of us being strong enough to admit where we were flailing and feeling incompetent, we both got aggressively independent. We took care of ourselves, and then took our frustrations out on each other.

If only I'd stopped long enough to tell Matthew that I didn't love anything as much as I loved him, and if only he'd found a way to tell me he felt he'd been taken advantage of, we might have learned how to handle a problem together.

But we didn't, and what happened next didn't just affect that night, it started a series of questions that drove us apart, and would continue to destroy the fabric of us over the next year.

It wasn't how we yelled at each other. It wasn't how we called each other names, or made accusations and judgments on each other's motives and character. We could have come back from all the words, I think.

But I said something that hurt Matthew enough that he raised a fist. He inhaled sharply just after he did it, staring at his hand, as if he had no idea what it was doing up by his head. He stumbled, and pulled his arm away.

He didn't hit me. He punched the table, right through one of my miniatures.

"Stop it!" I pushed him away from the table, and started moving my things.

"Don't be dramatic," he said. "It was an accident."

"I don't think so. You're drunk, and you're pissed at me."

"Charlotte, if I wanted to break them, I'd just do it."

And then he did. He grabbed a tiny playground piece, and threw it against the wall. I still remember the sound of all the pieces skittering across the hardwood floor.

He went for another one. An apartment building, my hipster dollhouse, a project I'd spent three months on.

"No!" I screamed, jumping at him as if he was a bully holding my schoolbooks over my head.

He opened the door and threw the scraps of my work out onto the porch.

I fell to the ground, empty, like I'd been tossed out, too.

Right there.

Right there was where my life stopped.

Where my marriage broke.

"Sorry," he mumbled as he urgently pushed past me to the bathroom. Not a physical push, not trying to hurt me. Just careless.

As I listened to him throwing up in the toilet, I couldn't move.

Instead, I stayed on the floor asking myself, "What do I do now?"

An answer came back, from somewhere both far away and deep inside of me, loudly and clearly. It demanded: *You do everything you can to forget this ever happened.*

41

W hat did you do?" Francesca asks, her palm making tiny circles against the curve of her cheek.

"Nothing, at first. Matthew went to bed."

"Did you cry?"

"No. I couldn't. I kept wanting it to have not happened, for me to have imagined it. And if it had happened, surely in the morning when he was sober, he'd apologize."

"Did he?"

"No. He said he didn't remember it, and that it must have been an accident. That he would never have done it if he hadn't been drunk and that upset with me."

"Oh, Charlotte. That's not your fault."

I shake my head. "The thing is, I don't believe him. And no matter what I've done in all this time, I can't seem to find a way to let it go."

And then I tell her a very dark secret. "Sometimes I wish he had hit me. That he'd really pushed me. Done something so I could say, 'There. That's unforgivable. Now I have to go.'"

"Some would say what he did *was* unforgivable. I think he's a jerk."

"He left two weeks later. I think he couldn't handle what he'd done."

"Or what he was told he did. If he really doesn't remember, that has to be a little scary, huh?"

I scratch the back of my head, feeling the heat of sunburn at the base of my scalp. "I know. And maybe now he thinks I'm a reminder of the worst that he's capable of."

Francesca crosses her arms and stares out at the view. "But what if you haven't seen the worst he's capable of?" she asks.

The question causes me to rub my chest, trying to get through to the ache inside. "Frannie," I say, my voice breaking. "Why do you think I moved out?"

Maybe if I'd taken his name. Maybe if he'd come home earlier that night, instead of staying for another round. Maybe if I were different, if I wanted different things. Maybe if I were the perfect wife. A million useless maybes.

I spin my empty beer bottle between my hands. "Some people work this stuff out."

"Some do. That's true. But some people can't. And that's okay. Nobody dies. Maybe you're both too messed up and hurt. I don't know. It sucks, but love isn't always enough."

"So I have to give up everything I wanted: him, our marriage, our home, our future that I wanted . . . He doesn't even remember it, and I have to be the one to walk away? Doesn't that seem incredibly unfair?"

"One hundred percent unfair. But if you stay with him, and things get worse, if something bad happens one more time, you'll never forgive yourself."

A wind has picked up around us. It's getting chilly. I hug my shoulders and twist my neck from side to side. "I'm still sore from practice the other day," I say.

"I bet that's why you like derby," she says. "All the rules.

When you hit someone, there's a right way and a wrong way. There's no weird gray area like in love, when sometimes you hurt someone and it's kind of okay, but kind of not. I don't know. It's like you're the Jammer in your marriage."

"Oh, God."

"I'm serious!" She punches me in the arm. "Shut up, I'm being profound. You played by the rules. You skated clean, made it through all the rough slams, found the holes and fought your way to the front of the pack, and now you don't know if you want to call off the jam."

I exhale, and it releases something I have been holding on to with all of my might. It releases the truth. "I have to call off the jam."

"Yeah."

"We were supposed to be on the same team."

No more looking back, no more trying to fix, no more worrying about where I'm broken. No more being cracked.

My marriage is over.

I think people assume there's a relief that comes from this realization, this decision, because something is done. That's not true. It never stops being sad.

You can't hide from it. You can't make it easier on yourself. And the worst of it is that no matter what you do, you can never, ever fall small.

42

Bang-Up finds me hiding in the back bathroom of the Wheelhouse.

"This is where the girls always go when they want to disappear," she says. "You'd think you guys would figure out we always find you in here."

"It's a warehouse, Bang-Up. It's not like there are a lot of places to go."

I'm the worst skater on my Rookie Rumble team. I'm always at the end of the pace line. Sometimes I have to get off the track entirely, just to catch my breath. I'm very frustrated with myself. I'm sure the others notice just how bad I am. The looks they quickly give themselves when I join the pack or come lumbering up behind say it all. They try to find my strengths, they try to be encouraging, but I know there must be a part of them hoping I will back down, skate away, and offer to be the girl who refills their water bottles instead of the dead weight on their team.

Bang-Up leads me toward one of the warm-up rooms. We move in lazy circles as she talks.

"You're doing much better," she says. "I know you can't see it, but it's true."

"I'm really struggling."

"So you have things to work on. We all do. Even the rock stars out there. But that's derby."

"Right, right," I say, dangling my helmet from my fingers. "I know. *Welcome to roller derby.*"

"You'll make it through this, Broke-Broke. And I don't mean the Rookie Rumble."

I look up to see the softness of her face, the empathy in her eyes. "Past'er told you I'm getting a divorce?"

"Yeah," she says. "But also I know what it looks like." She sticks out her hand. "Welcome to the club."

I take her hand, as she pulls me into a hug. I wasn't expecting it, and topple over, taking her with me.

"Oh, no!" she shrieks. "Your tailbone!"

I'm laughing too hard to tell her that I'm fine.

43

I'm so nervous waiting for Matthew to arrive that I just cleaned the toilet.

It was a dumb move, because now I'm a little sweaty from anxiety, and I smell like bleach, so if he hugs me when he gets here I'm going to smell like a housekeeper. I feel a little pang of nostalgia remembering the bleach spill the first night at his place. It's different this time. This isn't the beginning. This meeting is to end things as quickly and painlessly as possible.

Every car that passes outside my window sends me running to check if it's him. I eventually force myself to sit down on the Fuck You Couch and open a book. But I can't focus on the words in front of me. I just sit there staring at the pages. Like a mannequin.

He knocks on the door, too loudly. I jump, halfway expecting to hear: "LAPD! OPEN UP!"

My knees are wobbly as I walk to the door.

Matthew is standing in my doorway. He's on my turf.

"Hi," he says. He's already looking over my shoulder. Is he checking for visitors, or instantly sizing up my home? I say hi back and open the door wider, taking a few steps back to let him into the living room.

He looks tall in my place, and I realize nobody tall has ever been in this apartment. I have never seen him here. It looks like a mistake, like there's a backdrop around him of my apartment instead of our house, where he's supposed to be standing in front of me. It must be awkward for him, too, because he hasn't moved from his position a few steps in. I have to gesture him farther inside so I can shut the door.

"You don't have very good parking out there," he says.

I guess I *am* being graded. And that's one point for Matthew.

"Oh," I say. "Well, I have my own parking spot, so it doesn't really affect me."

He grunts at this, and starts taking in my apartment, looking like he's making an inventory. His eyes go over each piece of furniture. He glances down at the rug and kicks at the corner, as if he's checking my apartment's tires. He scans through the books. Then he stops at one, pointing at it. "That one's mine," he says. He grabs the book, flips to the front page, and shows me his initials scrawled in the corner: "M.P."

"Oh." But I stop myself before I apologize.

He slides it back into its place. "It's okay," he says, assuming I needed forgiveness. "I didn't like that book anyway. Not sure if I even finished it."

And that's *two points* for Matthew Price!

"Do you want something to drink?" I ask him.

"Um, yeah, I guess. What do you have?"

"Water. Wine. Scotch. Beer. Maybe a Diet Coke, I'm not sure. Tea. Um—" I stop myself again, as I'm starting to sound like a waitress.

"Water's fine," he says.

He follows me into the kitchen, staying a few steps behind me, to survey my home. "Did you paint this place yourself?"

"No, it came this way."

"Oh. I was going to say."

It's like I walk right into his traps.

"I heard you quit your job."

"Yeah, I did."

"Must be nice."

Three points. This man is on a roll. You aren't even going to try to play defense?

He's wearing new sneakers. They are blindingly white, and if we were still together I wouldn't have let him out of the house in them. The shorts and white socks pulled up toward his knees make him look like my grandpa on his way to a golf course. Maybe he isn't seeing anyone. If he is, he did not see her this morning. Or perhaps she's blind.

I hand him a glass of water. "Where'd you get that bookcase?" he asks.

"Pretty much everything came from IKEA."

. . . which is Swedish for Fuck You.

We make small talk until we're approximately halfway through our drinks.

Then Matthew says, "Can, um, I . . . Can *we* talk for a second?" He rubs his thumb around the rim of his glass. "About us."

"Yes."

I wonder what you'd find if you compiled all the words said between a couple at the beginning of their relationship and compared them to all the words said when they're at the end. I'm pretty sure that the harder a relationship gets, the shorter the words become. I don't know if we're too afraid to articulate and become vulnerable, or just too exhausted to do much more than grunt and nod.

Matthew is sitting on the couch opposite me. He takes one of the pillows, puts it in his lap, and then puts it back where it was. He rubs his face and swallows twice.

He says, "Can, um, I feel like . . . we should, um."

Usually when Matthew struggles like this, I help him out. But not this time. It breaks my heart to watch us act like we never used to be madly in love. Like our shells are talking. We've hired other people, horrible people, to fill our flesh and be here because our real selves are too wounded to look each other in the eye.

I don't want to get emotional, but I can already feel my muscles tugging at the corners of my mouth. As he gags on syllables, it dawns on me that the reason he's struggling is because he wants to tell me something he thinks I don't want to hear.

He rubs his face again. And that's when I notice he isn't wearing his wedding ring.

I gasp. I actually gasp, as my hand reaches out and I touch his naked finger. Matthew jumps like I've cursed him and he's about to have a limb fall off. Then he figures out what I mean and quickly shelters the back of his left hand with his right.

I've always kept my rings on. Maybe it's silly, but to me they were a reminder that I'm still a part of someone else until we officially call it quits. They helped keep me from feeling like I'd become a completely different person who slipped away into a different life. I also didn't want other people out there to think I was available. The ring gave me a silent barrier from the rest of the world. I belonged to someone, no matter how complicated the situation.

Now I know what's coming. The naked finger said it all.

When Matthew finally speaks, it's too late. I feel the words before I hear them.

"I think it's time we moved on."

Game, set, match.

Matthew excuses himself to the bathroom, and I sit stunned.

He beat me to it. I couldn't do it first. Matthew just did exactly what he said I shouldn't expect: he just told me what was going to happen to me.

When Matthew comes back from the bathroom, he asks, "Did you know your hallway light is out? You should fix that."

44

*Charlotte Goodman watches her friends Andy and Jonathan help
each other with another large box. They struggle in the doorway,
the box digging into Andy's thigh as Jonathan hikes his side up
higher. They quietly joke between them about what's inside, gently teasing that it must be Charlotte's anvil collection. From the
bedroom, Francesca runs over to join the men, opening the box
and peering inside. "Kitchen stuff," she says with authority.*

*Charlotte feels slightly numb as she watches her old life join
her new one. She's still feeling dazed as she rubs the tender ridge
of skin on her left finger where her rings once lived. Francesca
quickly found a buyer for the engagement ring; Charlotte doesn't
have to worry about finding a new job for at least a few months.*

*The boys return from the kitchen with glasses of ice water. They
sweat and pant, but they do not complain. They just keep working until the job is done.*

*Afterward, Charlotte stares at a cold slice of pizza that sits
untouched on a plate she once parted with, but now owns again.
But her friends sitting around the coffee table have no problems
finishing their hard-earned dinner. Charlotte watches Andy eat
as he sits on a chair that he's sat on before, but in another house.
In fact, Andy sat on that chair in a different apartment even*

before that. Charlotte realizes as long as that chair and that man can find a way to reunite no matter where life takes her, she will be able to find a way to be okay. She hasn't left earth's atmosphere; she just changed her position in it.

Her fragmented life has reassembled.

Francesca notices Charlotte's gone inward again, her gaze unfocused, soft. "You okay?" she asks, never seeming to tire of checking on her friend.

Charlotte gives the smallest nod before she quietly asks, "What did you do with my wedding gown?"

Her friends take a moment to share glances, deciding who will answer. Then Andy says, "We're never going to tell you."

Charlotte picks at a piece of rubbery pepperoni as she whispers, "Thank you."

• • •

It's strange when a voice in your head starts becoming more and more a part of your daily life, when you rely on it to get you through the bad times, the boring times, the times you're supposed to be turning to someone with the perfect joke but you find you are alone. But it's an even more surreal experience to know that the voice in your head is packing up to leave.

Charlotte Goodman is just starting to get the hang of letting things go, and she knows her narrator is a terrible enabler. It lets her hang back and observe instead of being out there in the life she's worked so hard to create. It's not that she doesn't want the companionship, it's that she no longer needs it.

So Charlotte is going to let John Goodman take a step back. Things will be okay if he can't speak for Charlotte anymore. She will miss him, and she'll be forever grateful for his warm cloak of protection.

Charlotte Goodman takes a moment to change the pronouns in her head.

I know it's been a while, but I'm ready to be the only one living my life.

First person, present tense.

45

I'm on the Jammer line, putting the panty with the little stars on each side over my helmet. I can feel my heart pounding against my chest, as if it wants to take off and start long before the whistle.

I see the pack in front of me. There are eight girls. The four on my team are crowded together, making plans. Francesca's one of them, playing jam assist. It's her job to help me through the pack, to make room for me, and keep me out of harm's way. Some of the other team's Blockers look back to size me up, just as my Blockers are doing to the other Jammer. It's Muffin Top, head titty twister. She's standing beside me on the Jammer line, rolling her shoulders as she bends into a squat. She nods at me and says, "Here goes nothing."

The whistle blows, and the Blockers take off, already slamming into one another, trying to create space for me and Muffin to get through.

The second whistle blows, and it's our turn. I run on my skates at first, turning my feet out so I've got some traction. I sound like a refrigerator falling down a flight of stairs, but I end up a few feet ahead of Muffin, and that's all that matters.

I spot Francesca on the high side, near the rail. She's leaning onto an opposing Blocker, her arm outstretched behind her, an invitation to whip me past this pack. I pick up my pace, but another Blocker hits me from the left, and for a second I slam into the rail. My momentum is gone, and I see Muffin skate past me, taking the lead on one of my Blockers. She quickly gets so far ahead of me I can no longer see her starred helmet. In fact, I can't see anything but the back of this other Blocker in my face. Some girl named HELL'S KITTEN, a name I don't have time to think about right now.

I use the angle of the track to pick up speed as I skate down toward the infield. It works and somehow I get past the kitten from Hell, and back toward my own pack. Two of my Blockers are on the ground, but Francesca is still skating. She sees me again and puts her arm out. I grab it with both hands, and she pulls me, whipping me forward.

Muffin has busted out of the pack in front of me, and as Lead Jammer, she's starting her lap to meet up with the pack again in order to score points. I have to get out of this pack and get in front of her. That's my only job right now.

Out of the corner of my eye, I see an opposing Blocker lean to the right, curling like a panther about to pounce. She takes a second too long, giving me enough time to know she's planning to hit me. I pull myself back, Matrix-style, in that same second. She misses and falls.

I haul ass.

I'm skating as fast as I can, all by myself, focused on Muffin. I'm allowed to hit her if I can get near her, and I think maybe I can get her to the ground.

My skates wobble because I'm going faster than I ever have on the track. My brain is battling with itself, telling me both to slow down and speed up. Slow down so I don't get hurt.

Speed up because *I can beat her, I know it; I just have to get there*.

Then: a miracle. Muffin takes herself out at one of the turns, tripping over herself during a crossover. I gain precious distance, so that by the time she's skating again, I am beside her. More importantly, I am on the high side. I have more power from up here. I take a few steps and throw myself into the flesh of her right arm, slamming her to the infield. She falls.

But I fall, too. We are both on the ground, and everybody else is yelling at us. Whoever gets up first and gets past one of the opposing Blockers will score a point. Then she can call off the jam before the other one gets to the pack.

I think about a skate to my face, even though there isn't one coming. I picture my nose exploded in blood and cartilage, and my body hurls itself back upright. I'm off, leaving Muffin in my dust.

I pass a Blocker, scoring one point.

I'm about to call off the jam, my hands ready to smack my hips, but then I hear Francesca scream, "Go high!"

There's a hole. I see it. A space where the other Blockers aren't covering, and if I can get there, I will pass two of them. That's two more points, but I can see Muffin's already back on her feet and getting closer. It's Francesca's style to go for the extra points. I'm nervous to risk losing the lead.

"Go high!" she screams again, and I know I'm running out of time, so I bolt up the track, sounding like thunder as I do. An opposing Blocker sees me, tries to get her shoulder into my arm, but I push myself forward three more steps, three baby steps that make all the difference as I push past her, scoring another point. But then, just as I'm about to call off the jam, I see it.

Another hole.

I can make it past the other two Blockers. I can score five points.

I start to glance back to see where Muffin is, but Francesca's suddenly giving me a push from behind, hollering, "Go, go, go!"

I skate harder than I could have ever imagined was possible and I shoot past everyone else, finding my way to the front of the pack, free and clear.

I whack my hips with both hands, calling off the jam. The whistle blows.

Five points. A personal best.

My teammates cheer. Someone pats me on the ass. Francesca shouts, "Broke-Broke, you're my hero!"

I know I'm in a warehouse in the middle of nowhere, playing a sport most people have never even heard of with a group of women whose real names I might never know. I know it's just a practice jam in a practice scrimmage for the rookie skaters of a much bigger league. But this moment, right now, is pure victory. I feel invincible.

46

I can't wait for the bout," Bruisey-Q tells me as we round the last turn back toward my apartment. My unemployed status allows me the kind of free time that lets me go for a run around four, and I found out Bruisey works freelance as a graphic designer, so she's become my semiregular running buddy. She's a little bit spacey, but her seemingly random thoughts keep our workout routine interesting.

"I can't believe it's almost here," I say, as we slow down to a walk. I check my watch, pleased to find we shaved four minutes off our normal five-mile time.

We've been working hard, training six days a week. To my relief, I'm no longer the worst one on the track. Nowhere near the best, but not the worst. I can't believe something I started on basically a dare has become so important to me that it's a daily part of my life.

"I'll be sad when it's over," Bruisey says.

"Me too. But my body will be happy to have some time to heal." I lean over to stretch out my side.

Bruisey takes a few breaths as she kicks out her legs, side to side. "I'm so jealous. You're like, this perfect free butterfly, getting to do whatever you want. Your whole life is ahead of you, and you get to decide what you want. I wish I could do that, sometimes. Be that free."

She trails off as we walk the remaining feet to the front of my apartment. It's hard to imagine anyone would be jealous of what I have, when I think about this past year. There were times when I felt like I'd never be able to get out of bed, much less run five miles. Bruisey's admiration of what I have makes me realize I haven't spent enough time appreciating what I've been able to do, both on my own and with the help of some really phenomenal people.

Bruisey sighs, tucking a pink strand of hair behind her ear. "See? Even your cute apartment. I'm jealous again." She points at the scooter illegally parked next to the trash bins. "Past'er's already here waiting for you, probably with a glass of wine. This never happens to me."

"Bruisey, it's happening to you right now."

"Only because I'm with Broke-Broke Superstar. That's the name you should put on your next gallery showing."

"I don't have a gallery showing."

"Sounds like you will soon!"

I had called Book's gallery out of curiosity, and learned a new Book owns the place. She goes by the very normal, humanlike name of Marcy. She remembered me from when I used to hang out there all the time. "I wondered where you went to," she said. "It was like you dropped off the face of the earth!" We set a meeting for next week.

My front door opens. Francesca is standing there, not with a glass of wine in her hand but rather a flute of champagne. But what seems to be of more importance is the envelope she's clutching to her chest.

"Yo," she says, handing me the glass. "You got served."

• • •

Twenty minutes later, we're sitting around my coffee table, going through the stack of paperwork that requires me to list all of my assets.

I laugh. "It shouldn't take all this paper just to write the word *None.*"

Francesca holds her glass of champagne up toward the window, rotating it by the stem in the light, like she's counting the bubbles. "I always wanted to say '*You got served,*'" she says. "It just wasn't nearly as much fun as I thought it would be. Why can't we serve Matthew?"

"Because he filed."

Bruisey's eyes widen as she rifles through the pages. "Look at this," she says, pointing, her normally brusque voice elevated in shock. "There are five different things you can check to claim what's happening to your house. There's one if you're selling the house and splitting it, one if you're keeping the house—"

"He's staying there for now."

"Right. That's what I'm saying. There isn't an option for that. It says, '*The wife will remain in the property until point of sale.*' Nowhere does it say the husband keeps the property and the wife moves out."

I close my eyes and nod sagely. "Well, I am a progressive woman."

"What a mess," Bruisey says, shaking her head.

"Still jealous?"

She smiles. "It's still kind of exciting. Paperwork. Court."

Francesca snorts. "Wow, lady. You are weird."

"One chapter closing so another can begin. Maybe now Charlotte gets to find her soul mate."

Francesca makes a face. "Don't. Charlotte gets testy when it comes to boys. Holden Wood has had a crush on her for months, but she won't do anything about it."

"Hi, I'm still holding my divorce papers. Just got served."

"Congratulations again," Francesca says, clinking my glass.

Bruisey's eyes are round with shock. "Holden is cute."

"I don't know his real name. Doesn't this seem doomed?"

Bruisey's tone gets very serious, like she's suddenly found her purpose. "But how do you feel about him?"

"I've given it exactly zero minutes of thought."

She dances in her seat. "Then here's what you have to do. The next time you know he's walking near you, hide behind something and watch him."

"You mean stalk him?"

Bruisey shakes her head, brushing me off. "I had a friend who was on the fence about this guy she was seeing. She asked him to meet her at the library, and then she hid behind a bush when he walked up so she could find out what it felt like when she first saw him."

Francesca refills my glass as she says, "That is the most ridiculous thing I've ever heard."

"He won't see you, and it gives you a moment alone to just see how you feel. Try it."

"I think I will not."

Bruisey downs the last of her glass, whistling in her seat. She's still in her sweaty running clothes, and her cheeks are flushed from the champagne. "I don't know," she sing-songs. "I think you will."

"I know you were making a joke with the champagne," I say to Francesca, "but it's still pretty good."

"It wasn't meant to be ironic," she says, sliding the papers to the side, topic adjourned. "I originally came with good news. Then I checked your mail and once again Matthew ruined everything."

"What good news?" Bruisey asks, immediately perking up. "I bet it's exciting."

Francesca stares at her for a second. "You really are trippy."

"I am drunk."

"Go ahead, Past'er," I say, taking away Bruisey's glass.

She smiles, lowering her chin to her chest demurely. "Jacob's moving to Los Angeles. Permanently. He got a transfer."

I sling an arm around my friend and congratulate her. "That's so great. How lucky for you guys."

"Lucky? No. I gave him just shy of an ultimatum. I asked him to make a decision about me, and then make a decision with me. He did both."

"You should give him a certificate."

"Charlotte," she says, dropping her head to my shoulder, "you know I did."

47

Okay, I'm going to throw up."

"You can't throw up," Francesca says. "I'm going to throw up and I need you to hold my hair while I throw up. Plus if you throw up I'll totally throw up because I have that thing where watching someone throw up makes me throw up."

The bout starts in twenty minutes. Francesca and I are decked out in our team uniforms, or "boutfits." The theme for the bout is "Cops versus Robbers." We're both dressed like hot lady cops, in dark blue miniskirts and collared button-up shirts that have patches that look like badges on the pocket. We're sporting dark fishnets and black thigh highs. Jonathan is going to have a field day when he finds out teams wear "boutfits," but I don't care. We look fantastic.

Francesca is pacing, the carpeting making her skates useless. She has to lift her knees high and prance like a pony, barely covering any ground. Francesca lurches forward, and her skirt flies up, exposing her hot pants with the words SEE YA! written across her ass.

"We need a goal," Francesca says. "You and me. Let's do something really badass together."

Partnering is key in roller derby. If you try to play by yourself, you pretty much end up useless. It's something I've grown to really appreciate about the sport. You always need someone, and someone always needs you. Even the Jammer, who looks like she's on her own, actually has an entire pack of girls who have her back. We are all in this together.

I quickly come up with our goal. "Let's promise we'll take out the other Jammer together, at least once. Let's surround her and take her to the rail."

"Deal. I'll get in front of her to slow her down, and then you hit her."

"Hammer and nail," I say, calling out the name of the play, as I tape my final certificate from Francesca on the wall over my space on the locker room bench. It reads: CHARLOTTE "HARD BROKEN" GOODMAN IS OFFICIALLY FIXED.

"Let's go kick some ass," says my best friend and super-badass Hot Wheels Derby Devil Blowin' Past'er, number 69.

"Hey," I say, taking her hand.

"What's up, Broke-Broke?"

I get down on one knee pad and look up to meet her confused gaze. "Now that I'm divorced, will you be my derby wife?"

She tackles me in celebration with such enthusiasm I worry I'm injured before the game even starts.

• • •

I've practically sprint-skated back to the dressing room because I decided I wanted an extra water bottle in the infield during the bout, and that's when I see Holden Wood adjusting his skates outside the referee dressing room. I quickly stop as quietly as I can and roll backward, tucking myself behind the entryway. I can't believe I'm about to follow Bruisey-Q's whack-ass advice, but I stay hidden and watch him. He's holding his skate laces in two fists, awkward around his own gear.

The feeling I get is like how when sometimes you're doing two unrelated things at once—like reading a book while listening to music—the two things can magically unite. You hear a word in the lyrics sung the exact time you read that exact word in your book. It's impossible, but it seems like you made that happen.

As I watch Holden untie and retie his skates, I yearn for a memory I don't have yet. I realize I've been missing something for a very long time, and it's up to me if I want it again.

I want to step out of a bath clutching a helping hand, one attached to a man holding a towel. I want that warm, steamy, loving embrace that happens where he wraps me up in terry-cloth and inhales me. I'm ready to find someone who wants to be there at that moment, to kiss my damp eyebrows and say, "You smell good."

It's a moment that illustrates how private love can be. You, standing there like a child: clean and new, in nothing but your skin, still wet at the ankles, hair dripping soap-scented water. And someone takes care of you. It doesn't happen that often in life. And I really miss it.

Maybe it won't be with Holden. But it can't be with anyone if I don't stop being too scared to look.

I round the corner to let him see me. He breaks into a smile. "Kick ass out there, Broke-Broke."

I try my best to stop right before I reach him, but I stumble on the tiled floor. He reaches out his hands, quickly steadying me.

"Sorry," he says, even though I'm the one who should apologize. "I had to touch you just now, but it was completely legal. You were going to fall."

"Maybe I fell on purpose."

He puts his hands on his hips. "I think you want me to think that, but I know you just klutzed out in front of me."

"I'm ready for you to ask that question now."

My heart is racing and I can feel the blood in my face rushing to my cheeks. I hope he can't tell how nervous I am. It's been a long time since I hoped someone asked me out.

He smiles. "Which question? Because you waited a while, and now I have so many." He rubs his jaw against his shoulder. "Where should I start?"

"How about I just answer all of them with yes."

"Wow." He kicks at my skate with his own. "*All* of them?"

"Call me and find out."

"Ooh, Broke-Broke. I like it when you're flirty."

• • •

Francesca and I are humbled by the size of our personal cheering section. I immediately spot Andy, Jonathan and Cassandra, my parents, and Francesca's parents, who look way more normal than I ever would have imagined. Francesca's mother is wearing a sweater set, for Pete's sake. And her dad looks adorably nerdy. I can't wait to meet them and tell them how awesome their daughter is.

Standing in front of all of them, holding an enormous sign that reads: "Faster, Past'er!" is Jacob, beaming with pride.

My mother has such a look of horror on her face, I'm afraid someone has just told her I've grown a penis. My father, on the other hand, looks so proud of me I want to burst into tears. He's pointing at me while talking to the person who made the unfortunate decision to sit behind him. It makes me immediately wish I'd done more sports growing up, so Dad could have come to my games, beaming with this kind of pride. He looks so happy to be a dad. I watch him hook an arm through my mother's elbow, bumping into her with a grin. She loosens up, but only a little. When this is over, I owe my mom one usually insufferable brunch with the ladies from her knitting group.

I turn around to take a good look at my team, at this group of women who have spent hours with me, training with me, learning who I am, both inside and out. These women not only know what I'm made of, they knew what I was capable of before I did. They literally beat it out of me.

The lights go out around the crowd, the track is flooded in brightness, and the sound of cheering rattles in my chest.

Francesca grabs my hand. "Here we go!" she shouts.

"Ladies and Gentlemen! Welcome to the Rookieeeeee Rummmmmble!"

* * *

There was a lot of falling. Especially at first. We're thirty incredibly nervous newbie skaters slamming into each other in front of a crowd of screaming people. But eventually we get used to the lights and the noise, and remember the game we've trained to play. We remember to look at each other, to partner up and focus on our goals.

Francesca and I are called to a lineup with Francesca jamming, and I'm the Pivot. Bruisey-Q, Stick-N-Stoned, and a refrigerator of a girl named Gigantasaur round out my pack. I quickly make a plan. Gigantasaur takes the back, knocking the crap out of anyone stupid enough to come near her, preferably the other team's Jammer. Bruisey, Stoned, and I will take the front, holding back the other girls.

I follow Francesca's gaze to the other team's lineup. She sees Bloodfist pulling a Jammer panty over her helmet.

"You can take her," I say.

"Quatro-Mama?" she says, beaming. "Not a problem."

The whistle blows, and we take off. I jut out my hip, keeping one of the other team's Blockers from getting past me, but my eyes are firmly fixed on Francesca, watching her practically gallop her way toward us. To my surprise, Bloodfist is keeping a pretty good pace with her.

The other team clearly had orders to keep their focus on Francesca. She's hit as soon as she gets near the pack. She doesn't fall, spinning herself off the rail and swooping back in. But another Blocker is gunning for her, and I slow down to protect her, to try to take the hit before she gets it.

When I get to Francesca, I reach back my right hand, offering a whip. I know I can throw her up the high side and she'll be home free.

Francesca takes my hand, but she doesn't take the whip. Instead, she's firmly placed her Jammer panty into my palm.

We're Passing the Star.

I turn my head, eyes wide, and find her intense stare. Sweat drips from her chin as she growls, "Go!"

New play, new plan, everything changes. I take off as fast as I can, pulling the panty over my helmet as I pass the rest of the pack, the ones who haven't realized Francesca is no longer the Jammer; that I'm the one they're supposed to be stopping.

As I break through the pack and round the bend, I glance back to see if Bloodfist is behind me. She's on the ground—Francesca and Gigantasaur took her out.

I skate so hard I can feel my legs trembling all the way up my body. I push myself harder than I ever have before because now I'm jamming for two. These are Francesca's points I need to earn.

I score five points before I have to call off the jam.

From the other side of the track, I hear Francesca scream, "Fuck, yeah! That's my WIFE!"

There were other plays, there were other moments, but that's the one I'll remember for the rest of my life.

We won, by the way.

• • •

Sometimes I can't believe this all started with someone asking me, "Do you have a mouth guard?" In what other world could the answer to this question be a good thing?

The rules of the track work well for life. Roller derby is life in a tiny circle. You can only go forward, even if you find yourself turned around, facing the wrong way. There's speed, unpredictability, and danger. You can't be sure what's going to happen, you don't always know when you'll stop, and it appears most people are out to get you. You will fall. You will get hurt.

But you will get up again.

Look, what's the worst thing that could happen? Anything that hurts eventually heals. You get back up. You keep going. You get stronger. You get better. Life goes on. That's it.

. . . Or you get a skate to the face. You know. Either way.

ACKNOWLEDGMENTS

Thank you twice: Alexis Hurley, Jennifer Heddle, Kim Witherspoon, Todd Christopher, Erin Searcy, Carolyn Sivitz, Allison Lowe-Huff (Marlo, you totally made your mother win Accountability Thursdays), Allison "Kiss M'Grits" Munn, Sara "Queen Elizadeath II" Morrison, Anna Beth "Dewit" Chao, Tara "Maimie Thighsenhower" Ariano, David "Tandoori Honeylips" Cole, Robin Shorr, Rafael Garcia, Don Todd, Angela "Risky A Go-Go" Bae, Kate "Agnus Die" Burns, Tara Armov, Trixie Biscuit, Shannon "Janis Choplin" Kobylka, Jessica "Tilda Whirl" Lasher, Katy "Tae Kwon Ho" Lim, Jennifer "Kasey Bomber" Barbee, Alex "Axles of Evil" Cohen, PITA, Haught Wheels, Kubonator, Terri "Helen Surly Frown" Murphy, Kelli "Kocoa Krunch" Hancock, Rachel "Sulfuric Astrid" Watson, Danica "Anya Handzaneez" Cleveland, Wanda B. Onya, Tandi Collisson and David Hawkins, Kate "Fantastikate" Gasparrelli, Thomas Refferson, Roger Assaultry, Rachel "Marina del RAGE" House, Cynthia "Cyntax Terror" Mazza, The Meteorfights, Hell's Belles, Merrill Markoe, Niya Palmer, Brently Heilbron, Vince Chao, Chris Huff, Brian Rubenstein, Daniel J. Rogge, Scott "Mister M'Grits" Holroyd, Liz Feldman, Jeff Long, Evany Thomas, Stephanie Markham, Jami Holland, my family, the good people who visit pamie.com, and especially Jason Wesley Upton . . . for all the gym socks.

ROLLER DERBY GLOSSARY

BAMBI—Referring to the Disney character's first time on ice, describes the stance of a nervous newbie skater.

BLOCKER—The skaters who make up the pack. These girls try to make holes for their Jammers while simultaneously keeping the opposing team's Jammer from getting through the pack by hitting or obstruction. Each team gets up to four Blockers per pack. The leader is called the Pivot.

BOOTY BLOCK, "HIP CHECK"—Hitting or leaning on an opponent with your butt, hip, or thigh. You can legally hit from the hip to the top of the knee, but not below.

BANKED TRACK—As opposed to "flat track" roller derby, banked track roller derby is played on an oval-shaped inclined circuit track. All skating is counterclockwise.

BOUT—A game of roller derby played in four quarters broken into one-minute jams.

BOUTFIT—What a derby girl wears to the bout. It could be a uniform, it could be not much more than a bikini, a feather boa and a pair of fishnets, but know that she put a lot of thought into this design. No matter what, never ever call it a "costume."

"CALL OFF THE JAM"—The signal that a Jammer is ending the jam. She places her hands on her hips, often repeatedly, furiously patting her pelvis, in order to get the ref's attention. Only the Lead Jammer can call off the jam.

"FALL SMALL"—To ensure you don't take out every other player on the track when you eat the ground, go fetal when you fall, or everyone loses.

FRESH MEAT—Term of endearment for rookie skaters in training. Skaters who've been in training for more than six months may refer to themselves as "Rancid Meat" or "Jerky."

GEAR—The protective wear that keeps a derby girl's important parts from breaking. Includes: helmet, mouth guard, elbow pads, wrist guards, knee pads, and/or shin guards and crash pads (pants with hip and tailbone protectors).

"HAMMER AND NAIL"—A defensive two-on-one strategy. One player obstructs the opponent while the second player comes from the side and hits her.

HEMATOMA—A nasty-ass bruise, usually clotted, that hardens and makes other people freak out when they see it. Worst fact ever: some hematomas have to be drained.

HOLE—An opening in the pack wide enough for a Jammer to skate through in order to gain position.

INFIELD—The area on the inside of the track. It is out of play.

JAM, "THE JAM"—Sixty seconds of game play.

JAM ASSIST—An assigned role for a Blocker, her goal is to help her Jammer through the pack.

JAMMER—The player who scores the points for her team. Jammers are identified by the stars on either side of their helmet panties.

PANTY—A nylon covering players wear on their helmets to signify their position. Jammers have stars on their panties, Pivots have a bold stripe through the middle.

PACK—The group of Blockers from both teams. This is what Jammers must break through in their passes, only scoring points after one completed pass. Blockers who are beyond twenty feet of the pack in either direction are out of play.

"PASSING THE STAR"—An offensive strategy where the Jammer passes her starred helmet panty to the Pivot during the jam, switching the Pivot's position to Jammer.

PENALTY—There are many ways to get a penalty in roller derby. But let's start with no punching, tripping, pushing, elbowing, hitting in the face, hitting from behind, fighting, biting, kicking, choking, stopping, cheating, or arguing with a ref. The penalized skater has to sit out the next jam.

"THE PINK"—A pink line signifying the edge of the legal playing area. (Cribbed from LA Derby Doll vernacular, as their track is pink and gray.)

PIVOT—The leader of a team's pack, this head Blocker will determine the pack's pace, plan strategy, and call out plays during the jam.

POINTS—A Jammer earns points for each opposing skater she passes once she is on her second rotation through the pack. At the end of the bout, the team with the most points wins the game.

"THE RAIL"—The high side of the track, identified by the horizontal railing. It hurts to hit it, but it hurts even more to go flying over it, as it's a long way to the ground.

SKATES—Roller derby is played on four-wheeled speed skates, or quad skates. They look like fancy sneakers equipped with skateboard wheels.

TRACK—The oval-shape playing area for roller derby. Can be banked (raised) or flat, depending on the game.

TRANSITION—The move a player executes to rotate herself 180 degrees in order to skate backward.

WALL—A defensive barrier formed by two or more Blockers . . . or one Blocker with an enormous, powerful booty.

WHIP—To fling a skater forward, improving her position by giving her speed and power. Skaters can whip another skater using their hands, legs, or even hips.

WIFE—The ultimate term of affection from one skater to another, a derby girl takes a wife when she has been shown exemplary dedication and care by another skater. At RollerCon, the annual roller derby convention held in Vegas, there is a large ceremony where derby wives can get "married." For the origins of the derby wife, please go to http://www.rollercon.net/register/derby-wedding-registration/

Going in Circles
Pamela Ribon

INTRODUCTION

Recently separated (while still technically a newlywed), heartbroken Charlotte Goodman must choose between a severely conflicted marriage and the terrifying prospect of single life. While searching for the "right" thing to do, she struggles to drown out the voices of her overbearing mother, self-righteous boss, and cynical coworker. In such an uncertain phase, Charlotte is desperate enough to try anything that will bring her strength, confidence, and answers. Under the guidance of an eccentric new friend, she finds that salvation in the unlikeliest of places—roller derby.

QUESTIONS AND TOPICS FOR DISCUSSION

1. Discuss Charlotte's tendency to imagine John Goodman narrating her life as a way of coping. Is this method effective? What does it mean that she is ultimately able to shed his voice and live in the "first person"?

2. In her first meeting with the psychiatrist, Charlotte insists, "Of course there's one right way. One way is wrong, and then there's one way that's right" (page 66). Does this prove to be true in the end? Which other characters might or might not agree with this statement? Do you agree with it?

3. Observing the results of Petra's plastic surgery at one point, Charlotte notes that, "Petra is trying to freeze herself as an image that exists only in her head, and unfortunately she is losing the battle" (pages 73–74). Do you think that Charlotte might be guilty of the same crime? What are the consequences of attempting to live in limbo?

4. Discuss Charlotte's assertion that the idea of "soul mates" is depressing because it means that, "We're all just human puppets dancing on the invisible strings of an unknowable creator" (page 76). Do you agree or disagree?

5. When faced with the task of creating a pseudonym for herself, Charlotte claims that there is "something intriguing about the concept of losing my real identity" (page 120). Discuss the ways in which this alter ego in fact helped Charlotte regain her "real" identity. What was particularly empowering about her experience as Hard Broken? What name would you choose for yourself?

6. Discuss Ribon's choice to make Matthew a character with obsessive-compulsive disorder. Do you see a larger theme of control recurring in the lives of other characters? Which ones? How so?

7. How does Jonathan's ability to salvage his marriage inform Charlotte's failure to do so? How are the two cases different? Similar?

8. In her description of a "transition" in roller derby, Charlotte notes that "When it's over, you're still skating in the same direction, but you're facing the other way. You're going forward, facing backward" (page 156). How is this process paralleled in her personal life?

9. Discuss the effect that both Charlotte's fight with Francesca and Andy's disappointment in her friendship have on helping Charlotte escape her overwhelming grief.

10. What is the significance of Charlotte's miniatures? How do they help her to find order amidst chaos? Why does Matthew's destruction of these miniatures lead to the destruction of their marriage? How does talking about this moment help Charlotte make her final decision?

11. Discuss the irony involved in Matthew's comment that the hallway light is out. How does it signify a finite end to the relationship for Charlotte?

12. In Francesca's and Charlotte's debut in the rookie roller derby tournament, Charlotte is able to successfully deviate from the "plan" and take the lead. How does this triumph mark a transition in her attitude toward life?

A Conversation with Pamela Ribon

1. Where did you get the idea for this novel? Was there a particular scene that you envisioned first?

It started out with a very different story, one still stemming from the concept of "Well, I don't have the kind of money needed to have my own *Eat, Pray, Love* healing experience. What do I do to get out of this sadness and confusion?" In earlier drafts, the main character had made a huge mistake, and was starting from zero with absolutely everyone in her life. That story was more about trying to discern good relationships from bad. At the time I'd just started up with the LA Derby Dolls, and my agent was fascinated with what I was physically and mentally going through just to learn how to play. She's the one who suggested that Charlotte's story could take a similar direction. I joked, "You mean I should write *Eat, Cry, Shove*?" And it sort of took off from there.

2. How is this novel different from (or similar to) your previous novels?

It's similar in terms of dealing with changes in your important relationships—with your partner, your family, your best friend. I'm interested in the roles we take on for other people in our lives, and what happens when the power shifts, when the players in the game disobey the rules. The biggest difference between this novel and anything I've written before is that I'm writing about sports. I have a whole new respect for people who can describe the action in a game both accurately and passionately—sports reporters, color commentators, J. K. Rowling. That woman invented an entire sport and we all read it and said, "Yep. Got it. Brooms and magical glowing shuttlecocks. *To the Quidditch match!*"

3. What drew you to roller derby? Are any of Charlotte's experiences in the arena based on your own?

My sister and I used to watch roller derby on cable television when we were kids. Back then, it was as fake as WWE, but we didn't care. We didn't understand a single thing that was going on, but we liked how fast they went on their skates, and how they'd knock the crap out of one another.

My introduction to *real* roller derby happened just like that of any other derby girl, I'm sure—at the opening weekend of the *Sex and the City* movie. I was there with two of my girlfriends, one of whom groaned as she took her seat. "Sorry," she said. "I'm so sore. I just started training with the Derby Dolls last night and my thighs are killing me." I was right there beside her at the very next practice. She somehow snuck me in without an orientation or audition (behold the power of a derby wife). In fact, I didn't see an actual bout until I was already in training for my first Baby Doll Brawl. Come to think of it, almost everything in my life that I love I somehow snuck into when nobody was paying attention. Roller derby, acting, writing, and at least half of the relationships I've been in.

I really did break my tailbone. I now know the meaning of the threat, "You'll never sit right again."

4. What inspired you to include Charlotte's passion for miniatures as a major theme?

The miniatures came out of a number of ideas that were circling in my head about solving a problem that has no right or wrong answer. Charlotte feels as if her life is beyond her control, that there's nothing she can definitely hang on to. At some point during the writing of this novel, I found this little clay doll of a girl wearing a backpack and a polka-dot dress. She's looking up to the sky, her fists clenched and pressed against her chest, just pleading with the world. And I'd been reading about Occam's razor, but I'm afraid if I explain that any further, I'll sound ridiculously pompous. The short answer is: Charlotte is afraid to take control. The miniatures are all hers, and they are her gift. She got scared of where they could take her, but the reality is she's the one who decides where *they* go. At first she thinks that a miniature, like Charlotte's job, has a right way and a wrong way to do it, but as she grows with her work and takes risks, she finds a new direction, a new way to express herself. That's how she takes control again.

5. Which scenes were easiest for you to write? Which were the most difficult?

It is hard to tell a story about two people not being able to make things work without someone appearing to be The Problem. I don't think that's realistic. People sometimes make the mistake of assigning "weakness" to characters who endure heartbreak. I never understood that. Don't we all often struggle much longer than anyone else in our lives can tolerate? Sometimes we do it to keep someone we love, sometimes it's to understand exactly what's wrong in an attempt to fix it, but I think often it's just so we feel like we have *won*.

I wouldn't call any of the scenes "easy" to write, exactly, but I had fun writing about how I think about roller derby. The only problem was, after I'd write about a jam I'd get amped to skate. Sometimes I had to miss practice in order not to miss a deadline. Then one time I jammed my finger at practice. I had to keep my finger in a sling for a couple of days, making it so that I could neither write about nor play roller derby. That was the worst.

6. How were you able to infuse a novel about coping with grief with such refreshing humor?

I'm worried that I didn't, but I'm even more concerned people will think I wrote that question. So thank you, Stranger I've Never Met Who Wrote Question Number Six. That's nice of you to ask. I assure you early drafts of this novel were quite devoid of humor.

The voice of John Goodman came out of this struggle. I was trying to find a new way to tell an old story—girl is sad over a boy—without making Charlotte sound either pathetic or bitter. Both Charlotte and Matthew deal with their emotions by detaching and distancing—which is why they're ultimately doomed. And for both of them we learn that the greater the distance they put between themselves and their problems, the harder they fall when gravity inevitably brings them back to reality. Wait, was this a question about how I made sad things funny? I don't know. Comedy equals tragedy plus time. I didn't come up with that equation, but it works.

7. Does your life have a narrator?

Sometimes. When I was a little girl and couldn't fall asleep, my mom would suggest I tell myself stories until I fell asleep. Somehow that voice continued into my waking life, and would keep me company when I was having some of my most boring moments. And if I'm being really honest, I suppose the narrator started approximately when I gave up my embarrassingly large clique of imaginary friends.

8. If you were in Francesca's place, what advice would you give Charlotte?
Get over yourself.

9. Do you have any plans for another book? If so, what will it be about?
I just stared at that question for thirty minutes and then had a panic attack. Thanks.

ENHANCE YOUR BOOK CLUB

1. Visit Pamela Ribon's popular blog at www.pamie.com. She started it in 1998, and was nominated for a Lifetime Achievement Bloggie Award in 2006.

2. Check out *Roller Warriors,* a seven-part documentary series covering the 2008 Kansas City Roller Warriors, as well as the recent Drew Barrymore film *Whip It,* based on the YA novel *Derby Girl,* written by fellow LA Derby Doll alum Shauna Cross.

3. Support your local roller derby league! Visit www.derbyroster.com to find out where the action is in your area.

4. Already a derby girl? Be sure to check out RollerCon (www.rollercon.net).